ond Twenty-Seven Vagabond Twenty-

D0657821

Series editor: Dana Keller

DOUBTING THOMAS

HEATHER RICHARDSON

VAGABOND VOICES

GLASGOW

© Heather Richardson 2017

First published on 26 October 2017 by
Vagabond Voices Publishing Ltd.,
Glasgow,
Scotland.

ISBN 978-1-908251-87-9

The author's right to be identified as author of this book under the
Copyright, Designs and Patents Act 1988 has been asserted.

Printed and bound in Poland

Cover design by Mark Mechan

Typeset by Park Productions

The publisher acknowledges subsidy towards
this publication from Creative Scotland

ALBA | CHRUTHACHAIL

For further information on Vagabond Voices, see the website,
www.vagabondvoices.co.uk

To John, Isaac and Leon –
the Richardson menfolk

DOUBTING
THOMAS

PART I
THE FABRIC OF THE HUMAN BODY

From Scotland we hear, that upon Review of the dead bodies after the fight on the twenty second of June last past, there are found about nine Hundred of the Rebels slain ... All persons, men and women, are prohibited to Harbour, Relieve or Correspond with any Rebels, upon pain of being esteemed and punished as favourers of the said Rebellion, and as Persons accessory to and guilty of the same.

Domestick Intelligence or News Both from City and Country, July 1679

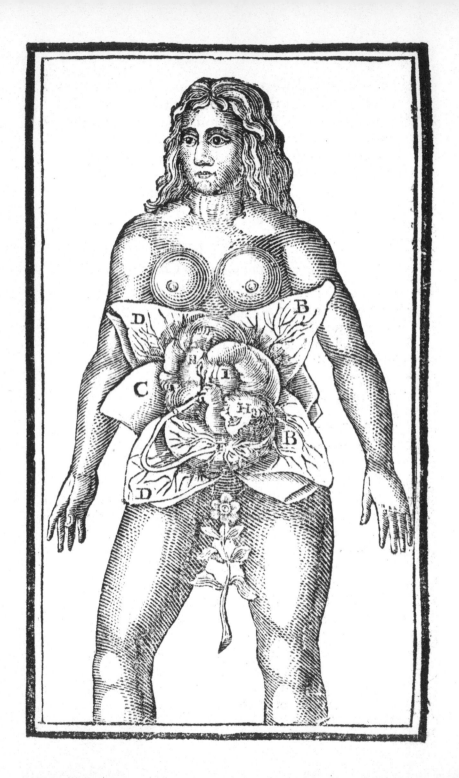

1682

Dr Carruth

The dead woman is covered with a sheet of thick-woven linen. I reach out and rest my fingertips on the table's edge. No one else is here yet. The porter suggested I stay downstairs by the fire, but I had a hunger to be first to the dissecting room. The air is so chilly that I can see my breath each time I exhale. There's a stove in the far corner, but it has not been lit. I cannot detect any reek of decay from the corpse. She's scarcely a day dead.

Somewhere below a door bangs shut. There's a slow, disordered drumbeat of footsteps on the stairs, accompanied by a deep voice that rarely pauses. I look down at the shrouded figure on the table. This will only be the third dissection I have attended, and my first of a female.

Dr Irvine enters the room like a galleon in full sail, still talking. Behind him comes a wan-faced fellow with a canvas satchel dangling from his shoulder. He is dressed like a down-at-heel Frenchman. Dr Irvine's two assistants follow.

"Here already, Carruth?" Dr Irvine says. "No sign of Maxwell?"

"I haven't seen him this morning."

"He was to join me for breakfast." Dr Irvine shrugs. "No doubt he has been diverted by someone more enticing."

Damn Maxwell. How is it that he is invited to breakfast with Dr Irvine, and I am not? And how can he so casually break an appointment, and not be thought any the worse for it?

Dr Irvine takes off his hat and wig and hands them to one of his assistants. The other comes forward to help him out of his coat. Thus divested he tugs his waistcoat and smoothes it over his substantial belly. "Signor Baldini is joining us this morning," he says, gesturing at the foreigner. Italian then, not French. "He will make sketches when my work is done. Such a rare opportunity – an *autopsia* of a woman dead of natural causes, and with a child in her womb. Worthy of record, do you not think?"

"Do you intend to publish your sketches, Signor Baldini?" I ask.

Baldini smiles at me, but does not reply, instead scuttling off to a corner of the room where he lifts up a stool that is nearly as tall as he is.

"Save your breath, Carruth," Dr Irvine says. "He hasn't a word of English." We both watch Signor Baldini struggle to carry the stool closer to the dissecting table.

Dr Irvine's assistants have laid his instruments on a bench. He studies them, reaching out to shift the position of a small saw. At last he turns and places his hand on the linen sheet covering the corpse. My heartbeat quickens. Signor Baldini looks uncomfortable, and murmurs something.

"*Sì, facciamo sempre*," Dr Irvine replies. "Baldini suggests we say a prayer for the dead woman and her unborn infant before we commence."

"Of course," I say.

Dr Irvine bows his head. The others do likewise. "Beloved Father," he begins, "within whose gift is life and death. We know that we are dust, and that one day we will cast off our earthly shackles and stand before you for judgement."

As he prays I notice Signor Baldini's hand creeping towards his satchel. His eyes are still closed and his face gives every sign of a man intent on prayer, but his fingers hover over the buckle. I suppose he must be itching to slide his sketchbook out, but he halts himself and clasps his hands together as if to restrain them. If he is so impatient for the dissection to begin then why did he suggest this delay? A show of piety, perhaps.

Dr Irvine finishes his prayer and looks up, blinking like a man new woken. "Now, gentlemen. Shall we begin?"

His assistants step forward, one on either side of the table. At a nod from him they each take a corner of the linen sheet and slowly peel it away to reveal the subject of our investigation. She is young, and utterly naked. Her hair… her face… like Isobel's. The floor lurches beneath my feet and there seems to be no breath in my body. A hand grips my arm and steadies me. I turn to see the anxious face of one of Dr Irvine's assistants. "Are you taken bad, sir?" he says.

"No, no…" I look again at the dead woman. Not Isobel, of course not. It's just that her hair is the same soft brown, and something in the shape of her brow…

"Nothing to be ashamed of, Carruth," Dr Irvine says, although the expression on his face does not console me.

"I assure you I am not usually so overwhelmed," I attempt a laugh. "Please do not delay on my account. I am quite recovered now."

We turn back to the corpse. How could I show such weakness in front of Dr Irvine? Worse still, how could this wretched girl put me in mind of Isobel? It was hardly a seemly comparison… *Be still. Concentrate. Study the cadaver.*

I obey my own instructions, and look properly, coolly, at the dead woman. I knew she would be young of course, given her condition, but knowing is a different thing from seeing. She's as yellow as beeswax. Her mouth is held shut by a strip of cloth looped from under her chin to the top of her head. One eye is half-open. Her small breasts lie flat. A day or two ago they must have been painfully plump as her body prepared itself for childbirth. The dome of her belly is strangely flaccid. There is little sign of the distension common in women near their time. I can only assume that the coming of death has caused the fibres of her body to ease their grip. Signor Baldini mutters something under his breath. His voice sounds full of pity.

"Poor lassie," Dr Irvine says. "The hangman made a widow of her last week."

"What was her husband's crime?"

"A Covenanter. The usual story. These fellows think they can overthrow the King with no more than a Bible in one hand and a pike in the other."

"And there's no explanation of why she died so suddenly?" This, after all, is why we are here. "There was no sign of fever or pain?"

Dr Irvine fixes me with an odd smile. "Her gaolers report that she was in as good health as one might expect for a girl that had spent the winter in the Tolbooth prison."

He walks to the foot of the table, places a hand on each of the girl's knees and gently pushes her legs apart. "There's certainly no sign that labour had commenced. Look for yourself."

I do as he suggests, and examine her perineum for a moment. Dr Irvine's assessment seems correct. I move back up the table and palpate her belly with my fingers, working thoroughly to study every inch of it. I should be able to feel the dead infant's skull through her skin, or the jut of his shoulder or knee, but I cannot. His position must be odd, or else he is terribly misshapen. "There seems to be no fluid in her womb," I say. "Had her waters broken, or did they leak away post-mortem?"

"Again, it is uncertain. Are you familiar with the Tolbooth prison, Carruth?"

"Certainly not."

Dr Irvine seems amused, as if by some private joke. "Covenanters are held in the worst of the cells. The floors are thick with filth, and it would take a rare genius to guess if any flux from her formed part of that cess. Her body is the only evidence we have of what befell her." Dr Irvine turns and lifts the largest scalpel from the side table. "And on that note, shall we see what story her womb tells us?"

I nod soberly, trying to disguise the excitement and dread that courses through me like a fever. Signor Baldini clambers up the rungs of the stool and perches on the top like a crow, sketchpad on his lap and pencil in his hand.

Dr Irvine makes a slow, shallow incision from the woman's navel to her pudendum, following exactly the dark line that nature draws on the belly of a gravid female. The flesh parts with an ooze of liquid fat. He makes a similar incision upwards from the navel to just beneath the breastbone. There's no doubting his skill. He makes another long cut, from side to side, passing once again through the navel.

"Our object today is investigation," he says, "so my incisions have been cautious. With a cadaver such as this, ill-fed and stretched by her condition, it would be all too easy to cut over-deep, and damage the womb." He sets the scalpel aside and edges his fingers into the lower incision, feeling his way along its entire length, probing more deeply as he does so. He does the same with the other cuts, and then turns to his two assistants. "Hold her steady now. One on either side."

We step away from the table to allow Irvine's men to come closer. When they have laid hands upon the body Irvine peels open her belly, tugging at each flap of skin until all four of them are opened out like the petals of a flower. Her womb is unveiled, the distended heart of the blossom, resting in a bed of congealed blood.

"Something is amiss here," says Dr Irvine. He glances up at me. "This is the first time you have seen a female opened, is it not?"

"I once witnessed a dying woman cut open to save her unborn child." I do not mention that the barber-surgeon who performed the procedure was my father.

"And what do you see here that is different?"

"The blood. Such a quantity is unusual. And the shape of the uterus. It is…" I reach into the body cavity and probe the thick walls of the womb. No. Impossible. This cannot be. "It appears to be empty."

"Let us lift it away. Hold it for me."

I take my jacket off and cast it to one side, then slide my hands underneath the uterus and lift it up to let Dr Irvine slice it free from the tissue that holds it in place.

13

"Och, sir," one of the assistants cautions, "let me roll your shirtsleeves up for you." His offer is too late. The frill of one cuff must have dipped into the blood, and a dark stain is spreading up through the fabric. Nevertheless, I keep still while the man turns my sleeves up, out of the way of further pollution. The uterus is slippery and heavy. A trail of fluid runs from my fingers to my elbow. The urge to wipe it away is almost unbearable.

At last Dr Irvine has finished his snipping and cutting. He lays down his instruments and takes the uterus from me. "Take a look inside her, while I inspect the womb," he says, laying the organ down on the bench.

I peer into the body cavity, observing the loops of intestine nestling in the pooled blood. There's a whiff of the slaughterhouse in the air, and I am thankful that it is too cold for the odour to ripen. A protrusion of dark-hued tissue catches my eye and I take hold of it and try to work it free from the tangle of innards, but it is larger than any bodily part that should be here. "Dear God," I say, "I believe this may be the placenta."

"But of course!" Dr Irvine exclaims. "See here – the womb is ruptured, and no sign of child or placenta. That's what has killed her." He leaves the uterus aside and comes to assist me, taking the placenta from me and cradling it as if it were the infant. The umbilical cord is still attached to it, and leads back into the body cavity. "Follow the cord, man!" he barks at one of the assistants. "See if the child is at the other end."

The man does as instructed with some show of reluctance, poking one hand gingerly into the body cavity. The air is suddenly foul with the stench of human waste, and he turns away, retching. He must have nudged the bowel. His colleague mutters something ill-tempered and brings forward a mop to clean up the vomit. Dr Irvine sighs in exasperation.

"Will you permit me…?" I say. He nods. I insinuate my fingers into the mess of organs, following the umbilical cord as if it were my guide through the maze of the dead woman's body. Gently now. I close my eyes and let my fingertips find their way along the cord until they feel a tiny ribcage. They continue up the foetal torso until they encounter a chin, the delicate nub of a nose and the dome of a skull. "I have him," I say, and begin to manoeuvre the infant out. When I have released him Dr Irvine and I move towards the bench, he bearing the placenta and me the tiny corpse. The cord hangs between us, connecting our two burdens. We must look like heathen priests, engaged in some dreadful ritual. My hands are greasy, coated with the first seep of putrefaction. We set child and placenta down side by side on the bench.

"The infant seems sound enough," he says. "You may examine it, if you wish." For a terrible moment I think he means to wipe his hands on his waistcoat. Thank God one of his men steps forward and offers us both towels. Signor Baldini, who I had quite forgotten in these last moments, scribbles away at his sketchpad from his eyrie atop the stool.

I step forward to inspect the baby. The cord is birled around the infant's neck, but not so tightly as to suffocate him had he ever been born. I unwind it. The child's eyes are shut fast. His arms are bent and his fingers loosely clenched, as if he is prepared for a fight. I turn him over, touching his damp skin as gently as I can. His spine is complete, and there is no sign of monstrosity. As I study him his limbs very gradually straighten, released now from the confinement of his mother's body. I sense Dr Irvine waiting for me to speak. "He seems physically sound," I say, laying him on to his back once more. My tongue feels dry. There's a sour taste in my mouth.

"Indeed." Dr Irvine is at my shoulder. "It is my deduction that there was some weakness in the womb. See, here—" He shows me the uterus. It has split apart like a ripe fruit. "Have you ever encountered such a thing?"

"Never. My expertise lies in the more everyday female

15

disorders. Excess or absence of flux, intimate mortifications, suffocation of the uterus…"

Dr Irvine waves a dismissive hand. "Yes, yes. Maxwell told me that."

"Maxwell?" The very mention of his name makes me bristle.

"Aye. It was on his recommendation that I invited you to view this *autopsia*. He tells me you are the man of the moment with the lady patients, and their *intimate mortifications*."

"That implies my reputation derives from fashion rather than skill," I say stiffly.

Dr Irvine smiles, fixing me with his keen eye. "He also said your temperament is as prickly as a whin bush."

I feel my face grow hot. There is little point in denying the truth of Maxwell's assessment.

The light is fading, another short winter day drawing to a close. Signor Baldini has requested that lamps be lit and placed around the dead woman so that he may complete his sketches. He is still perched on the stool, scratching away with his pencil. The sound is like a mouse scuttling behind a wainscot. Dr Irvine's assistants have soaked up the blood and reassembled the woman's body so that the infant is inside her once more, lying cushioned on the dissected womb with his head resting on the placenta. The lamplight disguises her waxy pallor, giving the illusion of sleep to her face.

I notice that there are deep indentations in her torso, where Irvine's men gripped her. She has become clay, and will bear the imprint of any who touch her. Once, perhaps eight or so months ago, her husband held her and begot the child that lies in her dead womb. His fingers must have pressed against her warm skin in a spasm of carnal passion. A brief, appalling surge of desire engulfs me. Not for this dead flesh, but for the living woman she once was. God forgive me. I remember the line from the book of Romans: *To be carnally minded is death.* I say it silently, over and over again.

Dr Irvine and I wash and dry our hands. The assistants help us back into our coats. Perhaps he will invite me to sup with him. That will present me with a dilemma. Isobel's mother and father are expecting me, but surely they would understand that I could not refuse Dr Irvine? He has influence. Connections that are quite beyond me.

"I trust you have found the day instructive, Carruth," Irvine says, settling his wig back on his head.

"Indeed, yes."

"Excellent." He takes up his hat. "Well, I'll not detain you any longer. I have an invitation to dine with Sir Andrew Balfour and some of the other Fellows. I suppose you're familiar with the Royal College of Physicians?"

"I know of it." I swallow down my disappointment and jealousy.

"Indeed. We are all abuzz with news of the soldiers' hospital the King is having built in London. Would that he would issue a similar warrant in Edinburgh, eh? These current troubles would ensure it had no lack of patients."

I mumble something non-committal. It's best not to say anything that might be judged as a criticism of the King.

Dr Irvine gestures back at the dead woman. "We'll keep her here for another day or so, until she starts to reek. I'll tell the porters to admit you tomorrow, should you wish to continue your inspection of her."

"You are very kind." I decide not to tell him that I cannot return to the dissecting table tomorrow. I have a more pressing appointment, in the Tron Kirk, where Isobel will meet me at the altar and become my wife.

Thomas

It's like I'm flying. Never moved so fast in my life. Out the door. Three big leaps along the landing. Down the stairs. Two at a time. Three at a time. Jumping and flying and never falling. Mother squealing up above. She'll not catch me now.

Into the close and bang-crash into the Keep-Count Man. He doesn't fall but thon book he carries flaps out of his hand and splatters into a puddle.

"Watch where yir going, yi wee skitter!" he gulders, but I'm away again.

Up the wynds, hopscotching over the middens, holding my breath through Bad-Smell Close, crossing my fingers past Dead-Bairn Close, and at last I'm up on the big road. Check over my shoulder in case Mother is after me. No sign of her. My heart's going thump-thump-thump. I suck in big deep breaths. When I breathe out it looks like I've got smoke coming out of my nose. It's that cold. Big men and women push past. They dinnae pay me any mind. They're too busy watching the soldiers march along, all tramp-tramp-jingle-jangle.

Along the big road. Cut across the kirkyard, fast as I can, dinnae look left, dinnae look right, dinnae look at the gravestones, fifty-three big steps from one side to the other. Nearly at Dada's shop. Slow past the coffee house, so as to sniff the air. It smells warm and – not sweet... something else. I don't have the word for it, but I like it. There's Dada's sign, swinging above his shop door. A painted green snake curled round a stick. I stop and look up at it. Squeeze my eyes almost shut. Makes it look like the snake is moving. Wriggling and wiggling. It's the best sign in the whole of Edinburgh. Dada says Mr Fenton across the way wishes he had a sign like ours.

I keek through the window. There's no one there. Dada must be in the back room. I push the door open and march in. "I'm a rich laird in need of physic!" I shout.

"Is that so?" Dada calls, and comes in from the back, all grand with his best wig on. He stops all of a sudden and stares at me. "Do you know, sir," he says, "you're the very spit of my son Thomas."

I'd like to keep playacting, but Dada smiles and grabs me up in his arms. "What brings you here, wee man? Have you been doing battle with your mother again?"

I hide my face against his jacket. It smells like the medicine he makes. "I let a man in the door, and Mother was cross and Katharine said to run."

"I cannae hear what you're saying, son. You're all muffled, talking into my coat like that. Come now, you know I'll not be cross with you."

I tell him again. Mother's always telling us to let no one through the door, but sometimes I forget.

Dada sounds sad. "Who was it? The butcher? The chandler? How much was he after?"

I dinnae know who it was or how much he was after. My eyes are all stingy. I dinnae want to cry. Crying's for bairns.

"There now, wee man," Dada says, and sets me down on the counter. "She shouldn't take the strunt with you like that. You're not to know." He pulls his handkerchief from his pocket and dabs my face. "I tell you what," he says, all smiling and twinkly now, "I've been selling a new cure. It'll mend our fortunes, and that's a promise. What say you help me make another batch?"

I'm grinding up salt of hartshorn in the mortar. It smells odd. Makes me cough. Feels like it's burning the insides of my mouth. There's been customers in and out all afternoon. Some of them pat me on the head and smile at me. It's quiet now. Dada counts the money. "What did I tell you?" he says. "You shall have a penny all to yourself today, Thomas. Don't tell your mother."

A man comes into the shop. He's all happed up with a muffler birled around his neck and his hat pulled down low so I cannae see his mouth or his eyes. I dinnae think I'd want *him* to pat me on the head. Dada steps forward.

"What can I do for you?" he says.

The man looks down at me, then back at Dada. "I heard tell of some tablets you make. For the women, you ken?" I have to listen hard to make him out. He looks at me again. "It's maybe not fit for a bairn's lugs."

Dada puts his hand on my head. "Take that hartshorn through to the back now, Thomas, and then give your hands a good wash."

I do as he says. When I'm done I climb up on a stool and keek through the wee window between the back room and the shop. Dada has it so as he can look and see if a customer comes in when he's at his work. The man is still there, and Dada is parcelling up a fancy pillbox. Dada hands it over to him, and he gives Dada some coins. I wonder what medicine the man has bought. Dada is hoking around in the drawer for change when the door to the shop opens and an old woman comes in, her shopping basket on her arm. The man gives a jump, puts the parcel in his coat pocket and heads for the door. "You're away without your change!" Dada shouts, but the man disnae hear him.

Quick as a flash I run out from the back room. "Shall I go after him, Dada?"

"Aye, there's a good laddie," he says, handing me the man's change. Out in the street I see him over on the other side. He's walking fast, big long steps like a horse, head ducked down. I call out, but he disnae stop. I trot after him, but he's too fast for me to catch.

I follow him down streets and up wynds. My legs are getting tired, and I'm too out of puff to call out. The shop signs are all strange to me. A picture of a black bull with a ring in his nose. Another of a golden-haired angel. Along another street and down another wynd and at last we're at journey's end in a court I didnae even know was here. I catch him up just as he's about to go in through a house door. "Here, mister," I say, and he gives another jump like he did when the old woman came into the shop. "You forgot your change." I hold out my hand, with the coins all hot and sweaty lying in it. He says something I cannae make out, takes the money and goes in the door. There's not even a bawbee for me, for my trouble. I bide for a moment in case he changes his mind and comes back. After a while I step away. There's a movement up above at a window, but when I look up no one's there. I take a keek around the court. It's bigger and cleaner than where we stay, but not much. I want to go back to Dada's shop and see if he'll still give me my penny. My legs are sore with running after the man, and my belly's griping with hunger. I'm not scared, though. I've been lost before, and I always find my way back.

Dr Carruth

I am being forced up the stairs by a good-hearted mob of kith and kin, few of whom I recognise. Most of them belong to Isobel. There are few remnants left of my family connection and they only appear at weddings, funerals and other such occasions where they will be well furnished with free food and drink. Indeed, the last time I saw them before today was at my father's funeral. We stop at the door of the bedchamber.

"Knock, sir, knock," some cousin of Isobel's slurs in my ear. His breath smells like ancient cheese. Other voices join in, and many hands slap my back in encouragement. I do as I am bid, and rap on the door. After a moment it opens and my supporters cheer. Isobel's mother peers out, blinking at the brightness of the lamp one of the menfolk is holding.

"You are impatient, *son*," she says, with a lewd smile that ill suits her thin, puritan lips. The tone of her voice makes my skin itch. Her eyes glitter like a bird's in the lamplight. "But fear not," she goes on. "Your bride is ready for you."

"Ready and willing, please God," someone behind me says, and hoarse, masculine laughter ripples through the air. All the solemnity that marked the earlier part of the day is quite vanished, submerged under a tide of whisky and port wine. I close my eyes for a moment and try to recall Isobel's face as she made her vows in the clear winter light of the Tron Kirk only a few hours since, before this day became a bacchanal.

My mother-in-law opens the bedchamber door wider and comes out, followed by two of the servant women. I am pushed into the room and the door pulled shut behind me. Thank God to get away from them all, the men with their crude advice and the women simpering and snickering as if they know my every weakness. Thank God for some relief from the airless rooms downstairs and the stink of sweat and burning lamp oil.

The bed looms before me, its curtains pulled tightly together. The only light and sound comes from the fire crackling in the grate. Then a rustle from behind the bed curtains. "Is that a mouse?" I say, feeling excessively foolish. Isobel will think I am drunk.

But she giggles, and says, "Perhaps."

I feel a ripple of delight at the sound of her voice. This day has been so long and strange. We have not had one moment alone, and have scarcely said a word to each other apart from the sacred promises we exchanged in the Tron Kirk this morning. All day I have been jostled and cajoled, my back slapped and base comments whispered in my ear. The menfolk of Isobel's family are a respectable collection of advocates and clergymen, but as the day has gone on their sober, Sabbath faces have reddened and contorted with unaccustomed merriment. I feel as if layer upon layer of filth and grease has coated me. Only now, in the blessed sanctuary of this room, with Isobel's clear voice tinkling like a silver bell in the darkness, do I start to feel clean again.

"Good Lord," I say, starting to creep towards the bed. "A mouse! What shall I do? Set a trap? Or perhaps I'd be better fetching a cat?" Our courtship has been one of earnest debate and common sense, and here I am babbling the foolish bairn-talk some lovers engage in. And yet I feel happier than ever before.

Isobel laughs again, but there is a nervous edge to it now. Of course. She must be even more anxious than I am. I feel a pang of pity for her. We are both innocents, but I at least understand the theory of what we must achieve tonight. "Don't be afraid, little mouse," I say. "I will do you no harm, for I am in grand good spirits."

"I'm glad to hear it."

I reach the bed and put my hand to the curtains, ready to pull them back. My eyes have adjusted to the dim light, and I can see the whiteness of my fingers clearly against the deep red of the bed curtains. "Aye, today I married the bonniest lassie in Scotland, and that has made me inclined to show goodwill to all creatures. Even to a mouse." More nonsense. I hesitate, my hand still on the curtain. Should I take off my wig, my coat? Will it not be odd for me to appear before her, full-clad in my wedding finery, and her likely in no more than a shift? And yet if I completely disrobe now it might take a good ten minutes before I'm ready. But if I do not do it now I must do it in view of her.

"Are you still there, Robert?" she says, her voice gently mocking. My mouth is dry and my palms are damp. No more delays. I can put it off no longer. My undressing will have to wait.

I pull the curtains aside so abruptly she jumps and lets out a squeal. She is lying atop the bedspread as naked as the day she was born, and in exactly the same position as the poor lassie I watched Dr Irvine cut apart yesterday. My head spins, just as it did when I first saw the dead girl and thought for a moment that she was Isobel. I sit down heavily on the edge of the bed, turning my back to her.

She sits and pulls a sheet around her so that she is no longer utterly exposed, moving closer to where I sit. "What is wrong, Robert? The expression on your face, it was so fierce." One hand clasps the sheet at her breast, the other lies on her lap. In the dim light her skin looks dark against the whiteness of the linen. Her eyes are bright with tears. "Do you not like me, then? Am I ugly? Too thin?" The hurt in her voice is unbearable.

"You're very lovely," I say. How can I tell her that what I see is not my slender young bride, but rather a cage made of bones and skin? "It is just that I did not expect… Forgive me, I do not know what I expected."

"It was Mother who said I should display myself like that."
There's bitterness in her tone, in the way she says the word
"mother". "I wanted to wear my nightgown, or at least to
cover myself under the bedspread, but she said it would
please you better if I was unhidden. It would not have been
my choice, Robert, but she told me I know nothing of the
minds of men..."

I embrace her clumsily. "Never mind that now," I say.
"From this day on you may do as you please, not as she tells
you." She rests her head against my shoulder. Her hair is
perfumed. I breathe in the scent of her.

"In that case," she says, pulling away from me, "I will put
on my nightgown."

"And I will ready myself for bed." I stand and move away
from the bed, keeping my back to it as I undress, hoping
that Isobel is too occupied with her own arrangements to
watch me. Once I am stripped down to my undershirt I
return to the bed and climb in under the covers. Isobel
turns on her side to face me.

"Well, husband," she says lightly, and waits.

I kiss her on the cheek, and then on the lips. She shivers.
Is she still chilled from lying naked – damn her mother's
recklessness! – or is she afraid? In spite of my own fears I find
myself stirred, then almost immediately am consumed with
shame. *To be carnally minded is death.* But this is our marriage
bed. Whatever lust I feel is sanctioned by the laws of God
and man. We kiss again, and Isobel wraps her arms around
me. She seems so fragile. I remind myself that the female
body – despite the nonsense written about weaker vessels –
is more robust than it might appear. Even those secret parts,
which are the source of so many afflictions, can withstand
the violence of childbirth. As I counsel myself in this way
Isobel insinuates one of her legs between mine. The sensation of skin against skin provokes a pang of desire, but just as
quickly I am gripped with a fear that if I place my hands on
her my fingers will sink into her flesh through the layers of

sinew and softness to the mess of bowel and blood. A tide of nausea rises within me. I pull away from her and dash to the washstand where I vomit into the basin. A second spasm grasps my gut, but nothing more comes out. The bitter stink from the basin clears my mind. It's the smell of the tavern, not the charnel house. Life, not death.

Isobel has risen from the bed and advanced across the room towards me. "There's water in the jug," she says.

I scoop a handful and swill it around my mouth to clean away the sourness. Isobel comes closer and dips a cloth in the jug. She tries to wipe my face, but I turn away. "I can do that myself," I say. She does not reply at once, but hands me the cloth, watching me with grave eyes while I dab away the sweat from my brow.

"I must have taken too much port wine," I say. Isobel looks unconvinced. "Perhaps if I could sleep it off for an hour or two?"

We return to the bed and climb in, lying side by side without touching like carved figures on a tomb. At last she says, "I had thought, with your profession, and having studied abroad..."

"I do not understand your meaning."

"Do not young men... I understand there are certain establishments... Have you not... experienced–" She stops, not having the words to continue.

I feel my face colour. "No," I say. "Not all young men are... debauched."

She takes a deep breath, and speaks. "Mother said you would teach me, but I suppose we must learn together." She reaches for my hand. "In a way, I am glad of it. I should not much like to be one of many."

The room closes in around me, and now feels as airless as the rest of this confounded house. I want to be away, back to my own cool, quiet home on the Pleasance. The place to which I am expected to take Isobel tomorrow. I shake off her hand and sit up. "I cannot stay here."

"What do you mean?" There's fear in her voice.

"I have made a great mistake."

"In marrying me?"

"In marrying at all. I am not made for it, is that not obvious?"

Isobel laughs nervously. "I thought it was the bride who was supposed to be fearful of the wedding night."

I get up and begin to dress. When she sees what I am doing she says, "You cannot leave. The house is full of my kin."

"Aye, and that's half the problem."

Isobel flies from the bed and grabs my arms, forcing me to look at her. "I will not be disgraced in front of my family. You will not walk out of this room until morning." Her face is ashen with fury, but her mouth is trembling. What have I done to my girl?

I try to calm myself by breathing deeply. She's right, of course. If I leave now my failure will be public knowledge by daybreak. Isobel's family will swoop down on me like corbies, to protect her reputation. Annulment of marriage, for reasons of non-consummation. My scalp is prickled with sweat. I go to the washstand and splash cold water on to my head. That's better. Control yourself, man. Settle your voice before you speak. "You are correct," I say. "I would not wish to expose either of us to disdain. Please accept my apologies."

She steps back from me, staring at me as if I am someone she does not quite recognise. "What shall we do now?"

"You should sleep. Or lie down, at the least. I will sit in the armchair here."

"And what of tomorrow?"

"I do not know."

She thinks for a moment. "Tomorrow we will do what is expected of us," she says firmly. "We will take breakfast with my family, and we will look as bashful as we might in response to any questions. Then you will take me to my new home." She waits for my response, and when I give none she climbs into bed, pulling the curtains shut. The bed creaks and I hear the rustle of linen as she slips beneath the covers.

I put on my coat for warmth and sit in the armchair. There's no sound from the bed now. Downstairs a cork pops and the gathered uncles and cousins cheer raggedly. Pray God they disperse soon enough to their own beds. It is long past midnight. Day will not break until near the hour of eight. I must wait here till then, for whatever the morning will bring.

Thomas

Mother walks faster than any of us. She has Anna by one hand and me by the other, and drags us along behind her. Katharine has to run to keep up. I look over my shoulder at her. "Are you running out of puff, Kat?"

"Sure it helps to warm me up," she says, and smiles, but I can see she's no breath in her.

"Stop your gabbing," Mother says, and hauls that hard on my arm I think she'll pull it off altogether. "Pick up your feet, Anna. You'll wear your shoes out, slithering like that." Anna starts to gurn, and that makes Mother more crabbit than ever.

I'm glad to see the shop sign up ahead. My friend the green snake. Mother will not be so hard on us in front of Dada. She'll tackle him instead.

Bang, crash, she's in through the door, and us three bairns stood on the street outside. I look up at Katharine. "Should we go in?"

She pauses, listening to the rise of Mother's voice inside the shop. "I suppose so. We came because we were starved with cold, so there's no point in biding out here." She reaches out a hand each to Anna and me. "Come on then." Katharine holds my hand nice and gentle. She disnae squeeze my bones till they crack.

The three of us shuffle in through the door. Mother goes on with her scolding, word after word after word. Dada looks over at us and gives me a wee smile. That puts Mother in an even worse twist. "Aye, you smirk away there, you grinning fool. That won't warm your bairns, and us without a lump of coal in the house." She pushes past him into the back room. "Oh aye!" she screeches. "You're keeping yourself all snug in here, with your stove burning!"

It's not fair. Dada needs the stove lit for making his medicines. I tug Katharine's sleeve.

"What is it, wee Tam?" she whispers.

The thoughts I want to speak are jumbled in my head. My eyes feel all stingy. Katharine hunkers down beside me. "Don't cry, Tam. She'll only be crosser."

The door of the shop bangs open and a grand-looking man comes in. He's wearing a coat with more shiny buttons than I can count, and he has a sealed letter in his hand. Mother's still guldering at Dada in the back room. The grand man looks down at us bairns. He stares hard at me. "I suppose you must be Thomas?" he says.

I nod.

There's a pause in Mother's shouting. Dada keeks out through the hatch. "Oh!" he says, and smiles. "Sir Patrick!" He bustles out into the shop, with Mother close behind.

The grand man looks very sad, or maybe very cross. I can't tell which. "I don't suppose you have the rent you owe me?" he says.

Dada keeps smiling, the way he does when Mother shouts at him. "I have a wee bit, Sir Patrick..." He opens the money drawer under the counter. "I could let you have two pounds."

Mother turns on him. "You've been holding two pounds by, and us with nothing but porridge to eat this last fortnight!"

Sir Patrick shakes his head. "It's no good, James. That's three quarters in a row you haven't paid a penny. I cannot let it continue, not when there's men of business aplenty would gladly take the shop on."

"Take the two pounds now," Dada says, "and I'll have more for you next week. Business is improved this last wee while."

"It's too late for that," Sir Patrick says. "I need a reliable tenant." He hands Dada the sealed envelope.

"And what's that?" Mother says.

30

Sir Patrick sighs. "It's an eviction notice."

"An eviction notice? Well, you've a brave cheek!" Mother marches over to Sir Patrick and wags her finger at him. "We're family! What sort of man treats his family like this?"

"We're only distant cousins," Dada says, trying to smile. "I can't blame Sir Patrick for wanting his rent."

Mother whirls round and gives Dada a box on the ear. "Would you listen to yourself! You'll stand up for anyone but your own wife and bairns." She turns back to Sir Patrick. "And as for you," she says, poking him in the chest, "you ought to be ashamed of yourself. That bairn there is your godson." Before Sir Patrick can speak she stops poking and starts slapping his chest. The buttons on Sir Patrick's coat jangle every time she slaps him and he looks most amazed. "Oh aye, you think you're most superior don't you? Well my people were every bit as good as the Aikenheads and don't you forget it." She stops slapping and points at Dada. "That fool there was lucky to get me."

"That's as maybe," says Sir Patrick, "but the fact remains that the rent on this shop has not been paid for near a year, and I cannot allow your husband to continue here."

Mother marches over to Dada, snatches the letter from his hand and tears it to pieces. "Here's what I think of your eviction notice," she cries. Sir Patrick shakes his head and turns to the door. "Aye, out you go, you dog!" Mother shouts.

His face is nearly as red as Mother's now. "I'll be coming back," he says, "and I'll bring the bailiffs with me. We'll see if you're so free with your fists then, madam, for they'll land a punch on anyone who tries to thwart them, man or woman."

He goes. Mother swaggers around the shop, hands on her hips. "I showed him, eh?" she says, not looking at any of us. "He'll not mistake me for a soft touch."

Dada opens the money drawer and piles the coins on the counter top. "You may take these," he says. "Split it between the grocer and the butcher. They'll maybe give us more credit then."

Mother stops swaggering. "What about the coalman? And the landlord?"

Dada sags down, like he's ready for his bed. "Dole it out whatever way you think best."

She goes over to the counter, pokes at the coins, and clamps her lips together the way she does when the notion of shouting has gone off her. My belly rumbles. I want something to eat, but I dinnae think this is the time to say so.

Dr Carruth

Isobel and I sit down to our meal of chops and stewed turnip. There is no conversation between us. No sound but the scrape of cutlery on our plates. The chops – sent in from the nearest cookhouse – are tough as boot-leather. I ordered them well done, for of late I can barely endure the flavour and texture of meat. Any hint of the flesh it once was makes the gorge rise in my throat. Isobel hacks at hers with her knife, staring down at the chop with a look of intense concentration. Her skin is winter-white, apart from the shadows of sleeplessness under her eyes.

Within a week of Isobel's arrival here as my wife, my housekeeper quit her position. I am still puzzled by it. The old woman seemed a steady sort, and had attended well to the domestic requirements of a bachelor such as myself. Her abrupt removal has cast Isobel's spirits down greatly. She tortures herself to think what she might have said or done to offend. My reassurances do nothing to console her, and have in no way thawed the frost between us. The upshot is that we are without a servant, reliant on a daily visit from my mother-in-law's maid-of-all-work to save us from squalor, and the local cookhouse to supply our eatables.

There's a rattle at the front door. I manage to cut a piece from my chop and put it in my mouth. It is stringy, tasteless. Isobel sets down her knife.

"I quite forgot," she says, "we have no one to answer the door. Shall I go?"

I nod in agreement, still chewing my mutton, and listen to the conversation drifting through from the hallway. A man's voice. Isobel returns, half closing the dining room door behind her. "It's a Mr Fenton to see you."

Fenton. It takes a moment for me to remember him. Apothecary and man-midwife. Respectable enough, but of no significance. "Does he not know it's dinner time?"

Isobel fixes me with a cool look. "Shall I send him away?" Her voice has a crisp tone I've not heard before.

I fling down my knife. "No, no. I'll go down to him."

Fenton is waiting in the hallway. He's a man of middle years, his face wizened as a walnut but with a bright intelligence in his eye as he watches me close the dining room door behind me. I decide against showing him into my consulting room.

"I'm sorry tae disturb you and your wife, Dr Carruth," he says, making no effort to soften his common way of speaking. "I wudnae interrupt you if it wisnae gie serious."

"Well then, you may tell me, if it won't keep."

"I was called tae attend a lassie called Jonet Stewart."

"I don't believe I know her."

Fenton smiles. "No, I'm sure you dinnae, for she's only a servant lass. In the house of William Dundas, the advocate." He skewers me with a look. "You've maybe heard o' *him*?"

I feel my face colour. "Of course."

Fenton nods, with a look of satisfaction that infuriates me. His face becomes more serious. "Poor Jonet's in a wild state. There's a fierce heat from her, and…" he glances down at the floor. "It's a wee bit delicate, Dr Carruth."

"Some female affliction, I take it?"

Fenton coughs, and shifts from foot to foot. "Her mistress tells me her private regions are all swelled up and blistered as if she'd been scalded. She has the bloody flux, and a leak of blood too, but I cannae be sure if it's her natural flow or some aspect of the malady."

"Her age?"

"She hasnae reached sixteen yet."

I consider the possibilities. It could be some ferocious manifestation of the pox, or the ill effect of a draught of pennyroyal tea taken to rid her of a misbegotten child. "What sort of young woman is she?"

"Decent, according to her mistress. There couldnae be suspicions of any carry-on with the same wee girl." Fenton shuffles closer to me. "She's been poorly this twenty days past, and shows no sign o' mending."

"Twenty days! And has no other physician attended her?"

Fenton squirms, as if his clothes have suddenly become uncomfortable. "They did call on Dr Irvine last week, but his cures made nae difference. It was him suggested we come tae yourself." Fenton looks at me, a cautious cast to his eye, waiting to see how I will react to this information.

"Twenty days is too long for a pox fever. Too long for almost any fever to persist." I keep my voice steady, non-chalant. "If the lassie's life is in peril I'd best take a look at her. Wait here while I gather my instruments and then we can be on our way." I go quickly to my consulting room at the back of the house and lift my bag. When I return I find Isobel in the hallway, engaging Fenton in conversation.

"I have offered your good lady my apologies for stealing you away," Fenton says.

"I am sure my husband will be able to help this poor lassie," Isobel says, favouring me with a smile. I feel my spirits lift, and remember why I fell in love with her. Tonight, perhaps, I will try again…

I would happily keep silence on our walk to the Dundas house, but Fenton seems determined to talk.

"Your wife is a fine-favoured lassie," he says. "I hear you're only lately wed."

"You hear right," I say, staring straight ahead to avoid his inquisitive eyes.

"And have you no servants about the place?"

Damn him! He misses nothing. "We are without a maid-servant at present."

"That must be a bother to you, and your lady."

I make no reply. We reach the crossroads and turn towards Cowgate where the town becomes busier. There are more

35

gentlemen on foot and horseback here. I scan each one as he approaches, regretting my decision to walk with Fenton. I have some apothecaries among my acquaintance – decent men who attend the Tron Kirk and are members of my lodge – but Fenton has no great standing. The sort who is best suited to selling powders for the cure of Grocer's Itch and Scrivener's Palsy.

The Dundas house looks well enough. It's not the best residence in Perrett's Court, but not the meanest either. In this part of the town you might find lairds and layabouts housed side by side. Fenton knocks on the door. A manservant admits us, and we walk upstairs to the very top of the house, to the sick-chamber.

The tiny room is in near-darkness, with the shutters closed across the window and one lamp burning by the bedside. There's a sharp smell, more like the rank scent of a wild animal than the more familiar sour sweat of a sick person. It takes my eyes a moment or two to adjust to the dim light, and make a first appraisal of my new patient. Jonet Stewart is a stout girl with a full, womanly shape to her in spite of her tender years. She twists beneath the coverlet in the narrow bed, as if she is trying to find comfort in a field of thistles. A woman I take to be the mistress of the house is sitting by her bedside on a stool. The room is so cramped that Fenton and I must stand in the small space between the door and the end of the bed.

Fenton introduces me. "Dr Carruth, Agnes Dundas, wife of William Dundas."

"I hear it was you cured the Laird of Desmond's wife of her trouble," she says, standing up as she speaks. There's a trace of rural Galloway in her accent, still making itself heard through her Edinburgh affectations.

I bow politely at her. "Fenton tells me the girl has been ill this twenty days past."

"Aye." She glances over at Fenton, and then down at the girl. There's something brittle in the way her head moves, as if her nerves are jangled. "At first it was no more than a—" She hesitates, pulls a lace-edged handkerchief from her apron pocket and dabs it at her face.

"Please be frank with me, madam. I am a medical man and you will not embarrass me."

Mistress Dundas holds the handkerchief in front of her eyes and speaks. "It started with a wild pain each time she made water, then a twisting in her guts. I boiled her up some barley water to drink, but her condition didn't mend. She's worse now than ever she was."

"Have you any notion what might have caused it?"

"None at all, Doctor."

"Think back, now. Three weeks ago. Did she, perhaps, eat something that might have been spoiled?"

Mistress Dundas stiffens. "Indeed not. I keep a good larder."

"Well, may I come closer?" She stands there by the bed like a guard dog, and for a moment I think she will not give way, but at length she moves towards the door, allowing me into the gap between the wall and the bed.

I walk to the bedside and sit down. The stool is unsteady on its rickety legs. "Jonet, I am Dr Carruth, and I am come to help you."

Jonet rolls her head from side to side and mumbles something I cannot understand. At least she is responding to the sound of my voice. I lay my hand on her forehead. "A dry fever," I say.

"I mixed a tincture to break it," Fenton says, "but it hasnae worked as yet."

I turn to Mistress Dundas. "I will need to examine her, madam. Do you consent to it?"

"If you must."

I stand again and unfasten the window shutter.

"Oh no, Doctor," Mistress Dundas cries out. "It would-nae be respectable."

I suppress my irritation at the woman's primness. "I can be faster about my work with the light of day shining through the window. Mr Fenton will quit the room while I conduct the examination, and you may stay with me." I speak in my sternest tone, and Mistress Dundas ceases her arguing.

With the shutters open and Fenton banished to the landing outside the bedroom I gently lift the coverlet off Jonet. Heat rises off her like the blast from a forge. Her nightdress is tangled in her legs, and stained with the leavings of the bloody flux. I pull the nightdress up to expose her lower body. Mistress Dundas whimpers quietly as I look more closely at Jonet's private regions. They are as distended as any I've seen on newly delivered women, and further bloated by water blisters as large as cooked barley grains. The blisters are at their worst around the girl's urethra, which suggests that the affliction is related to the urine rather than any amatory misdeeds. "You say she is greatly pained when she makes water?"

"Aye, Doctor."

I lay my hand against the girl's belly. It is tight and swollen. Her bladder must be filled to bursting. I feel her flinch, although my hands are soft and I hope my touch is gentle. "When did she last make water?"

"Not for a good few hours now. It was such agony for her, I think she must be afeard to go at all."

"Is it still in the chamber pot?"

"Certainly not, Doctor. I keep a clean house."

"Do you recall what colour her water was?"

"A sort of pinky-brown, sir. Not natural." She peers over my shoulder at Jonet, then moves quickly back. "I'd have kept it if I'd known it was important."

I make the girl respectable again. This is a puzzle. I have never seen a female pudendum with quite such an affliction. Undoubtedly she is in agony from the swelling and blisters. It is almost certainly the urine that is the cause of it. What agent could have made her natural water so poisonous? Sour in, sour out, the old wives say. It *must* be something she has eaten.

"Mistress Dundas, are you quite sure that Jonet hasn't eaten or drunk anything these last weeks that might have upset her constitution?"

Jonet turns again on the bed, and tries to speak. Mistress Dundas motions for me to stand, and I exchange places with her. She sits, and leans in close to Jonet. "What's that, lassie? What do you say?"

Jonet speaks again, but her voice is so low and hoarse that I can't make her out. Mistress Dundas looks up at me. "I think she said something about sweeties."

"Sweeties?"

Jonet speaks again, louder this time, but her words are still incomprehensible to me.

"Aye, I think so," Mistress Dundas says.

"Would you know what sweeties they might be?"

"She's had no sweeties I know of since Handsel Day."

I glance around the room. Apart from the bed and stool there is no other furniture. A small jug and basin sit on the floor in the corner behind the door. "Is this Jonet's bedchamber?"

Mistress Dundas looks flustered. "Aye, and it does her well enough. What more would she need?"

"Where does she keep her belongings? She must have a change of linen? A gown for kirk-going?"

"There's a chest below the bed there." She gives me a sharp-eyed look. "Do you want to hoke through it, Dr Carruth?"

I dislike her turn of phrase. It makes me sound like a sneak. However, that is indeed what I want. "It may be that we'll find some solution there to what has made her so ill."

"You think if you ken that then you'll ken better how to mend her?"

"That's it exactly, Mistress Dundas." She's shrewd. I'll give her that. I kneel down and reach under the bed.

"Mind the chamber pot," Mistress Dundas says tartly.

It's awkward trying to pull the chest out with so little space in the room. I grow hot and flustered in the attempt, conscious of Mistress Dundas's eyes on me. "Perhaps Fenton and I could carry this out on to the landing," I suggest. "It may disturb Jonet less if I inspect it there." Mistress Dundas opens the door and ushers Fenton in to help me with my task.

Together we lift the chest and carry it out on to the landing. The light is poor, so Mistress Dundas shouts down the stairs for someone to bring a lamp. For a few moments the three of us stand there, an uneasy silence settling on us. A girl comes up the stairs carrying a lighted lamp.

"Hold it up high, Mary," Mistress Dundas says. I take Mary to be her daughter. They share the same nervous movements.

I open the lid of the chest. Its contents are disordered. "Och, Jonet, you clarty girl," Mistress Dundas says, as if the servant girl were present to hear her chastisement.

I begin to remove Jonet's belongings. First a dress – the fabric is well worn, but respectable enough for her weekly visit to the kirk. I hand it to Fenton. There's a tangle of petticoats, chemises and stockings. I turn to Mistress Dundas. "Would you be good enough to take out these garments?" Mary gives a little snigger, which ceases abruptly at a glance from her mother. Mistress Dundas gathers up the underclothes and hugs them firmly to her bosom.

With the chest empty of clothes we peer into it. There is a bundle of papers tied up with a length of twine, and a plain lacquer box. The sight of the box makes me stop short. It is the very mate of the one Isobel brought with her when she came home with me the day after our wedding day. For a moment I think I will lose my composure at the memory.

Mistress Dundas throws down her bundle and snatches out the papers. She unlooses the twine and inspects them. I steady myself and glance over at the papers. They seem to be nothing but song sheets and penny handbills. Mistress Dundas mutters vague, disapproving comments as she leafs through them. I take a deep breath, reach into the chest and lift out the lacquer box. It is a little more than half a foot in length. The contents rattle, but it feels so light that it could be empty. Isobel's contains an ivory comb and a collection of the strange items women require to dress their hair.

"Where did Jonet come by this box?" I say.

"I couldn't tell you." Mistress Dundas gathers the papers back together again. "I can't understand why she has taken to this sort of vanity."

I open the box. Inside are several hairpins, along with a small pasteboard carton. The carton bears some similarities to the ones the apothecaries use to pack their pills and powders, but it is an unusual shape: a hexagon, rather than the more usual square or circle. I turn it upside down, but there is no mark or signature on its underside. When I open the carton I find a residue of what looks like sugar. I lick my finger, dab it into the pale dust and taste it. Yes, sugar right enough, but with some curious aftertaste.

"Do you know what this carton contained, Mistress Dundas, or where Jonet might have come by it?"

"Indeed I do not." She looks from the carton to the unsuitable song sheets and back again, as if she cannot quite believe that Jonet has kept secrets from her.

I glance up at the daughter. "What about you, Miss Dundas?"

"Me?" The girl looks startled to have been addressed.

"Aye. Did Jonet make any mention to you of anything out of the ordinary?"

"No," she snaps.

"Perhaps I may take a wee keek at it?" says Fenton. He puts Jonet's Sunday dress back in the chest and extends his hand towards me. Much as it irks me to do it, I can see the wisdom of letting him inspect the carton.

"The boxes you pack your pills and powders in – where do you get them?" I say. "It strikes me that if I could find the apothecary who prepared whatever was in this carton, I might be closer to knowing what ails Jonet."

"There's only the one supplier of pasteboard cartons in the Burgh," he says. "Some apothecaries may order theirs in from further afield, but the most of us go to McAllister the boxmaker, at the bottom of Hackerston's Wynd."

I stand up and let Mistress Dundas put Jonet's other belongings back in the chest. "Very well. I will prepare a soothing poultice for young Jonet which I will have carried to you here. Then I'll seek out this McAllister and see what he has to tell me."

Fenton hands the carton back to me, then tilts his head and clasps his hands together like a beggar on the prowl for spare change. "I have a fine supply of medicaments in my own place of business, Dr Carruth, if I can be of service to you."

"I have a receipt of my own devising for the poultice, I thank you."

"Ah, yes, I understand." Fenton knows – like all in his trade – the importance of preserving the secrecy of our special formulations. "Then perhaps I can approach Mr McAllister on your behalf, to save you the bother, you being so busy."

I pause before speaking, fearing that my irritation with Fenton will be too obvious in my voice. "Forgive me, Fenton, but I would rather resolve these matters myself."

Mistress Dundas leads us down the stairs, with Mary to the rear, lighting our way. As we reach the second landing a door opens and I catch a glimpse of a girl's face and a gleam of red hair. Mary sets the lamp down on a table and slips into the room, closing the door firmly behind her.

"How many daughters do you have, Mistress Dundas?"

"Just the one," she says. "The other lassie is Elizabeth Edmonstone, the Laird of Duntreath's daughter. She lodges with us, what with the troubles being as they are just now in Stirlingshire."

"Aye, the countryside is a dangerous place these days."

"Murder and outrage in every corner. My husband complains of the additional expense of her biding here, for we'll get no benefit from it."

"Still, it must be pleasant for your daughter to have a companion."

Mistress Dundas does not reply.

Thomas

I clap my hands over my lugs and stare as hard as I can at the book before me. "*Amo, amas, amat,*" I say to myself. "*Amamus, amatis, amant.*" It's no good. Mother's voice finds its way past my fingers, past my Latin, and goes right into my head. She's not screeching, but she's giving Dada a right chewing. I look across the table at Katharine. Her face is all screwed up as she studies her book. She moves her lips as she reads, and disnae seem to hear Mother at all. Anna shifts beside me on the bench. She stares out the window into the close.

There's a rap at the door and Mother stops her blether. "Who's that now? Eh? Someone else looking for money?" She stomps over to the door and opens it a crack. I keek round, but I cannae see who it is. She slams the door and birls round to Dada. "It's a Doctor Someone-or-other to see you. Do you owe money to them now too?"

Dada straightens up. "He might be here to buy something."

Mother does the laugh that means she's not really laughing, but she disnae stop Dada going to the door. He opens it wide, and now I can see the man standing there, although it's so dark on the landing I cannae make much of him out, except that he's tall and disnae look poor. Dada talks to him a minute, and then brings him in.

"Now children, wife," says Dada, "this is Dr Carruth. He is a very important medical man." Dr Carruth stands all stiff and still, but his eyes flitter around, looking at everything – the room, the furniture, Mother's gown, me. I've never seen any man with a face like his. You wouldnae know what he was thinking.

Dada coughs, the way he does when he's serving the gentry. "I have established a small pharmacopeia in the side

44

room here," he says, leading Dr Carruth across the floor and into the wee room. *Pharmacopeia*. I like that word. I practise saying it in my head. Then I slither off the bench and follow them, juking in past Dr Carruth.

I clasp Dada's hand. "May I watch, Dada?" I look up at him, watching his face.

"Of course you may, Thomas," he says. "Remember, you must call me 'Father', not 'Dada'. You are not a baby any more."

"Yes, Father," I say, and wait for his smile, but he's looking at Dr Carruth.

"Do you have children yourself, Doctor?"

"No," Dr Carruth says, with a snap in his voice. "I am not long married."

"Time enough, then," Dada says. He picks up a wee jar of ointment from a shelf and polishes it with his sleeve then sets it back. "Our space here is a bit confined, as you see, but the lease on my last shop was not satisfactory, so…" He looks up at Dr Carruth, and his eyes are going blink, blink, blink. "I beg your pardon," he says. "You wanted to talk to me about…?"

"I have a patient, a girl called Jonet Stewart. Do you know of her?" Dada shakes his head and Dr Carruth takes a carton out of his pocket. It's an odd shape, like the cartons Dada uses for special medicines.

Dada looks at it and his face goes all pale, and then all pink. "Oh," he says. "That's one of mine, is it?"

"There's no mark on it to indicate so, but McAllister the boxmaker tells me you recently ordered a number of them from him."

"Aye, well…" Dada shrugs. "If you would be so good as to tell Mr McAllister that I will be in a position to settle my account with him very soon. Within the month."

Dr Carruth looks none too pleased. "Do you take me for McAllister's debt collector?"

"No, no, of course not…" Dada looks confused.

45

"Tell me, Mr Aikenhead, do you use this shape of box for some particular treatment?"

Dada laughs. "Well, yes." He looks down at me. "You run back out to your sisters, Thomas."

"Och, Dada... Father... I want to stay here and learn the medicines."

Dada sighs. "Promise me you won't carry tales to your mother."

"I promise."

"He's bright as a button," Dada says to Dr Carruth, "and I don't want to be handing the wife any more weapons to beat me with."

"The carton, Mr Aikenhead. What did it contain?" Dr Carruth's voice is like a minister's, all sober and serious.

Dada laughs again, and that seems to make Dr Carruth sterner still, so Dada stops laughing and says, "Well, it is a little combination of my own devising called a *pastille espagnole*."

"A pastille? You mean something like a... sweetie?"

"Aye, they're not unlike sweeties, but not as... sweet."

"Mr Aikenhead, my young patient lies dangerously ill. She is in the grip of a dry fever, and her private regions are afflicted with the most ferocious blistering I have ever encountered. Is there a chance that these pastilles of yours might have been the cause of her condition?"

"Oh, dear, dear, dear..." Dada's all of a fluster. He turns to the shelves of jars and bottles and hokes around, clinking them all together so hard he'll crack them. Then he lifts out a wee shiny jar with a big, wide cork for a stopper. He opens it and holds it out to Dr Carruth.

The doctor leans over to inspect the contents, but jumps back straight away. "Dear God," he says, and pulls a handkerchief from his pocket to cover his nose and mouth. "The stench of it is foul."

"Aye, it's sharp, right enough," says Dada, "but it's beautiful to look at, don't you think? See how it gleams." He tilts the jar, and I stand on tippy-toes so as to see inside it. It's full of dull brown powder, but when Dada rocks the jar from side to side the powder shifts and changes colour. One moment it's green, the next gold, the next brown again. A magic powder.

"What in the name of heaven is it?" says Dr Carruth.

"You're not familiar with it, Doctor?" Dada smiles. I smile too, because Dada knows something that Dr Carruth disnae. "Crushed blister beetle," Dada says. "Known to some as the Spanish fly."

Dr Carruth goes all pink in the face. "You make and sell such… aids to concupiscence?" he says. That's a new word for me. I've not heard it before. *Concups…* I can't say it, even inside my head.

"There's many a respectable married couple have need of it, and there's no sin in matrimonial delight, is there, Doctor?"

Dr Carruth opens his mouth, but no words come out. His face goes all red. "And what need has an innocent young girl, scarcely sixteen years of age, of such an item?" he says. His minister's voice has gone ever so quiet, but he's all a tremble as if he's angry.

Dada shrinks down, like he does when Mother is in a rage. "I wouldn't know that, sir."

"For God's sake, put the filthy stuff away. What were you thinking of, selling such a thing to a child?"

"I am certain, sir… well, as certain as I can be… that I did not sell my *pastilles espagnole* to any young girl. I cannot rightly recall who…" He puts the jar back on the shelf, then opens the cupboard where he keeps the ledgers. "I keep records, you see. There'll be a note of my customers in here somewhere." I remember the tall man who came to Dada's shop to buy tablets, and how I followed him to where he stayed. Maybe there was someone in the house waiting for him, waiting for the tablets. I saw someone keeking out the window, I'm sure I did. Maybe it was this servant lassie that's so ill, who Dr Carruth is trying to save.

"Never mind that now," says Dr Carruth. "What of an antidote?"

"An antidote? Well, I couldn't be sure. Perhaps, if I had my books about me, but they're packed away at my cousin's house. Lack of space here, as you see."

Dr Carruth shakes his head. "I have no wish to waste my time here any longer, Mr Aikenhead. You may pray that I can devise some treatment for my unfortunate patient. If I do not, you may find yourself in worse straits yet." He strides out of the room, and Dada and I follow after him.

"She must have eaten them all down in the one go," Dada says. "If she'd taken them one at a time, as advised, she'd have come to no harm."

Dr Carruth disnae say anything back. He marches straight past the table where Katharine and Anna still sit at their books, and disnae even look at Mother. As soon as the door closes behind him I clap my hands over my lugs. There's bound to be screeching now.

Dr Carruth

The reading rooms of the university's medical library are bright with the natural daylight flooding in through the tall windows, but it is a different matter among the bookshelves. Each aisle is like a dim cloister, kept dark and dry the better to preserve the books. I avail myself of one of the library lanterns and search the shelves reserved for the newest medical publications. At last I find the book I am seeking: the most recent volume from Thomas Sydenham. It is a slim book, for which I am thankful. There is no time to spare in finding a treatment for Jonet. I have come here directly from my visit to that wretch Aikenhead, pausing only to send a brief note to Mistress Dundas telling her the cause of Jonet's illness. Now I take the book from the shelf, find an empty desk in the reading room, and apply myself to Sydenham's clear accounts of the symptoms and treatments for the most novel afflictions torturing the population.

I am so absorbed in my reading that I am only vaguely aware of the other people moving about the library. After a time though I grow conscious of someone standing behind me, peering over my shoulder. I turn in some annoyance, and see that it is Dr Maxwell.

"Ah, Carruth, I thought it was you," he says.

"What the devil do you think you're doing, watching over me like a schoolmaster?"

Maxwell smirks. "Now, Carruth, don't condemn me for taking a scholarly interest in your reading matter." He pulls out a stool from a nearby empty desk and sits down. The whole movement is conducted with an effortless animal grace, like a cat stretching before settling on its favoured cushion. "What is it you're puzzling over?"

"I'm looking for an antidote for an excess of… the Spanish fly."

He laughs loudly enough to draw censorious looks from several of the other readers in the room. This does not appear to concern him. He leans both elbows on the desk and rests his chin on his hands. "Never had the need of it myself. Surely not you, Carruth? Is your lovely wife demanding more than you can supply?"

I will stay calm although my face must be aflame. He knows nothing, after all. I suppress the memory of my most recent humiliation only a night or two ago. I was so determined to overcome my weakness, to make my marriage a true one. But no. All hope was dashed again. I persuade myself that Maxwell means nothing by his comment. It is no more than the flippant crudity of one who fancies himself a wit. "I know that these matters give you great amusement," I say, "but I have a young patient in grave danger of her life, so if you can contribute something wise on the subject I beg you do so now."

Maxwell considers this for a moment. "The Spanish fly. *Lytta vesicatoria*. Spirit of camphor, as I recall, can ease the inflammation." His mouth twitches with a smile. "Did I ever tell you about the time I was called to treat the Laird of… let's call him Laird N. An old man with a young wife. The poor old lad had taken such a dose of Spanish fly that he rose up and couldn't droop down, if you get my meaning…"

"Spirit of camphor, then," I say, cutting off his reminiscences.

He points at the book in front of me. "That's Sydenham's latest, eh? He's a great advocate of camphorated tincture of opium. The opium will calm the agitation and ease the pain. That might do the work for you."

"I've not used it before."

"Keep the dose low – only a drop or two in watered wine. You don't want to kill the girl."

50

I rise and put the book back on the shelf. Camphorated tincture of opium is a novel treatment, and one I do not have in my own dispensary. I must find an apothecary – I suppose it is only fair to give Fenton the custom – and equip myself with this new medicine.

Maxwell follows me out of the library. "I may as well keep you company, Carruth. I only came to the library in search of some diversion."

"Have you no work to attend to?"

Maxwell shrugs. "There's some dull meeting of the Royal College later," he says. "I suppose I must show my face. Have you not been invited to become a Fellow?"

"No." I jog down the library steps and out on to the street.

Still Maxwell follows me. "I'll put in a word for you, if you like."

I cannot trust myself to reply with civility, and stride on in the direction of Fenton's place of business. Maxwell looks unconcerned at my silence and keeps pace with me, nodding at acquaintances as we pass them, raising his hat to an inordinate number of ladies. At last a group of younger men hail him, and invite him to join with them in a nearby coffee house. "It grieves me to abandon you, Carruth," he says, "for you do interest me greatly. These young fellows are much simpler souls, but their hunger for my company is gratifying. They will, no doubt, be full of ideas on how to pacify Scotland – who should be hanged, who should be spared. If the King but knew there were such military geniuses in the coffee houses of Edinburgh the country's troubles would be over in a trice." He parts from me with an exuberant bow and continues with his new, more admiring companions. Their laughter drifts across the crowded street. It seems that all heads turn in his direction.

Fenton seems pleased to see me, and anxious to hear what I have discovered about the cause of Jonet's trouble. "James Aikenhead, eh?" He shakes his head sadly.

"Do you know him?"

"He used tae have his shop just across there. A decent enough body, but no sense with money."

He listens carefully as I describe the noxious blister beetle and the suggested remedy. I say nothing about Maxwell being the source of the suggestion regarding camphorated tincture of opium.

"I can make some up readily enough," Fenton says. "Shall we proceed?"

When I return to the Dundas residence I find Jonet badly agitated, although Mistress Dundas declares that the poultice I prepared earlier has given some relief. The girl tosses on the bed, wide-eyed and frantic as if in the grip of a waking nightmare. A brief examination shows that there has been no improvement in the blistering of her secret parts.

"Fetch a pint of weak wine," I order. "I will lace it with a new treatment recommended by the best Cambridge men."

Mistress Dundas does as she is bid. When she returns with the cup of wine I take it from her and add two drops of camphorated opium. The room fills with the clear, healthful forest smell of camphor. "See if you can sit her up, Mistress Dundas."

The girl is raised readily enough and I hold the cup to her lips. She drains it thirstily, and I signal for Mistress Dundas to lay her back upon the bed. Within a few minutes she has calmed, her breath slowing into the deep, easeful rhythms of sleep. "That's a marvellous draught you've given her, Dr Carruth," Mistress Dundas says, leaning over and stroking Jonet's hair.

"It should subdue her disturbance of body and mind for some hours, but we must then see if it has eased the terrible inflammation of her more delicate regions."

Mistress Dundas leads me down from Jonet's attic bedroom. "I told my husband the news you sent me about this apothecary and his vile pastilles," she says. "He said he wanted to have a wee word with you." She shows me into a cramped study with a desk piled elbow-deep in documents, and her husband, William Dundas, barely visible behind them. He rises to shake my hand. His face is an angry red, made fiercer looking by a jet-black wig in the London style.

"I'm minded to take this Aikenhead fellow to law, Dr Carruth," he says without pausing for any niceties. "He has cost me dear. I've had to engage a new servant in Jonet's stead, and no doubt you'll have a bill for me one of these days."

"You are the advocate, Mr Dundas," I say. "I can't imagine you need my advice on matters of law."

He fixes me with a beady look. "Aye, but should not Aikenhead be pursued for selling dangerous medicines? Surely you have a view on that?"

I think of Aikenhead, cringing and tittering as he showed me his wretched collection of treatments. Nothing would please me more than that his type be held to account for their recklessness, and it might advance my standing with the Fellows of the Royal College. Still, it will not do to have William Dundas think he can direct me. "You make a good point, Dundas," I say. "Let me give it some thought."

Dr Irvine will find nothing exceptional in my calling on him. It will be no more than a courtesy to thank him for referring Jonet Stewart's case to me. We can discuss her progress. I can tell him about the treatment I devised for her. I walk straight from Perrett's Court to his residence, and am advised by the servant that I will find him at the Royal College of Physicians. It is less than a quarter-mile from Dr Irvine's house; long enough a walk for me to compose myself, and prepare my words.

The college is still half covered with rickety scaffolding. A stonemason is perched like a crow on the highest part of the structure, chipping with his chisel at an architrave above one of the windows. My feet crunch on brick dust as I walk up the front steps, and the building echoes with the rat-tat-tat of the carpenters' hammers. A grim-faced porter signals for me to follow him up the stairs to the first floor. "Now, sir," he says when we turn into the comparative peace of the corridor. "How may I help you?"

I explain my purpose, and he nods. "Dr Irvine likes to come here for his noon refresher, although if I had my choice I'd stay well away until these labouring men have finished their work." He leads me further along the corridor, up another flight of stairs, and stops in front of a half-opened door. "I've a visitor here for you, Dr Irvine. It's a Dr–" He turns and looks at me questioningly.

"Carruth," I repeat.

"Dr Carruth."

"Send him in, man," Dr Irvine calls. He sounds in good spirits.

The porter ushers me into the room. As I walk in Dr Irvine rises from his seat at a small table and reaches out his hand to me. "Young Carruth!" he exclaims. His handshake is crushing. "You find me labouring at my papers, and sustaining myself with a drop of *uisge beatha*." There's a bottle on the table with a well-filled tumbler beside it. "You'll join me, of course?" He doesn't wait for my reply, but lifts an empty snifter glass from the windowsill, rubs it clean with his pocket handkerchief, and pours a generous measure of whisky into it. He hands me the glass, raises his own, and we drink each other's good health. The whisky scalds its way down my throat. "Sit down, Carruth, sit down. What think you of our new premises, eh?"

"Most impressive."

"And what brings you here this fine day?" He turns his face to the uncurtained window and basks in the sunshine like a cat. It is a fine day, I realise. I have been so preoccupied I have not even noted the mildness in the air.

"I wanted to thank you, sir, for recommending me to William Dundas in the case of his unfortunate servant girl."

Dr Irvine nods. "She'd quite defeated me, and I recalled

your interest in – *intimate mortifications*." He gives a little smile as he speaks, but it does not irk me as it might have done on any other man's face.

"I've treated her with an array of medicaments, but the thing which has been most efficacious has been tincture of camphorated opium. Her pain is greatly lessened. I am hopeful she will live, but whether or not there will be lasting damage I cannot say." I swallow down the rest of my whisky.

Dr Irvine refills my glass. "An odd malady, don't you think?"

"And I know who caused it." My face feels hot. I wish he would open a window, but then I suppose we would be troubled by the sound of hammering from the workmen. "She consumed a dangerous tablet made by an apothecary called Aikenhead."

Dr Irvine raises his eyebrows. "And what ailment was this treatment intended to cure?"

I drink some more of my whisky. I scarcely notice its burning in my throat now, although it sits uneasily in my stomach. "Aikenhead called it his *pastille espagnole*. The Spanish fly, in the form of a sweetie, the better to appeal to young women."

"Designed to heat the blood of the lassies, eh?"

"Indeed. But ill-judged. Ill-made. This Aikenhead is a reckless fellow. On his uppers. I fear he has put profit before the health of his customers."

Dr Irvine stares into his whisky tumbler, frowning as if in deep thought. "If these pastilles are so dangerous I'm surprised we haven't seen more cases such as this one."

That had not occurred to me. I curse my own stupidity. "Perhaps they disagreed with the girl's constitution," I suggest. "That will be the case with one in every hundred medicaments." As I speak I hear the flaw in my argument, and see the prospect of bringing Aikenhead to law recede. None of us – physician or apothecary – wants to encourage every dissatisfied patient to seek redress. We would all be the worse for it.

"And yet," says Dr Irvine, "it seems to me that a powerful substance such as the Spanish fly should not be sold willy-nilly to any that ask for it."

"You think there should be some... control over it?"

"Aye. Only a qualified man should have authority to pre-scribe it, don't you think? There are other considerations too. Morality, decency... It should only be made available to married people. God made such substances as an aid to conjugal felicity, not as a tool of debauchery." Dr Irvine drains his tumbler and sets it down on the table with undue force. "Let me give this some consideration, Carruth. You may know we've been troubled by apothecaries selling all manner of medicines they know little about. Our misguided patients flock to them, thinking to save themselves a doc-tor's fee. It may be that Mr Aikenhead is the very man to be made an example of."

By the time I reach home I am hot and perspiring. It is past lunchtime, and my head is light with hunger and throb-bing from the effects of the whisky. I climb the stairs to the dining room and find the table laid but no food served. When I step out of the room I see Isobel, peeping round the door of her parlour. "Will you come in, Robert? There's a girl come about the situation. Her name is Susan."

In my muddle I think at first that she means the situation with Jonet Stewart and Aikenhead's *pastilles espagnole*, but then I realise she is referring to our search for a servant. I follow her into the parlour.

The young woman rising from her seat to greet me is clearly from the lower classes. Her cloak is cheap, albeit reasonably clean, and I suspect she is not the first owner of her bonnet. Her hair, I note, is black as a raven's wing. There's something impertinent in the tilt of her head. "I heard you were after a housekeeper," she says.

I can't place her accent. Ayrshire, perhaps? "How did you hear of this?"

Isobel touches my arm. "I had asked Mother to keep an ear out for a reliable girl in search of a place."

"We servants talk to one another," the girl says. Her face is expressionless. No hint of insolence now, but there is something unreadable in her eyes. "I have a letter of reference. A good one." She nods over to Isobel, who I notice is holding an opened letter.

"Well, let us all sit down," Isobel says, "and I shall read what this letter reports."

"I am from the north of Ireland," the woman says, settling herself in her chair. "I was in service there, near Carrickfergus."

"Why did you leave?" Isobel speaks without raising her eyes from the letter.

"I thought I'd have better chances in Scotland."

That can't be the whole reason. There'll be a faithless sweetheart, or an ill-tempered laird, or some other cause. Perhaps the lady of the house mistrusted those dark, watchful eyes.

Isobel puts the letter down and looks at her. "So, Susan," she says. "You must work hard in this house, for you will be the only servant."

"Yes, miss."

I glance over at Isobel. She has made this decision without reference to me. Of course. It is for the wife to manage the servants. I must shape myself to what it is to be a married man. "Might I suggest," I say, and hesitate when both women turn to stare at me, "that we engage Susan for a trial period. Let us say a week."

Susan looks down at her hands. For a moment I think she means to object. But no.

"That seems sensible, sir. But I'll get a week's pay, even if I don't suit you?"

"Of course."

She nods. "Then we are agreed."

Thomas

I'm sitting on the warm step out in the close. I close my eyes and look up at the sun. All I can see is red. Dada says that's because my eyelids are thin as paper and full of blood, and the sun shines right through them like it shines through coloured glass. He says I must never look at the sun with my eyes open, or it would burn my eyeballs clean away. I open my eyes just a wee bit, and then a wee bit more, but the light hurts me, so I look down. Every time I blink I see a flash of that light again. I've maybe blinded myself. How will I tell Dada, after him telling me not to do it? I'll need to be led about for the rest of my days. Katharine will have to do that. I blink some more and my eyes come back to normal.

Keep-Count Man is sitting beside me, writing in his wee book. He mutters to himself. Only stops when he licks the tip of his pencil. Mutter, mutter, mutter. I cannae make out what he's saying. The pages in his book are all covered in marks and lines. He sees me looking. "Aye, *regardez vous*, wee lad," he says. "Do you ken what I'm keeping tally o' here?"

"No, mister," I say.

He points a grubby finger at the pages. "It's all those as is killed," he says. "Right-hand page for our ones, and left-hand page for their ones."

"What's 'our ones' and 'their ones'?"

"You should pay more mind to the state of the country, wee lad. Their ones are the Covenanters, and a wheen of bad articles they are."

"What do they do that's bad?"

"They'd overturn the King, son, if we let them."

I look closer at the book. Both pages are near full of marks and lines.

"Do you ken your numbers, wee lad?"

"Aye."

"Tell me how many is killed, then." He hands me the book.

"Does each mark mean one killed?"

Keep-Count Man cackles with his mouth wide open so I can see the gaps where he used to have teeth. He wags his head and pokes me in the shoulder. "You dinnae ken as much as you think you do, eh?"

"I'm only asking. How else will I find out?"

He stops laughing and snatches the book back from me. "Each of these is one dead," he says pointing at a row of four marks. "When the tally comes to five, I put a line through the four, like I've done there." He runs his finger along a line of marks. I can see that they're in sets of four, with a line drawn through each one.

"They look like wee gates," I say. "And each one means five killed?"

"Aye. You have it now."

I count the gates on the right-hand page. "Forty-four of ours killed? Is that right?"

He nods, his eyes all full of light and glitter. "And what about their ones?"

Quickly I tot the numbers on the left-hand page. "Only thirty-five." I feel like I do when I'm losing a game against Katharine. "Does that mean they're winning?"

"Dinnae worry, wee lad. The score will be better balanced by the end of this day, for there's three of their ones tae be hanged in the Grassmarket."

Just then a window opens in the tenement up above us. We both look up. Dada pokes his head out the window. "Thomas," he hisses. "Take this for me, will you?" Dada ducks back in, and the next thing I see at the window is a big satchel with a bit of rope tied around its handles. It tips over the edge and dangles for a moment, then slowly, slowly, gets lowered down. I jump up and run over to take hold of it when it gets near enough for me to reach. I steer it to the ground. Dada keeks out again. "Untie the rope, son," he says. I do as I'm bid, and Dada pulls the rope back up.

Keep-Count Man has been watching the whole performance. "Are youse for flitting, wee lad?" he says.

"I dinnae know." I hope not. I hate flitting.

Dada appears at the door. He's come down the stairs so quietly I didn't hear him. I run over to him, but stop short when he puts his finger to his lips. He takes me by the hand and we creep along, staying close to the wall of our tenement. "Run over and pick up the satchel," he says when we get near it. Keep-Count Man is watching us. He catches my eye and winks. I pick up the satchel like Dada asked and bring it back to him. It's heavy – so heavy it near tugs the arm off me. Dada takes it, and we carry on with our creeping until we reach the entry. "Good work, Thomas," says Dada. "Out we go."

We slip out the entry and into the wynd. Once we're up at the big road Dada walks faster with me trotting after him holding his coat-tail. I start to cry, thinking I'll never see Katharine or Anna again. Dada stops, sets the satchel on the ground and hunkers down to talk to me. "What's wrong, Thomas?"

"Can we not bring Katharine and Anna?"

"Sure they've work to do helping your mother." He looks at me all sad and serious. "We're not running away, Thomas," he says. "You don't think I'd run off and leave your mother and your sisters behind, do you?"

I stare down at the pavement, for I don't want him to see that that's what I did think. He takes hold of my chin very gently and lifts my face up to look at him. "I'd never do that, Thomas, no matter how bad things get." His eyes look all watery. Then he smiles and springs up. "Today, son, we're going to make some money." He lifts the satchel and marches off.

I run along behind him. "How will we do that, Dada? I mean, Father?"

"Watch and learn, my boy. Watch and learn."

We reach a crossroads where a wide street and a narrow street meet. There are people everywhere, pushing and elbowing. A preacher is standing on one corner, guldering about Jehovah and damnation. Beside him there's a man selling brandy by the spoonful. He takes a penny pay and holds the spoon to a customer's lips like Mother does when she's giving us a purging medicine. The customer slurps the brandy down. Then the man wipes the spoon on his breeks and turns to the next in line.

"Here's a fine spot for us," Dada says, pointing to a grand building with a wide, low wall around it. "Up we go!" He jumps up and reaches to pull me after him. "Open up the satchel now, then stand up straight and look appealing."

I unfasten the satchel. It's packed with wee bottles and cardboard pillboxes. "The best physic in Edinburgh," Dada shouts. "Only sixpence a cure, ladies and gentlemen. Sixpence a cure! Yes indeed, Aikenhead's Universal Medicine promises regularity of stool, relief of all known pains, prevention of fever, calming of the nerves and lifting of the spirits. And all for sixpence! I have it in tablet form. I have it in liquid form. Whichever your preference is, that I can supply."

Some of the passers-by stop and listen. Dada has told me to look appealing, but I'm not sure what that means. Should I put on a happy face, or a sad one? A woman smiles at me and nudges her companion. "Look at thon bairn," she says.

"Och, he's like a wee angel," her friend replies.

I have an idea. I reach into the satchel and take out one bottle and one pillbox. I hold them both up, one in each hand, so that the crowd can see what they'll be getting. The smiling woman hokes out her purse and presents a coin. "How often must it be taken?" she calls up to Dada.

"Once a day for prevention, madam, and three times a day for cure. Is it the tablets you want, or the liquid?"

"Liquid will go down easier," she says, and hands him the money.

"Give the lady her medicine, Thomas," Dada says, and I pass the bottle over to her with a little bow. Dada winks at me, quick and clever, so that no one in the crowd can see. He's pleased with me.

We sell another bottle, and then some tablets, and then I lose count of what we sell. But as quick as it began, the selling stops. Everyone starts moving away, turning up towards the far end of one of the wide streets. It's as if they're being sucked up into it. The preacher stops preaching and follows them. The brandy-man serves one more customer – it's a tall man. I think I know him, but I cannae mind from where. He takes his spoonful of brandy and walks off, with big long steps like a horse. I mind him now. The man who came into Dada's shop to buy the special tablets, the man I followed. He has his hat pulled down low, same as he did that day. He turns around and looks at me and Dada. I'm glad when he's out of sight. He goes the opposite way to everyone else.

"We may pack up now," says Dada. "We'll hardly sell anything more."

"Where are the people all going?" I ask.

"They're away to the Grassmarket."

What was it Keep-Count Man said about the Grassmarket? I peer up towards the end of the street, but I can see nothing but people, packed even tighter than they are on market day. Drums are thundering. There's another sound that starts quiet and gets louder, like the wind roaring over our roof on a stormy night. I realise it's the crowd – they're making all that noise. Oh, aye, the hanging. Three of their ones are to be hanged, that's what the Keep-Count Man said. My insides are trembly. I feel like I could step off this wee wall and skirl up into the air like a bird. "I want to see the hanging," I shout.

"You don't, Thomas, you don't," Dada says. He has the satchel closed up. "Come on now. We can buy bread on the way home, and some sugar candy."

I jump down from the wall. "Please, Dada! Let's go up to the Grassmarket." I grab his free hand and try to pull him.

"No, Thomas." He's not moving, no matter how hard I tug. "Stop that now, afore I get cross with you." His voice is louder than I've ever heard it – angry-loud, like Mother always sounds. I look up at him and his face is all frowns and lines. I've never seen that face on him before. My eyes feel stingy.

He bends down and takes me by the shoulders. "Don't cry, Thomas. Crying is for bairns." He's not so angry now.

"Why can't we go to the Grassmarket? Just for a minute. Just to see."

"To see three poor men dance from the end of a rope?" Dada shakes his head. "It would give you bad dreams, Thomas. And me too. Come along now. Let's see what your sisters say when we come in the door with a bag of sugar candy."

Dr Carruth

I wake early and ill-slept. The room is still dark beyond the bed curtains. My mouth is dry and my head heavy. Too much port wine last evening. Another vain attempt in the marriage bed. Tonight I will abstain from strong liquor.

There's a tap on the door. I hear it open, and the soft tread of feet on the floorboards. It must be Susan, I suppose. She's at the fireplace, redding out yesterday's ashes. Somehow she manages to complete the task quietly. The rasp of the brush and the scrape of the shovel are strangely soothing. A few moments more and I hear the crackle of a new blaze. The arctic chill in the air thaws a little, and I am suddenly very glad to have a servant again. I suppose Isobel must have instructed her to set the fires in the morning. With a pang of embarrassment I realise that Susan must therefore be aware of our sleeping arrangements – Isobel in the main bedchamber, and I skulking in the return room at the top of the stairs. Pray God she is discreet. She has a closed-up look, like a woman capable of keeping a secret, but looks mean nothing. What was it she said that first day she came to us? Something about servants talking to each other?

Isobel and I sit opposite each other at the table, each with a bowl of porridge in front of us. I take a spoonful. It has a gritty texture and barely any taste. Isobel grimaces as she samples hers.

"Didn't her letter of reference say she was a good cook?" I whisper.

"A good plain cook," Isobel whispers back, with the ghost of the old sparkle in her eye.

I force myself to eat more, watching Isobel as she does the same. I can't help but stare at the movement of her throat as she swallows, and imagine the food sliding down into the hollows of her gullet, her stomach, her gut. Her collarbones jut beneath her fine skin, so sharp and well defined that I can see them as clearly as if they were laid before me in the dissecting room. Last night, with the benign glow of port wine heating my blood, I was able to embrace her, kiss her, before those accursed images flashed through my mind. The dead woman's belly opening under Dr Irvine's knife. My own unnatural moment of lust for her. The slippery weight of the ruptured womb in my hands. And once more I had turned away from Isobel, my ardour reduced to ashes and shame.

I clear my bowl in haste and rise to go. "I'll call at the Dundas house this morning, and see how young Jonet fares."

"Stay a moment, Robert," Isobel says. Her voice is calm but there is an urgent look on her face.

I freeze, and rest my fingertips on the tabletop. I am unsure whether or not to sit down again. "What is it?"

She looks up at me, and for a moment I see a flicker of impatience. It is sufficient to make me lower myself back into the chair.

"This… way of living. Is it to remain so always?"

"What do you mean?"

Isobel takes a deep breath. "I have little experience in the ways of the world, but I know that this is not what a marriage should be."

I curse myself for sitting. The chair is like a cage now. I am trapped. "Last night… I was not at my best…"

"You cannot bear to touch me unless you are half drunk. I would not mind that so much, but each time I hope that all will be well and then… it isn't."

"I am sure that, given time…"

She looks up at me, with a strange, brave look in her eye. "Is there something in me that you find repugnant? You are familiar with… the female form. More so than I am…"

"The fault is mine." I know she will not be comforted by such empty gallantry, but I cannot find the words to explain my weakness. "We get along well enough, do we not?" How feeble my voice sounds.

She fixes me with a look from those clear eyes. "Was this perhaps always your intention? That we should live as... mere companions?"

I shake my head. A memory intrudes. One day, during our courtship, we found ourselves alone as we walked the land around her father's parish in Lauder. We came upon a fallen tree. I sat myself down and was surprised and delighted when Isobel sat on my knee. The nearness of her, the warmth of her body and her sweet, musky smell had my head spinning as if I were the worse for drink. I could not help but kiss the bare skin of her neck and bosom – even the thought of it now throws me into a kind of swoon. I cannot bear to look at her.

"Robert," she says now, "I want to be your wife – your proper wife. To bear your children, if it is God's will. If that is not what you want then we must... attempt to undo the mistake."

"How so?"

She shrugs, and looks down at the table. "Separation. Annulment. We have grounds for it."

I stand up again, stung into action by this last barb. "I would have come away on our wedding night, but you would not let me. You could not bear the shame, you told me, the humiliation. Will it not be so much the worse now that near a month has passed?" I hesitate for a moment, imagining the response of all our acquaintance if we took such a course. Isobel might be an object of pity, returning dejected to her father's house, but the true mortification would be mine to bear. Non-consummation through lack of the virile spirit. That would be how the courts would frame it. How Maxwell and his ilk would laugh. Dr Irvine and all those other gentlemen physicians at the Royal Society – would they ever countenance me as one of their own? And my patients – those genteel ladies who looked to me as the very exemplar of all a man should be... I would be ruined.

I am so absorbed in my thoughts that it's a moment before I notice Isobel has not replied. She is staring down at her half-finished breakfast. "I will not go on like this," she says quietly. "When we had no servant... at least then it was a matter between the two of us, but now–"

"You mustn't worry what Susan thinks. She'll mind her own business if she values her position."

"Share my bed tonight," she says. "Not for... Merely as bedfellows. Perhaps if we become accustomed to each other..."

"I know this is a matter of great importance to you," I blurt out, "as it is to me, but I really must attend Jonet Stewart. May we discuss this later?" It is a coward's escape, and from the look she gives me she knows it too.

Jonet Stewart is greatly improved, propped up on her pillows and sipping from a posset pot with Mistress Dundas's assistance. Now that she has her wits back she is reluctant for me to examine her secret parts, but Mistress Dundas upbraids her until she consents. I find the blistering much diminished, and cover her up again. "Have you made water today, Jonet?" I ask.

"Aye," she says quietly, not meeting my eyes.

"And did it cause you pain to do so?"

"Not so much as afore, doctor."

"Then I'd say you're mending well." I pat her hand. The skin is rough and flaking. Her hair hangs in dry hanks about her shoulders, and I see that a great number of strands have been shed on to her pillow. I fear that the poison of James Aikenhead's *pastilles espagnole* may yet be inflicting damage on her body. "Now, Jonet, I must tell you that I know what has caused this affliction."

She looks up at me, her dull eyes suddenly bright with fear.

"You ate some tablets."

"I never did, sir."

"Och, Jonet," Mistress Dundas interjects. "Don't add lying to your sins. Dr Carruth found the carton in your trunk, and he's tracked down the very man who made them." She gives me a sharp glance.

"Don't be afraid, Jonet. You are not in trouble – you've already paid a heavy price for any foolishness."

"I didnae eat any tablets, sir."

"You may have thought that they were sweeties."

"Oh!" she says, lifting one hand to her mouth.

"Did you eat some sweeties, before you became ill?"

She nods.

"How many did you eat?"

"The whole package. I didnae want to share."

"Greedy girl," scolds Mistress Dundas.

"And how many were in the carton, Jonet? Do you recall?"

Her voice when she replies is so low I can barely hear her say, "A dozen, sir." Mistress Dundas tuts in disgust.

"Jonet, how did you come by these sweeties?"

She turns her head away from me.

"Were they a gift from a sweetheart?"

"Oh no, sir," she says in alarm.

"But a gift from someone?"

She falls silent again.

I judge that she is in no state to be further pressed on who gave her the pastilles. I could force the matter, bully her into offering up the name, but that would be unkind. It can wait until she is stronger. "Well, whoever gave them to you, did they warn that you should only eat them one at a time?"

"No, sir." She closes her eyes. Her face is more pallid than before. My questions have exhausted her. It is clear, though, that whoever gave her the tablets – and I am not sure that I believe her denial of a sweetheart – they either did not know of their danger, or they knew and did not care. If the former, then more blame must fall on James Aikenhead, for selling such an item without adequate precaution.

I advise Mistress Dundas to continue with the treatment at a reduced dosage, and take my leave. Mistress Dundas follows me out of Jonet's room. "Is your wife receiving visitors?" she says, without preamble. "I would be pleased to call on her. Her mother and I know each other a little."

"I am sure she would be delighted," I say, although I am sure of no such thing.

If I could find a way of delaying my return home I would do so, but I cannot. I have two patients with appointments to be seen in my consulting room before noon. At least that will give me good reason to avoid conversation with Isobel for a little while more.

I let myself into the house and go straight to the consulting room to prepare for my patients. The fire is lit, and the room smells of lavender and beeswax. Susan must have been at work. I ring for her, and sort through my papers while I await her arrival.

There's a soft tap on the door – I am beginning to recognise it as hers – and she comes in. "Ah, Susan. I expect two patients this morning. When the first arrives – it will be a lady with her daughter – please show them in to me here. If the second patient should arrive before I am done with the first, you must seat her in the dining room."

"The fire's out in the dining room, sir," she says. "Madam told me not to set it until dinner time."

What is it in that tone I don't like? Some hint of criticism of Isobel's household management? I look directly at Susan's face. It is closed. Or not closed exactly... Perhaps I am reading too much into it, and she simply exemplifies the dumb, bovine demeanour of the servant. "Indeed I would not want a fire lit in the dining room when in all likelihood there will be no need for it. This is a comfortable household, Susan, but not a wasteful one."

"Yes, sir." There's a flicker of something – a challenge? – in her eyes as she speaks.

My patients arrive in due course. The first is a mama with her daughter who has not yet experienced her menarche in spite of reaching the age of eighteen. I diagnose suffocation of the uterus, and prescribe a daily infusion of certain herbs renowned for their power to provoke a woman's courses. The second patient is a merchant's wife who has brought forth eleven offspring – of whom eight are still living – as well as at least half a dozen miscarriages. She is suffering a continual flux of blood, which I deem little wonder. When I have finished with her I sit on at my desk, writing up my notes. I consider if there is any other way I may respectably avoid Isobel for another while, but every option smacks of cowardice, so I rise and make my way upstairs.

As I walk along the landing I hear voices from the parlour. I open the door and both Isobel and her mother turn to look at me. "Is that the time already?" Isobel says lightly. "Mother, will you stay to dine with us?"

"Indeed no," my mother-in-law says. "From what you tell me that new girl of yours hardly has the wit to make a meal for two stretch to three."

"Well, we must give her a chance." Isobel still has a slight air of awkwardness in her role as mistress of the house. I glance at both women, trying to assess if there has been any confidential discussion between them. The idea of Isobel's mother being privy to our difficulties – to my failing – is unbearable. My only consolation is that Isobel is as mortified as I am by the situation. I doubt that she would wish to share our shame with anyone – even her mother. Still, I wish that my in-laws would make an end of their visit to Edinburgh. They took a house off the West Bow for the weeks before and after our wedding, and show no inclination to return to Lauder.

My mother-in-law rises. "You may be reassured, son," she says to me, "for I had a word with her when I came today, and let her know that she'll have me to deal with if she tries any shortcuts." She sets her mouth in a firm little pout. The skin around her lips puckers like a wrinkled apple.

Isobel sees her mother out and we sit down to our meal. We are silent as Susan serves us, and I feel a sense of relief when she leaves the room. I must, as Isobel says, give her time, although I doubt if she will ever become like the old servants in Isobel's father's house at Lauder, who fit as comfortably there as if they were family.

We make desultory conversation as we eat, never approaching the topic that occupies both our minds. I have a sense that she will not open it again – not today, at any rate. "Isobel–" I begin, although with what end in mind I do not know. I've no sooner said the words, and observed the manner in which her body suddenly tenses, when there's a rap at the front door.

Isobel sighs – whether in relief or exasperation I cannot tell – and we await Susan's arrival with word of who is calling at this time of day, when every respectable family will be at table. At length she comes into the room.

"It's a Mr Aikenhead to see you, sir," she says.

James Aikenhead twists his hat in his hands, smiling anxiously down at his son. We are all three standing awkwardly in the hallway. "I knew you were most anxious, Dr Carruth, to know who it was had bought my *pastilles espagnole*, and it was my deepest wish to oblige you, which I would have done if my books had been in their customary order, but what with my recent reversals…"

"To the point please, Aikenhead," I snap. "Though it hardly matters now, as the girl's life is saved. Still, I should like to know what rogue tried such a wicked trick on an innocent young lassie."

Aikenhead places his hand on his son's head – the lad has no cap, I notice. "It's thanks to my Thomas that the mystery is solved, sir. He recalls an ill-favoured fellow who bought some of my pastilles. Wee Thomas has sound instincts, Dr Carruth. He's what the countryfolk would call canny. I've learnt to rely on him this long while. Such a judge of character!"

"And who is this 'ill-favoured fellow'? Can your son name him?"

"No, sir," the lad pipes up, "but I can lead you to where he bides." He is abominably self-assured for one so young.

"I have no wish to traipse around the streets of Edinburgh behind a bairn," I say to the father. "If you'll be so good as to tell me…"

Aikenhead wrings his hat even tighter – it will be completely destroyed by the time he has finished with it – and offers me his infuriating smile. "Ah, that I cannot, Dr Carruth. I would if I could–"

"You want money, I suppose?"

He looks shocked, affronted even. I see a flash of long-crushed pride. "Indeed not," he says. "It's only that young Thomas, clever and all as he is, couldn't *tell* you where the man bides – he wouldn't know how to describe the directions to you – but he can *show* you, if you care to follow."

"I'll guide you there, Doctor," Thomas says, boldly taking my hand. "Come with me."

His fingers feel damp and warm, and his grip is surprisingly firm for a child. He pulls me towards the front door. "Now, Thomas," Aikenhead says, "Don't treat Dr Carruth so roughly."

"Be so good as to wait for me outside," I say, shaking myself free of the child. "I must make my apologies to my wife, and then we will see how sound the boy's instincts really are."

"Och, Robert," says Isobel, who has descended the staircase as I spoke, "don't make the poor child wait out in the cold." She reaches out her hand to him. "Shall we go to the kitchen, my dear, and see if there's any cake?"

The boy considers her offer for a moment, then takes her hand and trots off with her down the hall towards the kitchen. The door to my consulting room lies open, and the child strays towards it, pulling Isobel with him. "You like books better than cake? Then you must come back another day and I will show you as many books as you please." Isobel says, with a lightness in her voice I have not heard these many days.

"Such a charming lady," says James Aikenhead, watching them go. "You are indeed a lucky man." His admiration only makes me dislike him more.

Thomas

So I lead them down the big broad street where the doctor bides. I run on ahead and Dada calls to me to slow down. "Look at him go, Dr Carruth," he says, "skittering like a dropped marley." He's all out of puff the same way Katharine gets. I take a hold of the doctor's hand again, though I know he disnae like it. He's forgot to put his gloves on. I wonder how he keeps his skin so soft and smooth, and him a man and all. Mother's hands are rougher than his are. I look up at him as we walk. It's an odd thing that his face is so cross and stern, and yet his hands feel kind. I dinnae think he would hit me, no matter how I vexed him. I dinnae think he would hit anyone.

I lead them back to Dada's shop – though it isnae his shop any more, and the sign with the green snake is gone, and the door is all closed up with a sign nailed to it – and then we set off the way the tall man who bought the tablets went that day. Up and down the wynds, past the sign of the black bull and the sign of the golden-haired angel. We turn into the court where the tall man went. The doctor says, "Are you sure this is the place?"

"Aye," says I, "for this is the very place I followed him to."

"And which door did you see him go in?" says he.

I march right up to the door and point to it. The doctor stands there all confounded. Then he turns to me. "Would you know this man again, if you saw him?" he says.

"Aye," I say. I start to feel a bit afeard. Dada strokes my hair.

"Don't worry, wee Tam," he says. "You're not the one in trouble."

The doctor raps on the door, all genteel. I like that way of rapping on the door. That's the way I'll do it, when I'm a grown-up gentleman. Someone opens the door, and the doctor speaks in for a moment, then we all troop through the hallway and into a room piled high with papers. I've never seen so many papers in my life. I wonder what's written on them all. There's a crabbit-looking man with a black wig and a red face stood behind the desk. The doctor says something to him about the man who bought the tablets, and that makes the crabbit man look even more crabbit and he goes out into the hall and lets out a gulder. And who should come running but the tall man, galloping intae the room with his big horsey steps.

"This is Chalmers, my manservant," says the crabbit man. He turns to me. "Are you certain he is the man you saw in your father's shop?"

"Aye," I say.

The bad man – Chalmers – speaks to his master. "Am I tae answer tae wee daft bairns now?"

"You'll answer to me," says the crabbit man, poking his finger in Chalmer's chest. "Was it you who bought those tablets that near killed poor Jonet?"

Dada chips in. "I'll have a record of the purchase somewhere."

Chalmers looks near as afeard as I feel. "I bought tablets alright," says he, "but I didnae gie them tae Jonet. Why would I?"

The crabbit man marches around him, head poking back and forth like a pigeon. "Well I would have thought that was obvious!" he cries. "You had designs on her, you filthy beast."

The doctor holds up his hand to the crabbit man. "If you will allow me, Mr Dundas," he says, all calm and steady. He turns to Chalmers. "You admit you bought the tablets?"

"Aye."

"But you did not give them to Jonet."

Chalmers shakes his head.

"You bought them, I assume, on someone's instructions?" Chalmers makes no reply. "So," the doctor goes on, "you bought them, and carried them back here. You cannot deny that, for we have a witness."

Chalmers scowls at me and I wish I could run away out of the room, but I want to see what happens next. "I dinnae deny it."

"Then you must have passed the tablets on to someone else, is that not so? Whoever it was that gave you the money to buy them," the doctor says.

At that the crabbit man starts jigging around again. "Who? Who?" he says.

"I cannae say." And with that Chalmers clamps his mouth shut and says nothing more.

The doctor strokes his chin. "Here's a strange coincidence," he says. "Jonet will not tell me who gave her the tablets. And now Chalmers will not tell me who he passed them on to." He turns to the crabbit man. "Who all resides in the house? How many servants?"

"Servants? Aside from Jonet and Chalmers here, there's only Miriam the cook."

"And your family?"

The crabbit man has stopped his leaping around. "Myself and my wife. My daughter, Mary. And young Elizabeth Edmonstone." He scowls so hard I cannae see his eyes under his great dark brows, and stomps to the door of the room. We all back away to the walls to steer clear of him. He hurls open the door and gulders, "Mary! Elizabeth! Come down here this instant!" I'm happy enough to be hiding behind Dada. No one is looking near me now. They're all staring at the door, listening to the rustle of skirts and the tap-tap of lassies' shoes coming down the stairs.

Two ladies come into the room. One has a face plain as cheese and hair that's dark like the crabbit man's wig. But the other one... Her hair is the colour of fox fur and she's bonny. The bonniest lady I've ever seen. I keek up to see what Dada and the doctor think of her. Dada's smiling, like he always does, only more so. The doctor looks as stern as ever, but there's a blush on his cheek.

The crabbit man stalks forward. "Now then, this is a serious business, and I want the truth from you." He glares at each of the ladies in turn. "We know that someone in this house sent Chalmers to buy those wicked tablets that made Jonet so ill. It wasn't me and it wasn't your mother. I very much doubt if it was old Miriam in the kitchen. So that means it was one of you. Come on now! Out with it!"

The plain-faced lady bursts into tears, and the bonny one gives her an ill-hearted look. "Surely Jonet and Chalmers can tell you who it was?" she says, her voice all cool and sweet. She takes a wee keek at Chalmers. He looks down at his boots.

The doctor steps forward. "They seem afraid to speak, Miss Edmonstone." The two of them stare at each other. I shouldn't like to have her stare at me in that way, no matter how bonny she is.

"How strange," she says. "Well, I know nothing about it. Do you, Mary?"

Mary sobs even louder, wrestling a handkerchief from her sleeve and covering her face with it. She tries to say something, but she's gurning that much I can't make out a word of it.

"Well, gentlemen," the bonny lady says. "I hope you're proud of yourselves, distressing poor Mary like this. I'll take her back upstairs before she is quite overcome." She hooks her hand into Mary's arm and guides her out of the room. All the men stand gawping.

At last the crabbit man turns to Chalmers. "You may pack your bags and go. And don't be looking wages or a letter of reference." Chalmers seems about to speak, then shakes his head and goes out. The crabbit man looks at

Dada. "You can be off too, and take that brat of yours with you."

Dada reaches down for my hand and we go out into the hall, leaving the crabbit man and the doctor in the room. The crabbit man closes the door in our faces. "Well, Thomas," Dada says as we go back out into the court and head for home. "That was an adventure, wasn't it?"

Dr Carruth

Isobel listens attentively as I explain the situation. "So, you see, by drawing Dr Irvine's attention to Aikenhead's recklessness I may have caused deep embarrassment to Mr Dundas."

"Was it not Mr Dundas who first urged you to action?"

"I suppose he did not know then that his own daughter and her friend were at the bottom of it."

"You told me he intended to lodge a case against Aikenhead himself."

"Aye, and he has done, not two days ago. Aikenhead doesn't know it yet – he's not had his summons. The wretched fellow would have been smiling less had he been aware of it."

"Poor Mr Aikenhead. I feel a little sorry for him."

"Save your pity," I scoff. "He has brought the greater part of his troubles on himself."

She looks sharply at me and seems about to retort, but instead she thinks for a moment before speaking again. "Perhaps Mr Dundas will withdraw his case, and it will all be hushed up."

"Dundas doesn't know which way to hop. He's still in a rage at the cost of it all – there's my bill to pay, and Dr Irvine's, and Fenton's." I remember how Jonet's hair was coming out in great hanks when last I attended her. "I doubt if the servant girl will be able to work again, and he'll feel obliged to compensate her, so that's another cost for him."

Isobel nods. "And he must balance that against the shame of Mary and Elizabeth playing such a cruel trick. Did they say why they did it?"

I feel the heat creep into my face at the memory of Elizabeth Edmonstone, and the look that burned from those hazel eyes. "Miss Dundas weeps and Miss Edmonstone denies it with such brazen lies..." I stop, conscious now that Isobel is staring at me.

"You're blushing, Robert."

Whosoever looketh on a woman to lust after her hath committed adultery with her already in his heart. The words sound in my ears as clearly as if I were hearing them in the kirk. Isobel continues to regard me in her clear, guileless way. In the face of such innocence, what can I do but equivocate? "I am angry at them – not only for what they did to Jonet, but for their refusal to acknowledge their fault. That Miss Edmonstone... She seems to have them all in thrall."

"And Dr Irvine has brought the matter to his friends at the Royal College. What do they intend to do?"

"I don't know." I sink miserably into my chair. We are in the front parlour, awaiting the summons to dinner.

"Why don't you write to them?"

"My views would carry no weight with them."

She leans over and touches me briefly, gently on the arm. "Dr Irvine appears to think well of you. Write to him and explain that there are some new circumstances come to light. If Mr Dundas withdraws his complaint too, then perhaps poor Mr Aikenhead will be spared from answering a case before the Privy Council."

"I've no wish to spare Aikenhead," I snap.

"But if he is summoned to answer for his actions, then so must be Mary and Elizabeth. In a public court before the whole town."

"Aye."

She pauses, seemingly deep in thought. "Why do you dislike Mr Aikenhead so?"

I struggle to find an answer. In truth, I hardly know myself. There is just something in the man's demeanour that grates on my temper. "Because he is... careless," I say at last.

Isobel raises her eyebrows at this. "It would be a shame if the family should suffer for the father's carelessness. The little boy is most endearing." She smiles at the thought, and I feel a sharp stab of jealousy that the wretched child should inspire this softness in her.

At that the gong is struck for dinner, saving me from making a response.

After dinner I excuse myself and go to my consulting room to write to Dr Irvine. I explain to him the complication: that two young ladies – one a laird's daughter – are at risk of ignominy if charges are pressed. In addition, I tell him of my finding that Jonet had consumed all of the tablets at once. This fact puts a different complexion on Aikenhead's wrongdoing. His negligence is not in the formulation of the tablets, but in his recklessness in selling them to all and sundry, without proper instruction as to their use. I sand and seal the letter, then ring for Susan. She slips into the room, soft-footed as a shadow. "See if you can find a messenger boy to carry this to Dr Irvine," I say, handing her the letter.

"There'll hardly be a boy around at this time of the evening," she says. "I'll be happy to carry it to him myself, if you wish. Should I wait for a reply?"

I hesitate. It is not usual for a housemaid to be roaming the streets at this hour. "Will you feel quite safe?" I say.

She smiles. "I can look after myself, sir."

"Very well then." I think for a moment. If I bid her wait for Dr Irvine's response it might look to him as if I am in a state of anxiety. That would not do. "There's no need to tarry for a reply, but when you return let me know that it is safely delivered."

A good hour passes. I occupy myself with attending to my accounts. My nerves are aflutter, but I resist the urge to fetch a bottle of port wine from the pantry. My abstemiousness is not entirely a matter of strong will. If I leave this room there is a chance I will encounter Isobel, and

I am reluctant to revive either of the discussions we have embarked on today. As if that were not reason enough to stay hidden in my consulting room, I have the beginnings of a sick headache. When I look at my accounts book the letters dance on the page. Every time I blink it is as if a flash of lightning jolts through my skull.

After a time Isobel taps on the door and peeps in. "I am going to bed, Robert," she says.

"Goodnight," I say, not looking up from my work. I sense her waiting for something more. She is, no doubt, weighing up whether to speak or to let matters rest. It is a relief when I hear the door close and her footsteps ascend the stairs.

At last Susan returns and steps into the consulting room, still wearing her cloak and bonnet. "Your letter was delivered, sir," she says. "The man told me Dr Irvine was at home, and he would give it him directly."

"Thank you, Susan." I hesitate before continuing, "You were a long time about your errand. I was becoming anxious." She does not offer any explanation. Pain throbs at my temples and I rub my forehead.

"Are you quite well, sir?"

"Just a headache, Susan."

She tilts her head to one side and considers me with her inscrutable, dark eyes. "My mother had a grand remedy for the headache."

I'm tempted to laugh. "I'm a doctor, Susan. If I need physic..."

"It's not a powder or potion, sir. It's a rub for the neck. I have some in the kitchen, if you would like me to apply it for you."

Before I can respond to her she's left the room. I sit listening to her footsteps recede and then quickly return. She has discarded her cloak and bonnet, and now carries a small tin in her hand. "Susan, there is no need."

"You may trust me, sir. It's most efficacious. Just loosen your collar for me."

I hesitate. All my life I have relied on my moral instinct to keep me from danger. In my student days in the Low Countries, when the wilder young men, like Maxwell, tried to urge me into taverns or even more disreputable establishments, this instinct had held me back. It was not always easy. There were many nights that I fought with myself before turning my back on the warmth and cheer of the inns of Leiden, and walking alone back to my lodgings. My feelings of loneliness had been profound but salved somewhat by a sense of pride in my own strength of character.

Now I feel again as I did on those nights, standing on the very threshold of something I know to be unwise. But my head is aching. I untie my neckerchief and unfasten my collar.

Susan opens the little tin and sets it on the desk in front of me. She pulls my collar down so that the back of my neck is exposed. "You'll feel the benefit of it, sir," she says, leaning over to scoop up some of the ointment.

She stands behind me and rubs the stuff into my neck. Her fingers are cool, and I am uncomfortably aware that my skin is prickling into goose pimples. The air is filled with the scent of herbs. I can detect lavender, but there are others I cannot name. The smell is familiar. Susan places a warming pan in my bed every night before I retire and she must infuse the coals with this same fragrance. She rests her fingers on my collarbone, and presses her two thumbs into my shoulder muscles, circling and pressing in such a way that I don't know whether I am feeling pain or pleasure.

"You're all tied up in knots, sir," she says. "No wonder your head aches."

No woman has ever touched me in this way. I feel drunk with the delight of it, even while a sharp pang of guilt jabs at me, knowing that Isobel is close by, sleeping chastely in her marriage bed. *To be carnally minded is death.* Susan raises her hands to my temples, and strokes them more gently. I sense the heat of her body, only inches from the back of my head. Without meaning to, I lean back until my hair brushes the bodice of her gown. I half expect her to step away, to remonstrate with me, but she does not. It seems to me that she moves a fraction closer. Each time she breathes in I feel her breast touch against me. She glows with warmth. I am a man held under an enchantment. I know I should break the spell but somehow I cannot.

She takes her hands away from my temples and begins to pull my collar up to cover my bare neck. "Has that eased you, sir?"

I try to answer, but the words will not come. It is as if I have been struck dumb and motionless with the delight of her touch, her soft female presence. I fuss at my shirt in the hope of gathering my senses together. "Much better, thank you, Susan," I say. My voice sounds thick. "Go on to bed now. It's late. I'll close up the house."

I wait until she leaves the room, then bank the fire. The lamp on my desk still has a little oil left in it, so I use it to light my way around the house checking that the doors and windows are fast for the night. Normally this ritual fills me with a sense of melancholy. It echoes the way in which the spirit retreats from the dying body and puts me in mind of final things. Tonight, though, is different. For the first time in weeks I yearn for my bed – not for sleep, but for the freedom to let my imagination play on the sensations Susan has stirred by her touch. I climb the stairs and hesitate before the door of Isobel's bedchamber. Could the flame that Susan has kindled warm my marriage bed? I am suddenly disgusted with myself. To even think of approaching Isobel with such thoughts seems worse than exposing her to some vile contagion. I turn from her door towards that of my own solitary room.

The next morning I am glad to be busy with house calls. The case of Jonet Stewart – stripped, no doubt, of the worst details of her affliction – has been a topic of conversation among the better sort of person, and my role in her survival has brought me more patients. In spite of all my anxieties I feel a certain feverish lightness in my spirits as I walk from one respectable house to the next, calling on my ladies and easing their discomforts. I decide against attending Jonet herself. She is well mended now, and after yesterday's contretemps I have no wish to return to the Dundas household until matters are more settled.

When I finally enter my own front door I see the coat stand is laden with capes and cloaks. My heart sinks at the prospect of company. No one was expected today. I am tempted to slink into my consulting room and hide there until the visitors leave, but that would be discourteous, and unkind to Isobel. My earlier good spirits are quite extinguished as I ascend the stairs to the front parlour.

Inside the room I am dumbfounded to find Dr Maxwell, Mistress Dundas and Elizabeth Edmonstone. Isobel is sitting bolt upright, and casts me a pleading look. Her copy of the *Edinburgh Courant* is set to one side on an empty chair. Susan is serving chocolate to the ladies. Maxwell has a glass of Madeira in his ungloved hand. "Good Lord, Carruth," he exclaims, "you look extremely vexed."

"Indeed not," I lie, forcing myself forward to greet him. "Merely surprised. We have so few visitors as a rule."

"It occurred to me that I had not yet made a visit to your new bride. Having no wife of my own to guide me I sometimes neglect these social niceties." Maxwell bows towards Isobel, with a sly smile on his lips. His glance strays towards Elizabeth Edmonstone. She looks away from him and up at me. There is something practised in her manner, so taunting in the way she deploys her allure. I become aware that Isobel is observing me. At the same moment I find Susan by my side.

"Will you take some chocolate, sir, or some Madeira wine?"

"Madeira," I say, and take a seat between Isobel and

Mistress Dundas. In truth, I have no desire for wine, but dread appearing womanish in front of Maxwell. Susan fills a glass for me, clattering the decanter against the glass. Elizabeth Edmonstone stifles a laugh. Susan's hand shakes as she gives me my Madeira. I glance up at her face and see that it is flushed with anger or embarrassment.

"I was just telling your good lady about my Mary," Mistress Dundas says.

"She is not unwell, I hope?"

"Unwell?" Mistress Dundas rolls her eyes. "Snivelling like a baby, and won't come out of her room."

"I am sorry to hear it."

"Indeed. I said to Mr Dundas, I said, 'Let us ask Dr Carruth to attend to her, since he's so good with young ladies.' Of course, it is her nerves that are out of kilter, rather than any physical affliction."

"I would be happy to call upon her."

Mrs Dundas shakes her head and shapes her mouth into a sad moue. "Alas, Dr Carruth, my husband won't hear of it. He says he'll have enough to pay you as it is. So I said to him, 'Are you telling me you'll pay for a servant to be cured, but not your own daughter? Shame on you sir,' that's what I said to him."

We all sit in awkward silence for a few moments. I turn to Elizabeth Edmonstone. "*You* are well, at any rate, Miss Edmonstone?" I hope there is enough ice in my question for it to find its mark.

"Thank you, yes," she says. There's just a hint of boredom in her voice. I can feel Maxwell's eyes on me, and sense the smirk on his face.

"And how is Jonet today?" I go on. Let her not think I don't know her role in this cruel business.

"Jonet!" Mistress Dundas interjects. "Why she's removed from us!"

"How so? She's scarcely fit to travel."

"Dr Irvine saw no obstacle. He sent his own coach."

As I struggle to make a reply Maxwell laughs. "Oh Carruth, if you could only see your face!" He glances over at Isobel. "You must school your husband better, Mistress Carruth. He must learn the art of hiding his jealousies."

"I do not think he is jealous of Dr Irvine," she says mildly. "Indeed, he admires him greatly. I imagine he is merely taken aback at this intervention, and concerned for Jonet's well-being." She smiles over at me, and I feel a rush of gratitude towards her.

"Where has Jonet been removed to?" I ask.

"Well, that we don't know." Mistress Dundas drinks off the cup of chocolate in one long swallow and licks her lips. "He said he knew of a woman by the waters of Leith who kept a lodging house for invalids, and that the fresh air would benefit Jonet's recovery." She sets her cup down. "It has been most pleasant calling on you, Mistress Carruth. I hope you will visit us some day?"

"Yes indeed," says Isobel.

Susan shows Mistress Dundas and Elizabeth Edmonstone out – not before Mistress Dundas draws me aside and whispers that her husband has withdrawn his complaint against Aikenhead. I feel a strange mixture of relief and frustration. Not so much that Aikenhead will go unreprimanded – for I am a little ashamed now of my antipathy – but there is a part of me that would like to see Elizabeth Edmonstone called to account. Still, it is for the best, no doubt. After a few minutes more Maxwell announces he must leave. We pass Susan on the stairs as we go down. "You're a lucky man, Carruth," Maxwell says, "though your blood must be stirred beyond bearing."

"I don't know what you mean."

"To have a maidservant with that air about her." He throws me a quizzical look. "I'd say the vital spirits pulse strong through her veins, eh?"

"She seems a respectable girl."

Maxwell lets out a scornful laugh. "Well, you have a fine young wife to keep your attention. I make sure to employ an old and ugly housekeeper, for if I kept a young one I'd be in all manner of trouble, bachelor or no."

My consulting room is quiet and cold, the fire long since died down. Isobel and Susan have both retired for the night. I have a book open in front of me, but I cannot take in its content. The question of why Dr Irvine intervened in Jonet's case whirls round and round my head. He has not responded to my letter, but I am sure that his action must be in some way connected with my communication.

There's a rustle on the stairs and a tap on the consulting room door – Susan's tap. When she enters I am astonished to see her dressed in her nightgown, her dark hair in a loose plait. She has a shawl wrapped around her, clasped together with both hands. Her feet are bare, and very white against the dark floorboards.

"Are you ill, Susan? Or has something alarmed you?"

"Forgive me, sir," she says. "I could not sleep for worry."

"I am sorry to hear that, Susan, but this is scarcely the time..."

"I did badly today, sir, when you had your visitors. Didn't the mistress speak to you about it?"

"No, not a word."

"Before you came home, sir, Miss Edmonstone complained that the chocolate was bitter. I'm only a housemaid, sir. Good for cleaning and plain cooking, not for waiting on gentry with chocolate and Madeira wine."

"Susan, please be assured that Miss Edmonstone's opinion counts for little with me. I believe she is a spiteful young woman, with too much leisure at her disposal."

"You are a good judge of character, sir."

Her praise is oddly gratifying, but I am conscious that Isobel is sleeping in the bedchamber just up the stairs.

What if she too is awake, and listening to the murmur of our voices? "You really must go back to your room, Susan. And don't worry about it another moment."

"Thank you, sir," she says, fixing me with those inscrutable eyes. "You are very generous."

I am in bed, but I cannot sleep. The night is very still. I wish there were a storm blowing around the rooftops. It would better reflect my state of mind than this heavy, airless calm. When I lie on my side I feel suffocated, so I turn on to my back and stare up into the darkness of the room. Dashes and dots of light dance in front of me, and when I close my eyes they do not disappear.

I might have dozed for a time – I cannot be sure – but I am suddenly wide awake again. There is movement in the house. The creak of a floorboard in the rooms above me. Is someone stirring? I calm my breathing, the better to listen. There is another creak, fainter this time. And then I hear the door to my room being opened.

Somehow I know it is Susan. Her bare feet scarcely make a sound as she crosses the floor, but I sense that she is coming closer. I can smell that strange scent of hers. The bed creaks as she sits down on it. Her hair brushes against my face as she bends closer and kisses me lightly on the mouth. For a second I am too astonished to move. I try to speak, but she places one finger on my lips and says, "It is only a dream, sir." She kisses me again, but when she begins to climb under the covers I shrink away from her.

"What the devil do you mean by this behaviour?" I whisper.

I sense her sit upright. In the darkness of the room I can just make out the pale gleam of her face.

"I'm sorry, sir. You are so kind and seemed melancholy. I thought you would like a little comfort."

"If I want comfort I'll find it in my work and my studies and–"

"And your wife?"

"Get away from me."

She stands, and it seems that the bed grows cooler as she retreats. A moment later the bedroom door squeaks open and then is shut again. As I lie listening I hear the creak of the stairs. There are other sounds from the rooms above me – she must be moving about, climbing into her narrow bed. And then silence.

I lie flat on my back, forcing myself to take long, deep breaths. The pace of my heartbeat grows steady again. Surely sleep will be impossible now? Every nerve in my body feels raw, as if a layer of skin has been peeled away. What can have prompted her to present herself to me in such a way? Does she feel it is the price she must pay for my support? Perhaps not. From what she had said it was pity moved her. True, she had shown concern for me these past days, but still... My innate caution makes me doubt it. She has seen that Isobel and I sleep apart, and come to her own conclusions about the reasons. Perhaps she thinks this will be a way to advance herself. Worse yet, blackmail could be in her mind. I imagine the consequences had I accepted her advances. A threat, perhaps, of revealing my behaviour to Isobel, or to my in-laws. Thank God I withstood temptation. For I must be honest with myself, there was a brief moment when my baser passions might have inclined me to respond. *It is only a dream*, she said. I could have pretended it was so.

Before my imagination continues in this line I admonish myself. I am a Christian man, and my objective has always been that my animal needs would be contained and sanctified by matrimony. Dear God, I am not yet two months married. How could I even think of breaking those sacred vows, and with a servant girl at that?

The next morning, Susan presents us with our breakfast in much the same manner as she always does, with a perfunctory "Good morning, sir, madam," and little more. I do not want to meet her eye, fearing I will see some sign of unwelcome familiarity or knowingness. Still, I cannot stop myself from observing her with repeated covert glances. Whether I hope or fear to find her looking at me I cannot say, but in either case I am to be disappointed. She keeps her eyes downcast, and leaves the room quickly.

I eat without relish, although I am hungry, and try to focus my mind on the business of the day. Isobel and I make desultory conversation. However, try as I might, I cannot stop my mind returning to the events of the night before. Should I dismiss Susan? Her behaviour is indicative of a lack of morals. If she is capable of attempting to seduce her employer she will surely have no qualms about making off with any valuables she can lay her hands on. Still, I have not noticed anything going missing about the house. In any case, what explanation would I give Isobel for the dismissal? I cannot let this matter pass though. When Susan clears the table I offer my excuses to Isobel and make my way down the hall to the kitchen.

Susan looks up from the basin where she is stacking the breakfast dishes. "Would you like a bite more to eat, sir?" she says.

"No, Susan." I hesitate, realising I have not fully thought through what I am going to say to her. "I wanted to speak with you about last night."

"Last night?" She frowns, as if she does not understand me. I feel flustered. "There must be no repetition."

"I don't get your meaning, sir. Repetition of what?"

What has got into the girl? I am on the verge of saying outright what occurred in my bedroom, and then realise how deranged it will sound when she is keeping up this pretence of innocence. I must take some other approach. "Tell me, Susan, after you spoke to me last night about Miss Edmonstone, did you have any cause to leave your room before morning?"

She stares at me, unblushing, an expression of puzzlement on her face. "Why would I leave my room, sir?"

This is insufferable. I indicate for her to follow me and march out of the kitchen, along the hall and into my consulting room. Once there I search on the shelves for the family bible. I do not read it as often as I should, and it takes me a moment to find it among my books.

"Here," I say, setting it on my desk. "Swear on the Bible that you did not leave your room last night."

Susan shrugs, and places her hand on the Bible. "I swear by almighty God that I did not leave my room last night." As she says the words she looks me in the eye, fearless.

I feel foolish. Ridiculous. She must think me a madman. "Very good, Susan. Get on with your work."

She makes to leave the room, but pauses in the doorway and looks back at me. "Did something disturb you in the night, sir?"

"Yes. I thought..." I cannot continue.

She stands watching me; her dark hair neatly tied back, her pale body concealed by the dull worsted gown. "Perhaps it was a dream, sir."

I stare at her. She has that same fearless look in her eyes. "Very likely, Susan," I say at last. "It was most probably a dream."

Thomas

It's all nice and quiet, for Mother is out doing the messages. Anna is feeling poorly, so she's tucked up in bed and Dada has her dosed with medicine. Katharine's staying by her side, to keep her company. I'm sitting at the table with Keep-Count Man, while Dada makes up a remedy for him in the wee dispensary. Dada's left the door open so that he can keep an eye on us. Keep-Count Man has got his book open. "Two more o' themmuns go today, young Tam," he says, making his marks on the right-hand page. He talks very soft, on account of his earache. He's prone to earache. That's good news for Dada, for the remedy costs tuppence a time.

Dada is grinding up herbs in the mortar, and then stops all of a sudden. "Och, what am I doing?" he says. "I've made it all wrong."

"You should mind your work, James," says Keep-Count Man. "Your head's away."

"Not a bit of wonder," Dada says. He comes out of the dispensary, opens the window, and throws the ground-up herbs out into the close. "I may start again." He stays by the window, looking out. "Ah now," he says, sounding happier, "here's my cousin coming."

"Which cousin?" I say. I used to like it when cousins called, but Mother has fallen out with so many of them that we scarcely see them from one year end to the next.

Dada turns round to me, and his eyes are all bright. "It's your godfather, Thomas. You remember the grand gentleman who came to the shop one day?"

"Him with all the buttons on his jacket?"

"Aye, the very one. Be a good laddie now, and charm him well. He's under obligation to you, in a fashion, being your godfather." He speaks to Keep-Count Man. "Don't you agree, that a godfather is obliged to do right by his godson?"

Keep-Count Man snaps his wee book shut and clutches it to his chest. He looks all around the room as if he's afeard. "I wouldn't ken that James, indeed I wouldn't. You may ask a minister if you want the answer tae that conundrum."

"Och, never worry," Dada says, all kind and calming. "You bide there and I'll make up this new powder for you."

"Oh no, James, I cannae stop here." He rises from the chair like one of those puppets being pulled up by a string, all dangling and shaky. I run to open the door to let him out. He hirples on to the landing just as my godfather rounds the turn of the stairs. The two of them look at one another – Keep-Count Man in his rags and wrappings and my godfather with his fine jacket and all its buttons – and I don't know which one's more afeard. Keep-Count Man pushes past him and staggers away down the stairs.

"Come in, Sir Patrick, come in!" says Dada, in the voice he used to use for rich customers.

"Well, James," Sir Patrick says, looking all round him. "Is it just yourself and the bairns?"

"Oh aye, you needn't be afeard of Helen. She'll be gone this good while." He smiles over at me. "Clear a chair for your godfather, there's a good lad."

I wonder what chair he means. The last good armchair went away last week when a man came to take it. He gave Dada a shilling for it. All we have left is a bench and two stools. Sir Patrick looks too grand to sit on a stool, but he must sit somewhere. I pick the steadier of the stools and brush the dust off it with my sleeve. "Will you sit yourself here, godfather?" I say, all the while looking up at him with my eyes wide open.

"Thank you, Thomas," he says, easing himself down. His buttons give a wee jangle as he smoothes his jacket. "Now, James," he goes on. "What's this new trouble?"

Dada goes to his own jacket that's hanging on a hook by the door. He searches through the pockets and pulls out a letter. "This came yesterday," he says, handing it to Sir Patrick.

Sir Patrick begins to read it. "A summons!" he declares. "Och, James, what have you been at now?"

"There was this servant lassie took my *pastilles espagnole* and they near killed her, that's what they're saying. It's hardly my fault if she ate them all at once, is it? Any medicine will hurt you if you take too much of it."

"The lassie in question being this Jonet Stewart who has made the complaint?"

"Aye."

"And who are these two women who are charged alongside you? I don't think I know Mary Dundas, but Elizabeth Edmonstone... I'm sure I've heard that name."

"They're saying she's the one that gave Jonet Stewart the tablets."

Sir Patrick read on through the summons. "And told her they were sweeties. That's a cruel trick."

"She's the Laird of Duntreath's daughter, and a right spoiled hinny she is."

"Jonet Stewart must have a stout heart in her to take action against a laird's daughter."

Dada sits down on the other stool. "Aye, she must." He rests his head in his hands. "What am I to do? I haven't a penny to pay for an advocate."

Sir Patrick sighs. "And so you call on me."

"You see how we're fixed, Sir Patrick. I can barely feed the bairns, and that hearth has been empty and cold this last se'ennight."

"Hmmm." Sir Patrick glances over at me. "Are you a good boy, Thomas?"

"I don't know, Godfather," I say. "Dada – I mean, Father – says I'm good, and Mother says I'm not, so I don't know which I am."

Sir Patrick gives me a tired smile. "Very well, James," he says, rising to his feet. "I'll pay for an advocate. We may hope he persuades the Privy Council in your favour."

Dada jumps up and grasps Sir Patrick's hand and starts talking so fast I can hardly make him out, but he's saying "thank you" and "God bless you" over and over again with a lot of other words tangled up as well.

As we show him out the door Sir Patrick says, "Have you told Mistress Aikenhead of this latest misfortune?"

Dada freezes. "No," he says. "Not yet. I know I must, but–"

Sir Patrick nods. "Aye, I understand. You must pick your moment."

When he's gone, Dada says to me, "Not a word to your mother, eh Thomas?"

"Cross my heart and hope tae die." I draw a big invisible cross over my chest.

Dada pats me on the head. "That's the way, Thomas. Now, will you help me make up a cure for earache?"

Dr Carruth

It is Sunday, and I am breakfasting alone. Susan enters the room.

"The mistress says she will not go to kirk this morning," she says.

"Does she say why not? Is she indisposed?" There has been an outbreak of chills and agues, as there often is at the turn of the seasons.

Susan gives a barely perceptible shrug. I assume that means she does not know the answer to my questions. She clearly cares little either. Is this hint of insolence new? Has it emerged since her night-time visit to me? – the visit she claims never happened. "Will there be anything else, sir?"

"You may clear the table. I have no appetite."

I go to Isobel's bedchamber before leaving for the kirk. She is sitting by the window looking out at the street, an open book lying face down on the sill. "Are you unwell, Isobel?" I say. "Would you like me to prepare something for you?"

"I am quite well, thank you," she says without looking at me. She sounds in low spirits.

"Susan says you are not going to kirk this morning. What reason shall I give for your absence if the minister asks?"

"Tell him... whatever you think best." She turns and smiles weakly. Her eyes are red-rimmed. "I do not think I could endure to be in a press of people today."

I walk over to the window. "It is a pleasant day. I had hoped we might take a walk after kirk."

"You go," she says. "Do not let me deter you." She turns away from me, and resumes her observation of the street.

And so to the Tron Kirk, where the minister devotes a good hour to explaining why it is God's will that the Covenanters be crushed without mercy. No doubt in the hidden fields of Galloway there are wild-eyed Covenanters telling their followers that it is the likes of me who should be put to the sword. Quite what the Almighty thinks on the subject I could not say. I'm not sure I follow the Reverend Crawford's theological arguments on the matter, although I can understand the practical reasons for suppressing the Covenanters. Religion is all very well until its more fanatical followers threaten our earthly leaders. The Covenanters call their fallen brethren "saints". Heaven will be a stern and silent place if they comprise the celestial choir. As the minister preaches on I steal glances around the congregation to see who is there that I know. There's no sign of my mother-in-law and father-in-law, for which I am grateful. I catch a glimpse of Dr Irvine.

The crush of the congregation leaving the kirk nearly thwarts my plan of crossing paths with him, but I elbow my way through – as genteelly as I can – and feign surprise at the encounter.

"Ah, Carruth," he says. "Forgive my not replying to your letter, but I have been rather occupied."

"I hope Jonet Stewart continues to mend?"

He smiles at me with an expression I cannot fathom. "Indeed she does."

"I was surprised to learn of her removal."

Now he laughs. "Not as surprised as that rogue Dundas. He'd have happily swept the whole matter under the rug once he found his own daughter had a hand in it."

"I understand he has decided against pressing charges."

"Happily not everyone is of the same mind. Jonet Stewart has made a complaint against them. Summonses have been served. All three come before the Privy Council next week."

The anxiety that has been twisting in my gut intensifies. "Was this the reason you removed Jonet Stewart? She would hardly have made her complaint had she remained in the Dundas house."

"Aye, that might have been a wee bit awkward."

For a moment I can think of nothing to say. My whole body feels heavy with despair. At last I gather sufficient composure to speak. "I must say I am disappointed that my appeal for discretion fell on stony ground."

Irvine puts his arm around my shoulders like a father counselling his son. I cannot help but observe the eyes of several parishioners take note of this sign of favour. "Let us walk together awhile," he says, and we set off together down the high street.

"I recall," he says, once the crowd has thinned, "that it was you who first drew my attention to Mr Aikenhead's involvement in this case."

"It was."

"And you seemed quite passionate in your disapproval of him."

My mouth feels dry. "Perhaps I was... too choleric."

"Your view of Aikenhead has softened?"

"A little, perhaps. I have no wish to bring about his ruination."

"Especially now that two young ladies – one a laird's daughter! – are tarred with the same brush. That makes you more uneasy than poor Aikenhead's prospects."

"I would rather not make enemies among the gentry."

Dr Irvine stops and looks hard at me. "Is that it? You should have no fear of any man, Carruth. We are all equal in the eyes of the Almighty."

His complacency infuriates me. "That is an easy view to take when you are secure in all your affairs," I say. "I am a young man without connections, and I cannot so easily disregard the opinions of..."

"Of your betters?" he says drily.

I cannot reply.

He speaks again, more gently now. "Tell me, Dr Carruth, what was your father?"

How to answer? Such a direct question leaves little room for anything but the truth. "My father had a great number of occupations. Sometimes an apothecary. Sometimes… it was he the midwives summoned when a child had died in the womb."

"Ah. A crotchet man."

I shudder at the memory of those tools of my father's trade. The hook for drawing out the dead child. The scissors, strong enough to cut through infant bone.

"But a medical man, nonetheless," he goes on, "and one who found the means to educate you well. You should take pride in that."

We are at the Netherbow, and Dr Irvine stops. "Well, Carruth, here I must leave you. The matter of Aikenhead and those two wicked lassies is out of our hands now. The Privy Council must decide the rights and wrongs of it."

I decide to pursue my early idea of a walk, in the hope of settling the turmoil in my mind. It is for the best that Isobel is not with me, for her presence would have compelled me to restrict our ambulations to the lower walkways of Holyrood Park, close to the palace. Isobel is not feeble, but a gentlewoman's attire does not lend itself to strenuous exercise. On my own I am free to climb up the steep paths of Arthur's Seat, and I set off with the notion of reaching the summit. Very quickly I am beyond the popular loitering places close to the palace and taking a wilder route. It still surprises me that one moment I can be among the few Sunday strollers – there are not many of them, for the great majority of the better sort deem it sinful to take exercise on the Sabbath – and the next completely alone, save for the birds that chirp and forage in the gorse. In places the whin bushes grow so high that I cannot see a single spire of the city. I stride upwards, walled in by wild shrubbery on either side. The sun beats down on my head and shoulders, unmitigated by any breeze. I loosen my neckerchief.

At length I reach the spot that I have always judged to be the summit, although given the strange geography of

Arthur's Seat there are arguments to be made for several high points. There is not another soul to be seen, and the moss is dry, so I sit down to rest myself, and look at the city spread out beneath me. The view is clear, the outlines of the buildings sharp as pen-strokes against the cloudless sky. The usual gauze of smoke is absent, what with it being Sunday. Most hearths will be cold today, sanctified by disuse. Looking over towards Leith I can see a cluster of ships anchored in the Firth of Forth. Whether it is the salubrious effect of the fresh air or the stimulation of the exercise, I begin to feel easier about the Aikenhead case. As Dr Irvine says, it is for the Privy Council to decide. If Elizabeth Edmonstone and Mary Dundas suffer some penalty as a result – and I doubt if any punishment would be severe – they have only themselves to blame. My role in the whole business, aside from attending to Jonet's illness, will scarcely be remarked upon.

But even while freeing myself from one anxiety, another takes its place. Isobel's well-being starts to prey on my mind. She seemed sound enough in body this morning, but cast down with melancholy. It may be nothing more than the natural despondency women are afflicted with at certain times, but I feel certain the fault is mine. Another more terrifying thought comes – a great number of more dangerous maladies first make themselves known in the same way. All manner of fevers and plagues. I am seized with a momentary panic, remembering one of my patients – a hale young lady who was expecting her second child. One fine summer's day she complained of feeling low in spirits. The next day she developed an ague, and within a week she was in her grave. I jump to my feet, determined to take better care of Isobel, to reassure her of my devotion, and to overcome – if I can – my incapacity.

I make my way down the hill taking a different, less trodden path. As I round a bend I see a lad and lassie reclining in the shelter of a cluster of whin bushes. Her bodice is undone and her pale breasts are bare to the sun. The boy has his mouth to her nipple, like a suckling babe. I freeze for a moment, fearing to move in case I should be noticed, but they are too engrossed to detect me. As I back away the girl looks up and sees me. Her eyes widen, but she does not cry out or cover herself. Instead she runs her fingers through her lover's hair and smiles at me, as comfortable in her sinfulness as a cat sprawled in front of a blazing hearth.

I stumble on, troubled and stirred by what I have seen. By the looks of her she was a servant girl, making ungodly use of her one day of leisure. I wonder where Susan is today. For one unwise moment I imagine her similarly engaged, and then push the idea from my mind. These impure thoughts are close to overwhelming me. I hurry home, determined to mend my marriage.

The house is silent when I return. There's no clatter of crockery from the kitchen, none of the bustle of housework. I walk through to the kitchen to find it tidy and vacant. A covered platter sits on the table. I lift the lid and find it contains a selection of cold cooked meats – sliced mutton, a disassembled fowl, fried bacon, stiff and white with congealed fat. A day-old loaf sits beside the platter, wrapped in a linen cloth. I am hungry now, so many hours after my scant breakfast, but I must see Isobel first.

I look in the dining room, then climb the stairs to the first floor and check both the main parlour and Isobel's own, private parlour. The rooms are empty, so I continue to the bedchamber. I tap on the door, but receive no response, then open the door as quietly as I can, in case she is asleep.

The curtains are wide open and the covers pulled up on the bed. Isobel's nightgown is draped over the chair, but otherwise there is no sign of her. I am puzzled, but not unduly concerned. If she is up and dressed she must be recovered.

I go out on to the landing and call her name. No response. I check my own bedchamber, and then make my

way downstairs again, for I doubt she would be in the servants' quarters at the top of the house. At length I am back
in the hallway. There's only my consulting room to look in
now, and I am almost certain I'll not find her there.

And so it proves. But there's a sealed note for me, written
in her hand, on the desk.

My dear husband, she writes. *Forgive my absence. After you
left for the kirk I had word from my mother that my father was
taken ill – nothing, I believe, that places him in real peril, but
enough for my mother to be uneasy and in need of my companionship. Do not trouble yourself on this account. I am sure
it will be a matter of days before I return. Your devoted wife,
Isobel.* She adds a postscript saying, *My own indisposition
seems quite banished by this more pressing concern. Such is the
mystery of the human frame.*

I read the note over several times. Is she telling the
truth, or is this a means to accomplish our separation? Will
this pretence be succeeded by another, and then another?
Better that, I suppose, than the public humiliation of an
annulment. I could not bear it. That would mean the end
of my life here in Edinburgh, for I could not show my face if
all the world had heard that my marriage had been undone
by my inadequacy. And yet, if this is to be the beginning of
gradual uncoupling then the world will notice soon enough,
and draw its own conclusions. I determine to put this right.
Let Isobel have her few days away from me. When she
returns I must – by some means – overcome my weakness.

The house is dark and silent apart from the scratching of
mice behind the wainscot. My accounts book is open in
front of me, but I cannot give it the attention it warrants.
The cause of my distraction sits close at hand in the form of
an empty bottle of port wine. Its erstwhile contents fill my
belly, heat my blood and muddle my brain. I close my book
and prepare to climb the stairs to bed. Susan has not yet
returned, so I am obliged to leave the back door unbolted.

The idea makes me uneasy. How can I rest knowing the house is vulnerable? In any case, she may already be back. It is possible I have been so absorbed in my studies that I have not heard her come in. It will be best to check.

I take the lighted candle and walk up the stairs, past the parlours and bedchambers. The final flight of stairs is narrow, the wood bare and unsanded. Up here, in the top floor of the house, are two servants' rooms, and a larger room meant for a nursery. My father found the means to buy this house when it was new built, by which time I was long beyond childhood. I wonder if any infants of mine will ever be nurtured here, or make the walls ring with their childish noise. The futility of such a notion in my current circumstances darkens my bleak night-time mood still further.

The door to Susan's room is closed, and I pause a moment, listening for any sounds that might indicate she is inside. There is nothing, save a few creaks and whistles from the wind around the chimney pots. When I place my hand on the door handle I find my palm is slick with sweat, and I am trembling. I take a breath and remind myself that this is my house and I can enter any part of it without permission. I open the door.

The room is empty, the curtains still open from when Susan pulled them aside this morning. There is a half-moon tonight. It is not visible through the tiny window, but its light spills over the bedspread. The room smells richly female. As I might have expected, there is a faint scent of lavender, overlaid with Susan's particular musk of sweat. There's a small willow basket at the end of the bed, untidily piled with linen. Of course. Tomorrow, being Monday, is washday. That must be her own soiled linen, ready to be cleansed.

A creak on the stairs makes me jump. "Who is it?" I call out, attempting to disguise my alarm as anger.

"It is Susan, sir," she says, approaching me out of the shadows. She stands in the doorway, her bonnet and shawl in her hands. Her eyes are dark and glittering by the light of the candle. "Did you want something of me?"

My mouth is dry. "I did not know if you were here or not. I didn't want to bolt the door if you were not returned."

"Well here I am, sir, and I have bolted the back door behind me, so you need have no fear." She walks into the room and hangs her shawl and bonnet on a hook that's been hammered into the wall.

"You were out late, Susan."

"The Sabbath is my day of liberty, sir."

I mumble my goodnights to her, and make my way down the stairs to my own bedroom. My bed is cold – there has been no strangely scented warming pan slid between my sheets tonight. Perhaps it is for the best. My blood is over-stirred. The penance of icy sheets on my skin might calm me.

Thomas

Dada is dressed in his best coat and wig. "Fetch me my hat, Thomas," he says. The hat has a dent in the crown, from when Mother crushed it in a rage. I hand it to Dada and he puts it on. "Well," he says. "How do I look?"

"How do you look?" says Mother, standing with her arms folded. "Like the bletherskate you are." Her mouth snaps shut and she presses her lips together so hard they turn white.

"Will you not come with me, Helen?" he says. He sounds all sad.

"I'll come with you," I say, but neither of them is listening. Katharine smiles at me from across the room, and then her face settles back to looking worried.

"Don't you 'Helen' me!" Mother says. "Anyhow, someone must look after the bairns. I may get used to being on my own, once they have you dragged off to prison."

"Are you going to prison, Dada?" My belly feels all trembly. I take Dada's hand. It's sweaty, but I keep a hold of it.

"Of course I'm not, Thomas," he says. "I have to go and see some important gentlemen. You stay here with your mother and sisters. If Anna's feeling better later you can read to her." He pulls his hand away from mine and nudges me towards Katharine.

He goes out then, without another word. I wait until Mother goes into the other room to check on Anna, and I'm off. Out the door, down the stairs, three at a time, into the close and into the street. I can see Dada walking up ahead, but he cannae see me.

I'm in the biggest room I've ever been in, apart from the kirk, and a kirk isn't really a room, is it? This room has a big long table at one end, and a whole crowd of cross-looking gentlemen sitting behind it. There are benches and chairs clustered in front of the long table, and behind that a great press of people standing. I don't think bairns are allowed in here, but I sneaked in at the back and hid myself in among the crowd. I'm that wee that most of them didn't even see I was there. One big man put his hand on my shoulder and asked me what my business was. I pointed into the crowd and said I had a message for my grandfather, and when he looked to see who I was pointing at I juked down and got away from him. Every time I saw a gap I slipped forward, weaving and ducking to avoid getting a dig in the eye from some gentleman's sharp elbow. And now I'm near enough at the front. Not so close as to be seen. I don't want Dada to get a glimpse of me.

I can see him, sitting in the front row. My godfather, Sir Patrick, is standing in front of him, and another gentleman beside him, his hands full of papers, who is doing a lot of talking to Dada. The two ladies are sitting at the front too, side by side. I know it's them, for I recognise the colour of the bonny lady's hair, and so I guess the other lady is her plain friend. They are staring straight ahead, not saying a word to each other. The tall man I saw in Dada's shop – Chalmers – is there too, sitting a bit away from the ladies.

Someone bangs on the table with three big knocks and everyone quietens down. One of the cross-looking gentlemen opens a big letter up and begins reading from it. There are lots of big words in it, and ones I haven't heard before, like "complaint by his Majesty's Advocate", and "Jonet Stewart, late servitrix". And then he says "James Aikenhead, apothecary in Edinburgh..." My Dada! The gentleman goes on reading but I don't pay much attention to the words until the crabbit man who was so cross with me when I led Dada and the doctor to his house springs up from one of the benches and walks forward to the table. He bends over and whispers to the gentleman. There's a lot of head-shaking and finger-pointing and then he goes back to his seat.

"Mary Dundas," the same gentleman says, "your father tells me you are no more than a witness to this wrongdoing. Is that the case?"

"Aye, sir," says the plain girl, so low I can scarcely hear her.

"And are you willing to tell us all you know?"

"I am."

The bonny lady turns to stare at her. From where I am standing I can only catch a glimpse of the look on her face, but I see enough to know I would not like anyone to glare at me in that fashion. My blood would turn cold as ice.

The gentleman at the table nods. "Then you may go and sit with your father until we ask you to speak."

She stands up and skitters over to her father as if she's being chased.

"James Aikenhead," the gentleman says, in a stern, booming voice like a minister. "It is complained of you that you made and sold poisonous tablets designed to work strange wanton affections and humours in the bodies of women. What do you say to that?"

Dada stands up, twisting his hat in his hands. "Not poisonous, my Lord, indeed not. At least, no more than any other medicament taken in overlarge amounts."

"But designed to inflame female lust?" The gentleman looks as if he's eaten something sour.

"Well, yes, I suppose…"

"And you do not deny selling these tablets to any who requested them?"

"That's true enough."

"Did you offer any warning to your customers that the tablets could be noxious if overconsumed?"

Dada fidgets. I cannot rightly see his face, but I'm sure he's smiling, the way he always does when trouble comes calling. "I believe I did, my Lord. At least, I'm almost sure…

108

But any person of sense would know to take only one at a time, don't you agree?"

"Hmmm. Tell me, Mr Aikenhead, do you recognise any in this room as bought these tablets from you?"

Dada turns and looks all around him. I duck behind a stout man in case I'm seen. "I couldn't tell you," Dada says. "There were a brave few customers. I can't remember them all."

The gentleman glances over at a thin, pale man dressed in dusty black clothes who is scratching away with a pen. When he stops writing the gentleman looks back at Dada. "You may sit down." He turns to the bonny lady. "Miss Edmonstone," he says. "We will hear from you now."

She stands up. The room is very quiet. There's a rustling sound when she smoothes her skirts.

"It is complained of you that you sent the servant man Chalmers to buy Mr Aikenhead's tablets, and that afterwards you gave these tablets to Jonet Stewart, saying they were a sweetmeat. Do you admit it?"

"Certainly not."

There's a stir of whispers around the room.

The gentleman looks perplexed. "You deny it then?"

The bonny lady gives a big, loud sigh. "Clearly I do." There's a sour tone to her voice, like Mother's when she's in a foul mood.

"Miss Edmonstone," the gentleman says, "I have a witness statement that says you did send Chalmers to buy the tablets, and you did give them to Jonet Stewart. What say you to that?"

"That your witness is lying. Many people do, to save themselves from blame."

I think about what she has said. She's right. I've lied more times than I can recall to spare myself a hiding. Then I wonder if she is the one who's lying, and her accusing others of it is only to put the blame on them. I feel all muddled in my head about it, so that I don't know who is lying.

The gentleman looks as confused as I am. He nods to her to sit down, then looks at all the people sitting at the front of the room. "Which of you is James Chalmers?"

The tall man stands up. "I am," he says.

"And you were formerly a servant in the house of Mr William Dundas?"

"Aye."

"Why did you leave his employ?"

He doesn't speak for a moment, then says, "I was dismissed."

"For what reason?"

"Because I bought thon poisoned tablets that Jonet took. Mr Dundas said I had designs on her, but I didnae."

"Why did you buy the tablets?"

There's another big silence. "Someone asked me tae."

"And who was that someone?"

He says nothing.

"Come along, man," says the gentleman. "The person accused has been named here in court. You have but to confirm what we already know."

Chalmers still doesn't speak, but he turns and points at the bonny lady.

There's a wee shiver goes around the room. The bonny lady is sitting bolt upright, looking straight ahead.

"Are you saying it was Elizabeth Edmonstone?" says the gentleman.

"I am." He stares at the bonny lady with the oddest expression on his face.

"Did you know when you bought them that the tablets were composed with the aim of provoking lust in women?"

"Aye."

"And what reason did Elizabeth Edmonstone give for wanting them?"

Chalmers swallows so hard I can hear the sound of the gulp. "She said her blood was cold, and she feared that when she came tae be married her husband's attentions would not please her, so she thought it wise tae stir her passion ahead of time."

All the people standing around me shift and shuffle and turn to whisper in each other's ears. The cross-looking gentleman bangs his hammer again, and everyone quietens down.

"I must observe, Mr Chalmers," he says, "that seems a queer sort of conversation for a laird's daughter to be having with a servant man. Did you not think that yourself?"

"I dinnae ken what I was thinking at the time, sir."

"But you must have known you should not have been buying those tablets – for her or anyone else."

"I'm a servant. I do as I'm bid."

The gentleman frowns. "And when you bought these tablets from Mr Aikenhead, did he give you any warning about how they should be taken?"

"I dinnae think he did, but I cannae mind rightly."

The gentleman sighs. "Then I bid you sit down," he says. When Chalmers has sat the gentleman says, "I'd speak now with Mary Dundas."

The plain lady gives a kind of yelp, and turns to her father. He pushes her up out of her seat.

"Now then, Miss Dundas," says the gentleman, "you claim you are no more than a witness to this carry-on. Tell me what you saw."

She starts to speak, but her head is bent and her voice very low, so that I cannot hear a word she's saying. "Speak up, Miss Dundas!" says the gentleman, sounding none too pleased.

She straightens up and speaks louder this time. "Elizabeth Edmonstone said to me, 'I've got a wee treat for Jonet,' and I asked her why, seeing as she was always teasing Jonet, and mocking her."

"And what did she say to that?"

"She said it was time to make amends."

"What happened then?"

"She showed me the box of sweeties, and I said it looked more like something from an apothecary, and she said they were special sweeties that were beneficial to the health."

"Were you with her when she gave them to Jonet?"

"Aye. We were in the parlour, just Elizabeth – Miss Edmonstone – and I, and Jonet came in to tend the fire. She said to Jonet, 'Here's a wee remembering for you,' and fetched the sweetie box out of her skirts. Then she said, 'Dinnae tell Mistress Dundas, for she'll only scold. And dinnae tell the other servants, or they'll all be wanting gifts.' And when Jonet went out Miss Edmonstone looked very pleased with herself, and clapped her hands together, and said, 'Now we'll have some diversion,' but when I asked her what she meant she wouldn't say."

"Did she give Jonet any warning that the tablets – the sweeties – were not all to be consumed at the one time?"

"No, sir. Not in my presence."

The gentleman pauses and waits for the clerk to finish his writing. "So, Miss Dundas," he goes on, "tell me what happened when Jonet became ill."

The plain lady seems unsure what to say. She looks over at her father, who does no more than shrug at her. "Why my mother summoned Mr Fenton, the apothecary, and when Jonet was no better my father sent for Dr Irvine."

"And did it occur to you that Jonet's indisposition might be related to the tablets?"

"No," she says, shaking her head. "Not at first. But then… Miss Edmonstone took me aside and told me to say nothing about the tablets, or else we would both be in bother."

"Miss Dundas, you have heard Miss Edmonstone here today deny procuring these tablets and giving them to Jonet Stewart. Who are we to believe?"

"Me, sir, and James Chalmers, and Jonet Stewart. That's three against one."

The gentleman raises his eyebrows. "Thank you Miss Dundas. Your grasp of numbers is commendable." He glances round the room. "Am I to take it that Jonet Stewart's state of health leaves her unfit to give evidence?"

A stout gentleman in the grandest wig I've ever seen rises up. "My Lord, I regret that is the case. However, I can confirm that Miss Dundas's testimony concurs with Jonet's."

"Thank you, Dr Irvine. May I enquire after Jonet Stewart's prospects for a full recovery?"

"Very poor, my Lord. She will live, but I fear she will never earn her keep again."

The gentleman slams his fist on the table. "Another drain on the charitable resources of the city!" He points at Dada and the bonny lady. "It's the two of you should be held accountable, eh?" Everyone starts whispering again, until the hammer is banged on the table.

A tall skinny man stands up and shouts, "Session adjourned while my Lord and the council consider their response." The people around me push and press towards the door, and I am carried by them the way a leaf is swept along the gutter when there's a fall of rain. We all pour out into the street. I can't spot Dada's among all the hats and wigs of the gentlemen, so I climb up on the steps to give me a better view. Still no sign of Dada, but I see one familiar face – Dr Carruth, standing stern and handsome, a good way apart from the crowd. The stout gentleman with the grand wig approaches him and pats him on the arm. Dr Carruth still disnae look happy. He glances over in my direction, so I wave at him. When he notices me he stops short, stares at me for a wee minute, then turns away and walks off. I jump down and chase after him, just for the devilment, because he looks as if it would annoy him. But once I'm off the steps I can't see him anymore. I push through the crowd in the direction he went, but there's no sign of him. Then I see Dada, standing with Mr Fenton by the corner, so I go tae him instead.

Dr Carruth

I am even more uneasy now that I've seen the Aikenhead boy, waving at me as cheerily as if I were a benevolent uncle rather than the instrument of his father's undoing. For a moment I consider taking my leave of the whole proceedings, but I am anxious to know the outcome. Dr Irvine is hopeful that Aikenhead will be censured, and the authority of the physicians strengthened. He murmured something about inviting me to dine at the Royal College tomorrow evening. I should be gratified, but the pleasure is lessened by the way my role in Jonet's cure has been overlooked. There was not a mention of me, when it was I who tracked down Aikenhead, and I who formulated the course of treatment that saved Jonet. I suppose I must be consoled that my lady patients know the truth of the matter, and their word carries more weight with other ladies than any posturing by Dr Irvine. Perhaps he considers an invitation to dinner (and in time – who knows? – the offer of admission to the fellowship) to be adequate compensation. Perhaps it is.

We have been summoned back into the Privy Council chamber. Once again I find a place in the gallery, far enough back not to be noticed. The Earl of Linlithgow resumes the presiding chair. Some of the other Privy councillors chat to each other, but his Lordship does not join in. Instead he frowns down at the many papers that sit before him on the table, leafing through them as if to refresh his memory of what they contain. A few minutes more pass. I can see Aikenhead, seated in front of the table in conversation with another man – his advocate, I presume. Elizabeth Edmonstone is straight-backed, but she turns her head from time to time as gracefully as a swan. Her russet hair is almost hidden beneath her bonnet, so that only a flash of it is glimpsed each time she turns. It seems to me that she is scanning the room to see who is watching her.

Lord Linlithgow bangs his hammer and the room comes to order. "James Aikenhead, James Chalmers and Elizabeth Edmonstone," he says, and waits as the three rise to their feet. "We find you guilty of an open and manifest crime, and conclude that you should be subject to exemplary punishment. However, before sentence be passed we charge the Royal College of Physicians to examine the case more thoroughly. You may all be called to the college for further questioning, and should you attempt to evade such investigation by departing the city, then you will be judged outlaw." He turns towards Dr Irvine, who is in his former seat at the side of the room. "Dr Irvine," he says, "May I have your assurance that this will be pursued with all vigour?" Dr Irvine stands and bows his assent. Another bang of the hammer and we are dismissed.

The sunshine is bright and the crowd from the council chamber seem inclined to loiter in its warmth. I catch sight of James Aikenhead standing slack-jawed at the bottom of the steps. His son has him by both hands, talking at him but – from what I can see – not being heard. I want only to be away, but find my path barred by Elizabeth Edmonstone. "So, Dr Carruth," she says, her eyes glittering with fury. "You will be content to see me ruined."

"Why would I want such a thing?"

"To punish my father."

I am bemused. I know nothing of her father, save that he is Laird of Duntreath. "You are quite wrong, Miss Edmonstone," I say. I could tell her how I tried to have the complaint withdrawn, but something about her temper and arrogance makes me disinclined to placate her. Her face is pale but I can see an angry blush on her neck.

"Liar!" she hisses back. "I've noted how you fawn over Dr Irvine. You would do anything to gain his favour."

"What has Dr Irvine to do with your father?"

"Do not pretend you don't know."

She tries to turn away from me, but I cannot let her insult go unanswered. "I am glad to see you suffer, Miss Edmonstone," I say, "but not for the nonsensical reason you suggest. You are a spiteful, mendacious girl. The type who delights in tormenting any who are unfortunate enough to serve her." I remember how she laughed at Susan, taking pleasure in her discomfort.

Suddenly her anger is gone. "My father will be written to," she says. "No doubt Mr Dundas is already scurrying home to sharpen his quill. And where am I to go? Do you imagine I can return to the Dundas house, to break bread with that simpering coward Mary?"

Her change of mood disconcerts me. "You must have other friends here."

"Precious few." She turns on her heel and walks off as briskly as her skirts will allow.

I trust I appear calm, but in truth I do not feel it. My heart is pounding at the injustice of her accusations and – what else? Is there some ignoble exultation at seeing such a girl humbled? I am still feeling unaccountably disturbed when I see Isobel, not twenty yards away. She is with her mother, and they are deep in conversation, casting occasional glances my way. I must speak to them of course – what could be more natural? – and am on my way over to them when I am accosted by Dr Maxwell.

"So, Carruth," he says, "I saw Irvine beaming at you as warmly as the sun in the sky. I take it an invitation to join the Royal College will be forthcoming?"

"I really couldn't say," I snap.

Maxwell smiles, as if at some private joke. "I suppose you're feeling sour that our role in saving that lassie's life was painted out?"

"*Our* role?" He has a damned cheek.

He narrows his eyes. "I believe it was I who dropped the hint about camphorated tincture of opium?" There's an uncharacteristic chill in his voice.

My face heats with humiliation. "Of course. I quite forgot." I pause and force myself to say, "Forgive me."

Maxwell's warmth returns as suddenly as it departed. "Consider yourself forgiven, Carruth," he says. "Let he who is without sin, and all that." He takes out his handkerchief and mops his brow. "It's insufferably hot, don't you think? And it only April! Will you join me in taking some liquid refreshment?"

"Thank you, no," I say, conscious of how stiff I must look and sound. "My wife and her mother await me here." Isobel and my mother-in-law have drawn closer while we have spoken. I catch Isobel's eye, but her expression is unreadable.

"Ah!" says Maxwell, turning to look at them. "The delights of feminine company must surely outweigh the pleasures of the tavern." He raises his hat to the ladies, and is on his way.

I stand in awkward speechlessness for a moment. At length I manage to say, "I had not expected to see you here."

"Indeed," my mother-in-law says, arching her eyebrows in that knowing manner that irritates me so.

"I recalled how concerned you were about this case," says Isobel. "What was the outcome?"

"They were all found guilty, except Mary Dundas. She turned evidence against Miss Edmonstone."

We fall into silence once more. At length my mother-in-law says, "Isobel, my dear, I do not like to leave your father unattended for so long." She gives me a steely look. "Will you escort us home, *son?*"

I am ushered into the front parlour, where my father-in-law sits sweltering before an unseasonably large fire. He has a rug tucked around his legs, but apart from an uncharacteristic pallor he seems quite well. It is a relief to me that his supposed illness was not an invention of Isobel's. "The womenfolk fuss so, Robert," he says apologetically. "I dare say if you had charge of my health you'd prescribe fresh air and exercise." I rather like my father-in-law. In theory he is a minister of religion, but in practice he spends as much of his time as he can away from his damp country kirk. The diversions of Edinburgh are more to his taste than the dismal fields of Lanarkshire. Isobel's marriage has offered him the opportunity of many weeks in town.

We exchange some banalities until the ladies come into the room. I feel myself tense, and wonder if my father-in-law detects the change in atmosphere. Isobel observes me intently, but I cannot decipher her mood from her expression. As we all sit I notice a glance pass between her and her mother.

Talk turns to today's sitting of the Privy Council. "So Elizabeth Edmonstone is to be punished?" Isobel's mother says. "What will they do to her, do you think? Not prison?"

"I doubt it," I say. "A fine, most likely."

"Her father will hardly have the means to pay her fine," my father-in-law says.

"Is he poor?" I say.

"No more than any other laird, but he's inconveniently detained in Stirling prison."

"What was his crime?"

"He harboured a Covenanter preacher in Duntreath Castle. More fool him. He knew what trouble that would cause him, in these times."

I remember Elizabeth Edmonstone's anger at me today. Her claim that she had no friends in Edinburgh. Perhaps fear lay behind that fury. "Do you know, sir, if there is some enmity between her father and Dr Irvine?"

My father-in-law frowns as he considers this. "Dr Irvine had a bad time of it from the Covenanters when he was a young man. Before your day, of course. He wouldn't sign the second Covenant. They threw him in prison for a time, deprived him of his land, chased him from the country for a few years. Perhaps some of the Duntreaths were involved. They've always had a fanatical streak."

And now the shoe is on the other foot. Covenanters are persecuted, and their former prey are in the ascendant. Dr Irvine did not appear to be a man driven by vengeance, but perhaps, when the opportunity presented itself, he could not resist.

The conversation lulls. There's no sound but the crackle of the fire. "And is all well in the Pleasance?" says my mother-in-law. "What of the new servant – will she satisfy?"

Sweat prickles on my forehead. "I do not know. We husbands must be guided by our wives in these matters."

"Very true. I have said to Isobel that our Hetty has a niece looking for a place. If this Irish lassie of yours does not please, you could do worse than young Agnes. But of course, I must not interfere in your household, *son*." My mother-in-law stands up. "And on that point, I must speak to Hetty about the mutton." She nods towards her husband. "You should lie down, or you'll overtire yourself."

"I've no need to lie down, madam," he says. She stands staring at him and something in her glance brings about a change of heart, for he casts aside his rug and rises. "Well, perhaps a brief nap would be beneficial," he mutters, and follows his wife from the room.

Isobel and I are alone, and the silence continues. "Dr Irvine has invited me to dine at the Royal College tomorrow evening," I say, to fill the emptiness.

"What of Mr Aikenhead?" she says. "What will become of him and his family?"

"I... I do not know," I admit. I long for some approving word or glance from her. These last days my vital spirits have been sinfully aroused – by Susan, by Elizabeth Edmonstone, by that shameless servant girl I saw with her

119

sweetheart – chasing away images of death and decomposition. I think I might be able to embrace Isobel – sit her on my knee, as I did on that golden day of our courtship. Of course I know – as any physician must – that beneath her pale skin the thousand animal processes of the human body continue, but that knowledge no longer renders me powerless. "Isobel," I say, reaching forward to take her hand. "Will you come home soon?"

Oh the look she gives me! There's compassion in it, and something like disappointment. She does not turn away, but the expression in her eyes tells me that some door in her heart has been closed. "A few more days, perhaps," she says. "When Mother is content to spare me."

I cannot face home. A dark house, a lonely bed. And Susan. These last nights since Isobel's departure I have lain abed, half dreading, half longing for another visit from Susan, another "dream". I dare not return there in my current mood. I turn instead towards that part of town where the taverns are respectable enough for me not to lose my name by entering them. Here's one that offers grilled chops along with liquor. I go in, intent on calming myself with port wine, but glad to cloak my thirst in the respectable desire for victuals.

What time it is I do not know. I bang on my own front door and wait a good ten minutes before Susan opens it and lets me in. She is in her nightdress, with a shawl draped around her shoulders. The candle in her hand nearly flickers out in the draught as she closes the door.

"You have no business going to your bed before the master of the house gives you permission to do so," I say, and realise, with some mortification, that my voice is slurred.

"The hour was very late, and you'll expect me up in a few hours to light your fire and heat your water," she says, staring at me evenly.

120

Insolence. Damned insolence. I sway towards her, and she puts her hand against my chest. At first I think she means to keep me at bay, but her fingers grip at my coat and she pulls me closer. She turns her face up to me and lets her lips brush against mine. This time I do not rebuff her. She kisses me as no decent woman would, and I return in kind. After a moment she stops and says, "The mistress told me I could go to bed, sir."

"The mistress?" I am shocked into sobriety. "Has Isobel... my wife... returned?"

"Yes, sir. Some three hours since. You have likely woken her with your battering of the front door."

"Why did you not tell me sooner?" I lower my voice to a whisper. "Before I... disgraced myself?"

She smiles. "I could have let things go further, sir, had I wished. Be thankful I stopped you when I did."

I have not the presence of mind to address Susan's behaviour now. I walk upstairs, pleased to find my steps are steady. I am not some drunkard staggering and stumbling through his own house. Down in the hallway Susan bolts the door and creeps up the stairs behind me. On the landing I pause for a moment looking at the closed door of Isobel's bedchamber, then turn into my room and close the door. I tear off my clothes, throwing them carelessly to the floor. Susan can tidy them tomorrow. I pull on my nightshirt and climb into bed, suddenly wearier than I ever remember being.

I must have slept – the brief, deep sleep of the drunken man. When I wake I have no sense of how much time has passed. The bedsheets are damp with sweat.

For a moment I lie there, gripped by a strange and thrilling impulse, and then throw the bedcovers off and climb from the bed. I have an odd sense that this scene is not real. I feel as if I am observing a painting – although it would be an odd work of art that showed a man stood stock-still in his nightshirt, and the looming bulk of a bed, and the dark distance of the floor between him and the door. Every pulse of my heart makes me conscious of the ebb and flow of the blood around my body. My skin thrums in time to my heartbeat.

I go to the washstand and splash my face with cold water. Slowly I walk across the room towards the door. Outside in the hallway I pause. In front of me is Isobel's bedchamber door, and at the end of the corridor lies the narrow staircase to Susan's room. I hesitate, unsure which path to take.

She has left the curtains half-open, and a moonbeam shines across the floor. I see her head turn on the pillow as I come into the room. There is an air of watchfulness about her that makes the hair on the back of my neck stand on end. As I take the few steps to her bedside she sits up.

"I hoped you would come to me," she says.

"I'm afraid I have not behaved as I should."

"Hush now," Isobel says gently, and pulls the covers back to admit me to our marriage bed.

Thomas

Me and the Keep-Count Man are sitting on our usual step in the sunshine. He's in bad form, leaning against the doorpost with one hand to his sore ear. Dada isn't well enough to make up his powder, and it's the Sabbath, so there's no other apothecary who'll provide it in Dada's stead.

I copy the Keep-Count Man and lean against the other doorpost. My eyes are heavy. Dada was coughing all night, and Anna was gurning, so none of us had much rest. I close my eyes. It's odd the way you hear sounds differently when your eyes are shut. There are wee birds nesting in the roof, and their cheeping and chirruping is very clear. Someone in hobnail boots walks along the wynd beyond the close. From somewhere inside our building I can hear the scrape of a spoon in a bowl, over and over again, as if the person holding the spoon is eating their cold Sunday porridge as quickly as they possibly can.

Katharine is standing in the space between me and the Keep-Count Man. I must have fallen asleep for a minute, because I didn't hear her come down the stairs. She hunkers down. "Can you go and sit with Father for a while?" she says. "He keeps asking for you."

I stand up and stretch. My arse is numb and my feet are tingling from sitting so long. I stamp my feet to bring them back to life. "Houl' your noise!" the Keep-Count Man says, jerking upright and glaring at me. He touches his ear carefully and makes a face as if it hurts him.

Katharine guides me into the hallway and we go upstairs. "Mind not to be prattling at Father," she says. "He's no strength for replying to your nonsense." She sounds cross.

"If he speaks to me, may I speak back to him?"

"Of course you may, you clout."

We go into our lodgings. Mother is sitting looking out the window, and Anna is asleep on the floor in front of the fireplace, tucked around with a quilt. I head to the bed-chamber where Dada is resting. He turns his head towards me and smiles. "Och, there you are, wee Tam," he says in a whispery voice. "Come and sit down on the bed."

I do as he says. I wish I could take his hand, but Katharine has him all happed up in his blankets so that all I can see is his face. "Are you cold, Dada?" I say.

"No," he says. "At least, I don't think so."

"Do you feel better?"

"Aye, I do."

"That's good," I say. His skin looks an odd colour. Like candlewax.

For a while he doesn't speak, and then says, "What day is it, Thomas?"

"Sunday, Dada. Father."

He smiles. "You may call me Dada if you wish, son. If it makes you happy." He shifts in the bed, wriggling his arms free of the blankets. "Did you go to kirk this morning?"

"Aye. Katharine took me."

"Good boy," he says, and starts to footer with the edge of his blanket, twisting and tugging it.

"I prayed to God that you would get better soon." I reach out and touch his restless hands. His fingers are cold and damp, like the wall beside the stairs is, winter and summer. He stops fidgeting and closes his eyes. His chest rises up and down as if he is running, as if every breath is hard to find. I feel sleepy again. There's a wee fire smouldering in the grate, and the window can't be opened. I lie down on the bed beside him. There's enough room for me. Mother will shout at me if she comes in, on account of me having my feet on the bed, and me with my shoes still on, but I'm too sleepy to care. Katharine will be pleased, though, for I'm keeping Dada company, but not bothering him with chat.

I decide to pray again, even though I'm not in the kirk. I think it's allowed to pray anywhere – even in bed – but I suppose prayers work best if they're said in the kirk. "Please God," I say, "make Dada get better soon." I know it will work, for the minister said so today. "Ask, and it shall be given you," he said. "Seek, and ye shall find; knock, and it shall be opened unto you." He said a lot of other things too, for he always talks for ever such a long time, and I fell asleep in the middle of his sermon and only woke when Katharine squeezed my hand. *Ask, and it shall be given you.* "That's what it says in the Bible," the minister told us, "and the Bible is always right."

PART II
ANATOMY OF AN ACCUSATION

PRIMA MVSCV-
LORVM TABVLA.

Quarta

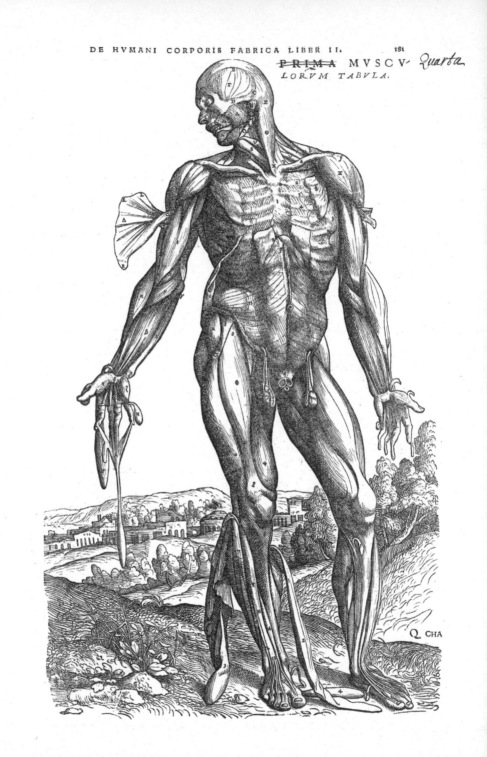

Q CHA

1696

Mungo

Hutchison has a fire blazing in the back room despite the season, and the sweat is blinding me though I am in my shirtsleeves. He's happy enough for us lodgers to freeze all through the winter, but now that his she-dog is about to whelp he'll spare no expense for her comfort. "Can we not open the window?" I say.

"And have her catch cold?" He looks down at the dog. She's worrying at a dirty auld blanket, snuffling it into the nook beside the hearth and then turning around and around on it as if she's taken the head-staggers.

"Are the pups coming, do you think?"

"Aye. Any minute now. If your friend Thomas hurries up he'll see it." He touches the sore on his cheek. "You told him to make me up a poultice?"

"I asked him. Thomas won't be told anything." The dog is half crouched now, still circling and making wee whimpering noises. "Should I call Patrick down? He might want to watch this."

Hutchison doesn't reply to me, but raises his head and gulders, "Mr Middleton! Come on down here and you will see something to your advantage!"

A clatter on the stairs and Patrick stumbles into the room, pulling on his coat. "What is it?" He looks all round as if he expects to see someone of importance.

"This lassie's about to pup." Hutchison nods over at the dog. She's rubbing her rump on the blanket, and I can just see a dark clot of something starting to nose out of her nethers.

Patrick stands gawping at the dog for a moment, then takes his coat off again and sets it on the dresser. The dog's sides are heaving like a bellows and the dark clot is pushed further out. I can see now that it is a tiny snout.

"Who's the sire?" Patrick asks.

Hutchison shrugs. "I'll know better when I see the colour of them. Is this first one black, do you think?"

We all hunker down closer to her and watch as the pup slithers free and lies like a stunned fish on the bloody blanket. She licks the pup so hungrily I think she's going to eat it, but her rough tongue stirs it into life and nudges it towards her teats.

"He's black as soot," says Patrick.

There's a rap at the door of the shop. Thomas. I go to let him in, glad to get away from the heat of the fire.

"Look at the state of you," he says, glancing head to toe at me. "You're like a hog roasting on a spit."

"Hutchison has the place well heated for the dog's lying in," I whisper.

I'm rewarded with a grin. "He'd make a fine man-midwife."

"Did you bring his poultice?"

Thomas pats his coat pocket. "He'll have a face as clear as an angel's in no time. Has he money to pay me?"

"You'd be as well to make sure and get payment before you treat him," I say. Hutchison can be a sleekit one when it comes to money. We go through to the back room. Another pup has been born. This one is brindled.

"It has the same coat as that mastiff the tapster at the Hart keeps," Patrick says.

"If that beast was the sire these pups would have burst her apart." Hutchison peers closer. "Anyway, the tapster keeps the mastiff chained up in the cellar. It would tear the throat out of his customers if he let it roam free."

"A sly dog will slip its leash," I say, "if the lure is strong enough." A third pup slips out. White, like its mother.

Hutchison stands up, his knees creaking louder than the snap of the fire in the hearth. He looks expectantly towards Thomas. "Well?" he says.

Thomas looks blank, and for a moment I think he's going to torture Hutchison. I hope he won't, for it will be

Patrick and I who'll have to bear his bad mood afterwards. I'm relieved when Thomas pulls the little parcel from his pocket. "That'll be sixpence," he says.

"Sixpence!" says Hutchison. "That's costly, and you not a doctor yet."

"I learnt the apothecary's art at my dear old father's knee," says Thomas. "This is a formulation of his own devising, never known to fail and worth every penny."

"I don't think I have change," says Hutchison.

Thomas puts the parcel back in his pocket. "Let me know when you do," he says, and turns as if to walk out.

"Hold on, hold on," Hutchison grumbles, reaching into his waistcoat. "Here, I have sixpence after all."

Thomas bows and pockets the coin. He retrieves the little parcel. "It needs heated," he says, starting to take off the wrappings.

The poultice is tied in a muslin bag, and Thomas sets it down on the griddle Hutchison keeps by the fireplace. He hooks the griddle on to the crane and swings it over the flames. An acrid smell hits the back of my throat and I start to cough. So too do Hutchison and Patrick. Only Thomas is immune. He bends over the fire watching the poultice. His hair hangs down so that I can't see the expression on his face, but I imagine his intent look. He has that gift of concentration. "Here's another pup," says Patrick, but I can't take my eyes away from Thomas.

"Is that thing not ready yet?" There's a catch in Hutchison's breath as he speaks. "It near has me choked."

"Patience," Thomas says. A moment more and he swings the griddle off the fire and picks the poultice up delicately, holding a loose end of the muslin between his index finger and thumb. He glances at Hutchison. "I'd advise you to sit, sir, before I apply this."

Hutchison pulls the good chair away from the table and plants himself in it. "Will it hurt?"

133

"Aye, at first." Thomas advances on him and presses the poultice firmly against the sore on Hutchison's cheek. He flinches and grips the seat of the chair.

"I think she's all done," Patrick says. He's the only one of us still paying attention to the dog. "Four pups. Two black, one white, one brindled."

"One less than last time," Hutchison says, without looking down at her.

Thomas stands for a moment, holding the poultice in place. "This needs to stay against the skin until it has cooled. Will you take it? I have an engagement in the Pleasance." He glances at me. "Don't look so put out, Mungo. You're invited too. And Patrick."

Hutchison takes over from Thomas in holding the poultice. "Will this one treatment be sufficient?"

"It may be, or it may not. The sore should dry out, and then come away in a week or so. If it doesn't we'll try again." He kneels down by the dog and her pups. "Look how they feed. I feel starved just watching them." The dog eyes him. She seems docile enough in her postnatal stupor, but I'm afraid that she'll snap if he puts a hand near the pups. I think of warning him, but something makes me hold my tongue.

"Who is it you know in the Pleasance?" Patrick says. Thomas just smiles and rubs the dog's head. She closes her eyes. The only sound is the crackle of the fire and the rasp of Thomas's fingers as he rubs them up and down the ridge of the dog's nose.

"Do you want a pup then, Thomas?" Hutchison says.

"That brindled one would make a fine companion, but my sister would go through me if I came home with a dog." He stands up. "Come along then, you two. It's time we were away."

"Am I properly turned out?" I pick fluff from my coat as we walk, and wish my clothes were not so shabby. The Pleasance is a respectable address.

"You'll do." Thomas's garments are in all likelihood older than mine, and are certainly more worn, but they have about them an air of faded quality and he carries them well.

"Are you not going to tell us what this is about?" Patrick scurries along, trying to keep up with us.

"I'm going to collect a debt."

That is his way. Never a straight answer. I am learning not to rise to it. Patrick hasn't attained that wisdom yet, but he is too out of breath to ask more. Thomas realises we aren't going to press him. That irks him. I can see it in the way the smirk fades from his face.

We get to the Pleasance. The houses are tall and thin, but the street is broad and airy, with the crags and green places of Arthur's Seat beyond. We come to one house at the end of a terrace with a fine set of steps leading up to the front door. Thomas looks up at it a moment. "It's smaller than I remembered it," he murmurs, then bounds up and rattles the door knocker. A raw-faced countrywoman in servant's dress opens the door. "Mr Thomas Aikenhead, to see Dr Carruth," he says loftily.

"Dr Carruth is at table," the servant says, taking in Patrick and I with a dubious glance.

"He and my father were... acquainted," Thomas says. "Please be so good as to tell him I am here."

The woman gives a curt nod, but closes the door in our faces nonetheless.

"What do we do now?" I look up and down the street. One gentleman is walking past on the other side. He stares at us. I feel my face heat.

"She'll be back, you wait and see." Thomas walks to the corner where a wynd runs down the side of the house. "As I recall his consulting room was towards the back of the house. I'm away to have a keek through the window."

Patrick and I exchange a glance. He looks as fearful as I feel. "Have a bit of wit, Thomas," I call after him as he skites down the wynd. "They'll have the town watch on us if they catch you snooping."

Thomas ignores me and stands on tiptoe looking in through the window. "He has a wall-full of books," he says. "How would you like to have so many volumes, Mungo?"

The front door opens again just as Thomas scrambles back up the wynd. The servant woman nods us in.

We are shown upstairs and into a parlour grander than any I've been in before. Dr Carruth stands before us. We passed the dining room on our way through the hall. The chink of spoons on platters and the voices of a woman and children drift through the narrow house. Dr Carruth is a man of around forty years of age, slender-built and quietly dressed. The only remarkable feature of his appearance is his eyes. They are dark and restless, and I feel my stomach tighten with anxiety. I cannot imagine feeling at ease in his company. He focuses his unsettling gaze on Thomas. "You were only a wee lad when I saw you last," he says. "Your father, is he...?"

"Dead," Thomas says cheerfully. "Mother too. I have been an orphaned bairn since the age of ten."

Dr Carruth looks as if he does not know what to make of Thomas's flippancy. "I am sorry to hear that."

"Poor Father," Thomas says, throwing himself into an armchair. "I gather he didn't have much sense. I remember little of him."

"He seemed very fond of you." Dr Carruth says. The expression on his face suggests an inner turmoil. He is irritated at Thomas's presumption in sitting without being invited to do so, but he is nervous too. "What brings you to call on me, after all this time?" he says at last.

"I am a student at the university."

"I had supposed as much."

"It is my hope to be a physician. A step up from dear old Father."

136

Dr Carruth nods. "That is most commendable. You have not yet answered my question."

Before Thomas can reply I hear the rustle of silk at the door of the room and a woman comes in. I take in the deep blue of her gown, the soft brown hair visible under her lace cap, the unblemished white of her hands and face. "The children and I have finished, Robert," she says, glancing at each of us as she speaks. "I've set your plate by the hearth, to keep it warm."

Thomas springs up and makes a bow. "Thomas Aikenhead, madam."

She frowns, as if presented with a puzzling question. At last she says, "You keep my husband from his dinner, Mr Aikenhead."

"It smells delicious. Mutton?"

"Mutton and barley broth. An old family recipe." She returns her attention to her husband, fixing him with a particular stare.

"You may remember, Isobel," Dr Carruth says to her, "that case some years ago where I spoke before the Privy Council?"

Mistress Carruth nods slowly. She turns to Thomas. "You are the apothecary's son?"

"Indeed." There is a trace of a blush on Thomas's face. He often boasts of the skills he inherited from his father, but there is something in Mistress Carruth's tone… condescension? He does not like it.

Dr Carruth stirs. "Perhaps Agnes could give these young men a bowl of broth? Downstairs. I'm sure she has plenty in the pot." He looks at Thomas. "Let me call one of the servants to show you to the kitchen."

"The kitchen?" Thomas raises his eyebrows, his annoyance more overt now. "You're very kind, Dr Carruth, but I wouldn't like to inconvenience your servants."

My stomach gurgles so loudly that everyone turns towards me. Patrick sniggers like a schoolboy. Mistress Carruth's mouth twitches as if she is suppressing a smile. "I believe your friend would be happy to eat Agnes's broth in any location, Mr Aikenhead." She looks at me, her smile undisguised now. "Is that not so, Mr...?"

"Craig," I say. "Kentigern Craig."

Thomas smirks. "Kentigern! A terrible mouthful of a name, don't you agree? Fear not, Mistress Carruth. We all call him Mungo." My face flames with mortification, and in that moment I wish Thomas to the devil.

"Come then," says Dr Carruth, ringing the bell for the servant. "Agnes will guide you to the kitchen and fill your bellies before you go."

"I did not call in the hope of a meal," Thomas says. "Rather I wished to have a private conversation with you regarding my prospects."

Dr Carruth broods on this for a moment or two. He glances at his wife, as if waiting for her guidance. Indeed, it is she who replies. "May I make a suggestion?" she says. "That you all return here a week hence to dine with us. Afterwards, Mr Aikenhead, you and my husband may have your conversation."

Thomas thinks about this for a moment, then bows his acceptance of her offer.

We leave the room, Thomas, Patrick and I following Mistress Carruth. The servant woman meets us at the foot of the stairs, and Mistress Carruth instructs her to show us out. As we pass the dining room door I see two young faces – a boy and a girl – peeking round it. Mistress Carruth chides them back in. "Your father is coming to finish his dinner, children. Stay where you are and keep him company." They do as they are bid, staring at us with great curiosity as we pass.

We troop obediently after the servant past the well-polished oak of the hallway and out on to the street.

"I could have done with a bowl of yon broth," Patrick says as we retrace our steps from the Pleasance to College Wynd.

"Did you see how he put me in my place?" Thomas makes no effort to hide his bitterness.

"Perhaps if you hadn't barged in…"

He cuts me off. "How else would I get in his company?" He kicks a loose stone across the street. It clatters against the wheel of a cart. The horse in the traces flinches and the carter shouts a curse at us. This seems to cheer Thomas, for he continues, "Still, we have an invitation to dine. And I believe Dr Carruth may be persuaded to assist my advancement." He gives a little skip, like a child at play.

"Why would he assist you?" Patrick asks. "You're neither kith nor kin to him."

Thomas gives Patrick a knowing look. "You wait and see, my friend. You wait and see."

We part from Thomas and go back to our lodgings. There is no sign of Hutchison in the back room, but the dog is still lying in her nest by the fire. A single pup – the brindled one – suckles at her.

Hutchison comes in from the yard, drying his hands on a cloth. "Where are the other pups?" Patrick asks.

"In a sack on the bed of the Nor' Loch," Hutchison says. "I've just come from there."

"You drowned them?"

He must not like the look on my face, for he rounds on me. "How would I feed four more animals? Would you have funded their keep?"

Patrick hunkers down to study the dog and her remaining pup. "At least you left her the one."

"Aye. He'll help clear her milk. I'll maybe find a taker for him, if folk can be persuaded he's half mastiff."

"He was Thomas's favourite," I say.

"It was Thomas's favour led me to spare him," Hutchison says, sitting down and stretching his legs out towards the fire. "You can tell him that when next you see him."

Isobel

I was married four years before I provided my husband with a living child, and my reward was a dainty writing desk – the sort the Spaniards call a *bargueño*. Little Henry was scarcely a week old when Robert carried the desk into our bedchamber, with the assistance of a red-faced Agnes, so that I could see it before it was set into place in my parlour. "It is to be yours, and yours alone," he said. At the time I thought him a madman, struggling up the stairs with a piece of furniture, when all that mattered to me in the world was the baby lying in the crib at my bedside. I was in the first delirium of mother-love, and all other things were trivial and absurd. Robert's face, aglow with delight at his choice of gift, looked almost grotesque. However, in the years that followed I realised how aptly he had picked. Other women of my acquaintance received jewels and new gowns – fripperies which they doubtless tired of quickly enough – whereas my desk has become more precious to me as the demands of my household hem me in ever more tightly. It is my haven: a private place where I can write my letters and journal. Each time I sit down at my desk it is as if I have entered another world, where I exist as a creature of thought, not of flesh.

But this evening duty brings me to my desk. A letter from my mother has sat unanswered for two days, and if I do not respond to it soon she will write again, complaining more bitterly of my neglect. I had always thought her one of those women who would excel at widowhood, but instead each year since my father's death has seen her retreat further into discontented solitude, with only old Hetty for company. She writes to me of little more than the weather and her own aches and pains, and at times I am hard-pressed to know how to reply. At least our unexpected visitors have given me something to write about – something more than the minutiae of the children's lessons or the price of mutton. *You may recall the court case Robert was involved with shortly after we were married*, I write. *The reckless apothecary, Aikenhead, who sold dangerous tablets, and Robert saved the life of one of the poor souls who had been poisoned by them. Well, now Aikenhead's son has turned up on our doorstep, craving an audience with Robert.* I pause as I remember Mr Aikenhead. There was a tender-heartedness about him, a sort of sad gentility. I could not dislike him as Robert did. And the boy, Thomas, – that delightful, bright-eyed imp – has grown into a man. He has his father's well-bred demeanour, but a sharper intelligence. After the trial I determined to help the family. I sent discreet gifts of money through old Fenton the apothecary. Robert knew nothing about it. But within a few months I miscarried our first child and had no compassion to spare for anyone but my own sorry self.

I stir myself from the memory and return to my letter. *The boy is a student of medicine at the university, and I think he means to cultivate Robert as a patron of sorts. He brought with him two companions, also students. One is an unremarkable fellow, but the other would be hard to miss, nearly as broad as he is tall – and he is taller than is usual – with a shock of black hair as coarse as a horse's tail.*

There's a tap at the door and Agnes comes in. "We're all gathered for evening prayers, Miss Isobel," she says. Although I was several months married by the time Agnes came to work for us, she has always called me *Miss Isobel*, taking her lead, I suppose, from her Aunt Hetty who served in my parents' house all through my childhood.

I follow Agnes to the main parlour, where the rest of our modest household is gathered: Robert, Henry and Margaret, with the addition of Alison, the children's nurse. Henry slips away from his sister to be beside me. We all kneel, bow our heads and listen as Robert reads the prayer from the book of Common Order. The familiar words are softened with use, like an old woollen cloak, and just as comforting to wrap myself in. I can always judge Robert's mood by the tone of his voice, and tonight I sense his tension. It is doubtful if anyone else would hear it, but I do.

"...furthermore, that our sleep be not excessive or overmuch after the insatiable desires of our flesh," he prays, "but only sufficient to content our weak nature, that we may be the better disposed to live in all godly conversation, to the glory of Thy holy name and profit of our brethren."

We all join together to murmur "So be it." In the moments of silent contemplation that follow I listen hard for the voice of God, but can hear nothing more than an infinity of silence. Perhaps it is foolish to expect Him to speak as mortals speak, but nonetheless I keep hoping.

Robert closes the book softly to signal that we are finished, and helps me to my feet. I ruffle Henry's hair. "Time for bed, my bonny laddie."

Alison steps forward. "I was wondering, Mistress," she says, "if I might stay here while you and the master read your chapter from the Bible?"

I glance at Robert. He looks as taken aback as I am. Our nightly ritual is precious to us. "I would not like the children kept from their beds," I say.

Alison's jaw has a determined set to it. "Agnes would be glad to see to them."

"Oh please, Mama," Henry says. "Let Agnes put us to bed."

I wonder that Alison is not affronted by Henry's eagerness for her substitute, but she does not seem to notice. How can I object without seeming thrawn? "Do you mind, Agnes?" I ask her.

"It's all one to me," she says, and leads the children out of the room.

Alison looks fixedly at the Bible on the table. "It's a fine, godly habit you have, Dr Carruth. Do you follow a particular method of reading, or go where the Holy Spirit guides you?"

Robert gestures for us to sit. "I'm a methodical man, Alison. We start at the beginning of Genesis and work our way through, a chapter a night, until the end of Revelation."

"And then we start again," I add. I try to remember when we began with this. Not from the first stuttering weeks of our marriage, certainly, but soon enough once we had found our feet.

"You have reached the book of Isaiah, I believe?" says Alison. Robert and I exchange a glance. How could she know that? Has she been listening at the keyhole?

Robert hands me the Bible, and I turn to today's chapter. "'Behold, a king shall reign in righteousness, and princes shall rule in judgement,'" I begin. I feel a slow burn of resentment against Alison as I read on. Isaiah is a book I relish – an unsettling alloy of comfort and threat, of poetry and catastrophe – and I would rather read it without Alison's gaze upon me. Her father was a Covenanter, and she has something of the fanatic's unthinking zeal in her eyes. "'Rise up, ye women that are at ease; hear my voice, ye careless daughters; give ear unto my speech.'" As I say the words I realise that Alison is reciting them along with me. She must know them by heart.

"'Tremble, ye women that are at ease;'" she murmurs, "'be troubled, ye careless ones: strip you, and make you bare, and gird sackcloth upon your loins.'" She is staring directly at me.

For the next few verses I am silent until, at last, she stumbles. I find my place in the Bible in front of me and finish the chapter. The three of us sit in silence for a moment.

"Is it your custom to discuss the meaning of the chapter after reading it?" she says.

"Indeed it is," I say, "but not until we are abed." I hesitate before adding, "I take it you do not wish to join us there?"

Alison's face darkens with a mottled blush, and she seems, for once, lost for words. She mutters something inconsequential and bustles out of the room, leaving the door ajar. I give the Bible back to Robert. He takes it from me absently, a frown on his face. "Close the door, Isobel," he says.

I do as he asks, first peeking into the hallway to make sure that Alison has truly gone. "I hope she does not mean to join us every evening," I say.

"You may have deterred her." There's the flicker of a smile on Robert's face.

"It's as well we have moved on to Isaiah. I fear the Song of Solomon would have been too much for her. 'Thy lips, oh my spouse, drop as the honeycomb: honey and milk are under thy tongue.'"

Robert reaches out his hand to me and I sit down beside him. "Do not tease her overmuch, Isobel."

"Why? I doubt the children would be heartbroken were she to seek another situation."

"Margaret is fond of her. As much as she is fond of anyone."

"But Henry is not."

Robert says nothing. He thinks I am too soft-hearted towards Henry, but how could I be anything else?

Mungo

"See here," Thomas says, in his special library voice – soft but clear. Quiet enough not to stir the library clerk from his midterm slumber. Thomas turns the book he has been reading and pushes it across the table towards me. "This Toland fellow says Christ deliberately chose his disciples from the ignorant classes. Do you see?" He traces his finger along the relevant passage. Thomas can read upside down, no matter how small the print.

I counter this idea with ease. "Was that not to show that his message was for all men? The humblest as well as the greatest?"

Thomas shakes his head with a smile and pulls the book back to his side of the table. "That's a pretty turn to put on the story. What Toland says, and he may have a point, is that those Christ chose were blockheaded fellows, and more easily gulled. Think about it, Mungo. When my poor old pa and I were out selling his worthless cure-alls, it wasn't the philosophers who were queuing up to buy them. Oh no. If you want an audience for nonsense you must pick one that has no schooling." He pushes the book towards me again. "Read for yourself. Tell me what you think."

So I read. Toland's book is notorious. It has been condemned by clergy, and copies burned by the public hangman in his native town in Ireland. But I am not afraid to look at such works for my faith in the Lord is strong. Know thy enemy. And yet, as I read, and argue, and oppose each contention with evidence from holy scripture, I am conscious of a thrill – a terror – that such thoughts have been thought, and committed to paper, and are now dancing through the summer air in this bright room. Toland's notions appal me with their cruel logic. The world tilts and trembles, as if its very foundations are an illusion. An idea once thought cannot be unthought. The book slides to and fro across the table between us, its cloth binding hissing against the oak with each exchange.

Some days later Thomas invites me to dine at his apartment after the day's lectures are done. I had assumed that he was – like me – in lodgings, but it emerges as we walk towards the Netherbow that he owns the property and lives there with his sister. He has so often bemoaned his impecunious state that I expect something meanly proportioned and humble, but the apartment is capacious, albeit sparsely furnished. I can stand tall in it without my head brushing the rafters. Stretch out my long, dockman's arms without touching a wall. What does it signify if the air is foul with the cess thrown into the close beyond the windows? The windows themselves are tall and broad. If they weren't so smutted with soot they'd let in as much light as the ones in the library. "I thought you said you were a poor orphan," I say.

"And so I am."

"But this–" I sweep my arms around the sheer, astounding space of it. "This must be worth a pretty penny."

Thomas crouches down at the hearth and studies the fire laid there in some perplexity. "Should I light it? If I do, Katharine will likely scold me for starting it too early. But if I don't, she'll scold me for letting her come into a cold house after her day's work." He smiles up at me. "What was it you were saying?"

I recall – just in time – that a gentleman does not discuss financial matters. "Have you lived here long?" I say.

"A while now. Katharine takes charge of all that. We are indeed poor orphans, as you point out, but we are in possession of a benefactor. My aged godfather. A relic from the glory days of the Aikenhead clan."

"That is fortunate." I hope that the poison of bitterness flowing through me at this moment is not apparent in my voice.

Thomas stands, gazing once more at the hearth. "I dare not light it. Can you bear the cold a while longer? Summer is turned, and no mistake. Take a seat, man. Be comfortable."

So I sit and we talk. Rather, Thomas talks, perching on a seat one minute, his foot tapping on the bare boards, then springing up and striding backwards and forwards like one of our livelier lecturers. Today's great news – the removal of certain books from the university library – is his sole topic.

"It's a bad business, don't you think?" he says again. "Are our minds to be kept shut up, like some maiden walled into a tower? It's as well we read Toland while we had the chance. And who are these men of the Privy Council who take it upon themselves to decide what we may and may not read?"

"I suppose the university..."

"Pah! Don't talk to me about them." He stalks over to the window. "Spineless. Craven. They should be defending our freedoms, not colluding with those dullards in the Privy Council." He speaks with his back to the window. His face is in shadow, but the weak daylight at his back surrounds him with a soft corona, picking out a hint of copper in his hair I have never noticed before. He turns to look out the window. "Ah," he says, "here is Katharine coming now. We shall have some heat at last."

"You must be the poet?" Katharine smiles. The smile is so like Thomas's. It is the clearest evidence of their kinship.

"I would not... dare to give myself that title," I stumble.

"My brother has shown me some of your little odes. Very deft."

My mind jangles. There is flattery in her words, admiration too. And yet I perceive a barb of condescension. But Thomas must have liked my scribbling well enough to show it to her. No condescension from him, at any rate.

"Poor Mungo," he says. "I've never seen a fellow less comfortable with attention. However will you manage when you're in the pulpit?"

Katharine is emptying her basket of its cargo of bread and eggs. "Light the fire, Thomas," she says. "I have a twist of tea leaves here. Have you fetched water for the kettle?"

Of course he had not. While he is gone to the pump I stand, awkward, too big in spite of the space. Katharine keeps moving about the room. Lifting crockery from a cupboard, cracking eggs into a bowl, flouring the griddle and swinging the crane over the fire. She has Thomas's restlessness, but all her movements are justified by practical intention. To tidy, to clear, to cook, to feed. Perhaps all women are like this. My mother is, in her slow, arthritic way. I have never been much in the company of women, I realise, and feel the sweat prickle on my face. I am relieved when Thomas returns.

Neither Thomas nor Katharine is a big eater. Their restraint inhibits me. Left to myself I would clear my plate and theirs too, but instead I pick genteelly at the strange hash of eggs, bread and scallions that Katharine has concocted. Thomas prefers to talk rather than eat. Katharine listens as he repeats his outrage at the removal of the books from the library.

"Atheistical, they call them," he says.

"Well," I dare, "I suppose they are atheistical." Brother and sister both stare at me. She is not bonny – no one would think that – but there is something... Handsome, that is the word. A face that will suit the middle years of life better than youth. "They find fault with Christianity. Pick holes in it."

"If Christianity cannot bear a little scrutiny, then it's a poor sort of religion." He is silent for a moment, pushing the egg mixture around his plate with a crust of bread. "Here's what perplexes me about the whole business, Mungo. The Bible tells us we are sinners, and therefore deserving of punishment."

"Aye, but God sent his son to became man and suffer that punishment in our stead."

He fixes me with a particular look I have never seen before. Sincere, his eyes dark with doubt. "That's what doesn't make sense. Let us say I was to commit a crime, and am lying in prison for it, and you go to the judge and say 'Punish me, in place of him.' Why, the judge would tell you to catch yourself on."

"You are applying the reasoning of this world to the workings of God."

"Believe me, Mungo, I have turned this over and over in my mind. What need for Christ to die? God is omnipotent. If he wants to forgive us he can do it, in the blink of an eye. No need for him to sacrifice his son."

"The problem with Thomas," Katharine says, "is that he thinks too much."

"Why would God give me the power of reason, if he did not intend me to use it?"

"Be careful, Thomas," she chides gently. "I heard today that there's a man taken up for blasphemy."

"Is he from the university?"

Katharine shakes her head. "Just a clerk, I think."

"It is, perhaps, a pity that we read that book," I say, "if it planted this seed in your mind." My words sound hollow, like lines spoken by an actor. The tendrils of doubt that burst forth that day in the library are growing stronger, probing through my own mind, like roots spreading and dividing in the darkness.

"You misunderstand the situation, Mungo. I used to wonder why no one else could see that the equation does not come out aright. I thought I was the only one, but since reading those books I know that others – Toland, Blount, Spinoza – are of the same mind. The Privy Council may take the books – burn them, confine them, whatever it is they mean to do – but they cannot confine the ideas contained therein."

Katharine goes over to the hearth and lifts the teapot that is warming there. "Will you take a cup, Mr Craig?" she asks.

Tea. A rare luxury in my mother's house, and likewise in my lodgings. "Thank you, yes." As she pours I study her. Older than Thomas, of course, by some five or more years, and older still in her actions. What does she really think of her brother's notions? Should I ask her? I do not know if it is usual to engage a woman in such a discussion.

"D'you know, Mungo," Thomas says, "I have been asking myself these questions for as long as I can remember." He takes a sip of his tea and continues. "All I have ever sought is the truth. But it seems the harder I pursue it, the more it eludes me."

The truth. Until I met Thomas, it never occurred to me to question it.

A week after our first visit to Dr Carruth's house we are seated at his table, which is spread more generously than any I have seen before. His wife sits, slender as a wand, shadows of weariness smudged under her eyes. Her blue gown rustles when she rises, or sits, or turns in her seat. The children stare up at us as they sup. The boy, a lad of ten or eleven, is particularly taken with Thomas. The girl seems fixed on me, watching me as a cat might stand guard over a promising gap in the wainscot.

The silence is wound tight as a spring following Dr Carruth's terse answer to Thomas's question. "What was your father, Dr Carruth?" he had said, his voice all innocence, enjoying the long moment until our host gave a sharp reply.

Odd that Thomas never tries to trip me with such a question. I wonder if this is how my future will be. Even if I find a kirk that will appoint me their minister, if I marry well, acquire land, will some whippersnapper still be able to topple me with that question? *What was your father?* Poor father.

The only favour he ever did me was to die young. His expiry was my free passport to the school for fatherless bairns.

"What of you, Mr Craig?" says Mistress Carruth. "Are you destined for medicine too?"

"The kirk, I hope." My words sound unclear, as if my tongue is too big for my mouth. What must she think?

"But Mungo has a freethinking streak in him," Thomas says.

"Does he?" Dr Carruth regards me with the first spark of interest he's shown.

I try to think of a suitable reply in order to keep his attention, but before I can Thomas moves the conversation on. "Look at Middleton, there," he says, drawing everyone's eyes to Patrick. "He looks as if he hasn't seen roast meat in a month." Patrick's mouth is stuffed with beefsteak, and he jaws frantically, growing redder in the face as he does so. I catch a glance pass between Thomas and Mistress Carruth – conspiratorial, mocking – and I feel a rare pang of pity for Patrick.

"Dr Carruth," Thomas says, turning back to our host, "how will I find my feet as a physician? Who will take me on as an apprentice, when I have few connections and precious little money?"

"There'll be time enough to worry about that when you have completed your studies," Dr Carruth says, a careful look on his face.

Thomas does not reply, but takes a mouthful of food and chews it a deal more elegantly than Patrick managed. He swallows, and says, "Do you remember, Dr Carruth, that odd court case my father was involved in? I recall very little." He glances around the table with a smile. "It was a disordered time in the Aikenhead family history."

"I remember it," says Dr Carruth in that same clipped tone as earlier.

Thomas leans back in his chair, looking up at the ceiling as if trying to retrieve some memory from the air. "There was a red-haired woman, was there not?" he says. "Bonny, in her way – that's why I remember her, no doubt." Another smile. "But still, there was something about her that scared me a little."

"Elizabeth Edmonstone," Mistress Carruth says, never taking her eyes off her husband. "The late Laird of Duntreath's daughter."

"Ah," says Thomas. "That accounts for her... air. What became of her?"

There's another awkward silence.

"She married well enough," says Dr Carruth. "One of the Ulster Montgomerys, I believe."

Thomas takes a mouthful of wine, then another. He dabs his mouth with a napkin. "How is it the gentry always bounce back, eh? Still, there's little to be gained from bitterness, don't you agree?"

Dr Carruth stands up. "Perhaps, Thomas, we should adjourn to my consulting room to discuss your prospects. It may, after all, be wise to plan ahead." He glances around the room at the rest of us. "There's no need to bore everyone else with our medical talk."

Thomas springs up and follows Dr Carruth out of the room. Mistress Carruth looks subdued for some minutes. Her sharp-eyed daughter regards her slyly. Patrick continues to chew stolidly, clearly thinking to make the best of the victuals while they last. At last Mistress Carruth rouses herself and turns to me with a smile that might convince a less perceptive man than myself. "So, Mr Craig," she says, "tell me about this freethinking streak Thomas says you have."

"The problem is," says Thomas later that evening, "lack of funds." We are all three of us in my room. He hands me the long-stemmed pipe and stretches out the full length of my bed, so that his boots touch one wall and his head the other. "How in the name of goodness do you fit into this cot, Mungo? You're twice the size of me."

I do not indulge in the tobacco but pass the pipe to Patrick, who is perched on the windowsill. He sucks on the pipe, holding the sweet smoke in for as long as he can, then blows it into the room before embarking on a fit of coughing and sneezing.

"Surely you could turn that rhyming of yours to profit," Thomas says, staring up at the ceiling. "There's a hawker on every corner selling pamphlets and song sheets. Couldn't you come up with some doggerel to please the common man?"

"Doggerel?" I feel a surge of grievance in my heart. He was not always so dismissive of my poetry.

Thomas laughs. "Och, poor Mungo. If you could see your face. You're like a beaten dog."

"You could make some money with your cures, Thomas," Patrick says. "That plook on Mr Hutchison's face cleared up right and well."

Thomas considers this. "What if," he says, "I invented a remedy for death?"

"That would sell well," I say, aiming for a sarcastic tone.

He sits up, eyes blazing, fingers drumming on his knee-caps. "A sovereign antidote," he declaims, like a street preacher. "It will cure a man though he be speldered like a haddock!" I can't help but smile, although I don't want to forgive him his slight.

"Anything else?" asks Patrick, joining in.

"A recipe for making the philosopher's stone, at a cost of only two Scots pounds. Just imagine it! The national debt would be paid in a trice. No need for taxes. The King could fight all the wars he pleases, and never ask Parliament for a penny."

"Very commendable," I say, abandoning my sulk, "but somewhat lacking in ambition."

Thomas springs up off the bed, beckons to Patrick for the pipe, and takes another deep inhalation. He blows the smoke in rings. They loop through the air, turning and

153

twisting until he waves them into nothingness. "A ship that can travel to the moon, and anywhere else you care to mention." He smiles benignly. "After all, if man can build a ship that travels through water, why not one that travels through the air."

Patrick claps his hands together. "Bravo, Thomas. Bravo."

Thomas gives him the pipe again, and hurls himself back down on my bed. There is an unhealthy series of creaks from its unsteady frame. "Seriously, though," he says. "We have to do something."

Isobel

"When will Thomas visit us again?" Henry asks at breakfast, his voice full of yearning. He is a child who forms swift, passionate attachments. Margaret is more composed, but I can tell she is as interested in the answer to Henry's question as he is.

I look over at Robert. He seems to be the only one of us immune to Thomas's charm. "We may invite him to dine with us once or twice a year, for charity's sake," he says, "but I would rather not be drawn into anything more frequent than that."

"Why not?" Margaret asks.

I begin to chide her for her impudent tone but Robert stops me. "It's a fair question," he says. He turns all his attention on Margaret. His indulgence of her is like a rebuke to me. "Mr Aikenhead is a young man in search of a sponsor. He is very pleasant, I am sure, but his intention is to make use of me."

"Do not all young men do the same?" I say. "At least those without family or friends to smooth the way for them. I recall that you were glad enough of Dr Irvine's support in your early days, and went to some length to secure it."

"I was not so impertinent as to inveigle my way into his dining room when I was a mere boy." He butters a crust of bread, but does not eat it. "I have more sympathy for his friend."

"Mungo?"

Robert nods. "He has come from nothing. One of Heriot's charity boys. The Aikenheads had fortune and influence aplenty. If they chose to squander it that's their own fault, not mine."

"It isn't Thomas's fault either."

Henry eats his porridge in silence, his emotions playing out on his face like clouds being chased across the sky. "I should like him to visit us again," he says shyly.

Robert sighs.

"What if I were to invite Thomas to come to take chocolate some morning," I say brightly. "You would be about your house calls, Robert, and would not be bothered by him." And, I am thinking, I would have better conversation from Thomas than from the other wives who make up my usual circle.

"Will this invitation be extended to Thomas's companions? Am I to feed and water half the undergraduates of Edinburgh?"

"Just Thomas," Henry says firmly.

I am making my way into the town with my basket hooked over my arm. There is no real need for me to go marketing, but I find a day pent up in the house leaves me in low spirits. I eke out my reasons for going – new bootlaces for Henry one day, a ribbon for Margaret's bonnet the next. Today I am in search of a twist of spice. The season will soon turn cold, and Robert enjoys a glass of mulled wine on an autumn evening.

As I make my way along Cowgate I pause at a shop at the head of College Wynd. I must have gone past it a hundred times and never stopped, but something makes me do so now. It gives no clear indication of its purpose – no sign swinging above the door – but there are often young men in scholars' gowns loitering about the door with parcels of books or papers in their hands. There are no students here today. I peer in the window, but a muslin curtain is pulled across so that I cannot see inside.

"Mistress Carruth?"

I jump at the sound and turn to see Mungo Craig standing staring at me as if he has been stopped suddenly in his tracks. "Mr Craig," I say.

"Were you–" He hesitates. "Were you looking for me?"

Why in the devil would he think such a thing? My puzzlement must show, for he continues, "This is where I stay. Where I have my lodgings."

I have a vague memory of some quip of Thomas's about Mungo's parsimonious landlord. "Plookie Rab", Thomas called him. "It must be a convenient spot. So close to the university."

"Indeed. Doubly so since he keeps a bookshop too."

"So that is what he has hiding behind the curtain," I say. And then, before I can prevent myself, "I have never been in a bookshop."

"But you are… I rather got the impression–" Mungo stops, conflicting emotions warring on his face. Confidence and inferiority, overfamiliarity and deference.

I take pity on him. "I am a great reader, and am fortunate always to have had books about me. My husband consults me when he is making purchases for our library at home."

"And yet you have never been in a bookshop," Mungo says. He looks pensive for a moment. "I would be honoured to escort you into this one. It is quite respectable, I believe."

I acquiesce, and allow him to open the door for me. It is warped, and scrapes on the floorboards with a sound that makes me shudder. The shop is no more than a small front room, but it is lined with closely packed bookshelves with cupboards beneath them. There are two trestle tables placed a little apart from each other in the centre of the room. One has several books laid open upon it, while the other displays samples of paper, pens and inkwells. A man comes through from the back of the house. Hutchison, I presume. He is taller than most men, and wearing an ancient velvet coat that is a little too short for him. There is a raised sore on his upper lip, the size and colour of a copper bawbee. It draws my eye, and he reachs up to touch it, as if self-conscious of my scrutiny.

"I see before me something outside my usual run of customer," he says, attempting a bow. "And may I say, it makes a pleasant change." There is something false in the way he speaks – not simply his laboured gallantry, but in the very tone of his voice. He is like a common actor attempting to mimic the accents of a gentleman.

"This is Mistress Carruth," Mungo says. "Wife to Dr Robert Carruth."

Hutchison strokes his chin and makes a display of giving this information some thought. "Dr Robert Carruth, Dr Robert Carruth…" He shakes his head and looks mournful. "I fear the good doctor does not favour this establishment with his custom, for I do not know the name."

"You will have to make do with me in his stead," I say, looking around me and drinking in the promise of so many books.

"Alas, we have very little that might interest the ladies," says Hutchison. "No poetry, nor romances, no no, that is not our stock in trade at all. The young men, you see–" and here he gestures at Mungo, "prefer to read more serious works. Natural philosophy, divinity, that sort of thing."

"I have very little interest in romances," I say, "although my children like such tales."

"Children, eh?" Hutchison brightens. "You don't want to fill their heads with too much nonsense. I believe I have something more improving here." He bends to open one of the cupboards and pulls out a small book. "Here we are," he says, and hands it to me.

The binding is pretty enough – a decent calfskin, dyed forest green. I turn to the title page: *A Token for Children, Being an Exact Account of the Conversion, Holy and Exemplary Lives, and Joyful Deaths of Several Young Children.* "I'm not sure they would much enjoy it." It would likely give Henry nightmares, though no doubt Margaret would read it with relish.

"Take it on approval," Hutchison says. "Look it over in the comfort of your own home. If it does not suit then send it back to me, and no harm done." There's a wheedling tone to his voice. He must be desperate for custom.

I do not want to pity him, but I do. "No, I think I will buy it," I say. I pay him and wait while he parcels the book up. Mungo is lurking by the doorway into the back of the house, staring at me like a lost puppy. "Thank you, Mr Craig, for this new experience." He mumbles some nicety I cannot make out.

"You must forgive poor Mungo," Hutchison says with an unctuous smile. "He is not much used to the company of ladies."

I escape the shop with my unwanted purchase and make my way up through Bell's Wynd to the high street. My favoured spice seller conducts his business from one of the luckenbooths that run close to St Giles' Cathedral. The air in the shop is a rich mix of all the many powders he stocks, the abrasive tang of pepper mingling with cinnamon, warm and comforting as a winter hearth. I make my selection, and as I am paying I feel myself observed for the second time today. When I turn to see who it is I find Dr Maxwell, a friend – or rather, an acquaintence – of Robert's, leaning in the doorway and smiling at me. He steps aside to let me out, raising his hat to me as he does so. "Good morning, Mistress Carruth," he says. "Does the day find you well?"

"Indeed it does. You have been away from town, I think?"

"Aye, in the Low Countries. I stayed with some old friends near Lieden. The climate there is more salubrious than Edinburgh in the summer. I've no fondness for the reek of the Nor' Loch in the heat of August."

"I envy you. Robert cannot be persuaded away from his work for any length of time."

He walks along beside me. "And how is that husband of yours? I suppose he's out tending to his lady patients?"

"They seem to keep him busy."

159

Dr Maxwell pauses for a moment. "If you were any other woman I would utter some frivolity about your husband's labours keeping you well supplied with bonnets."

"I'm as fond of a pretty bonnet as any woman."

"No doubt." He runs an approving eye over my attire. "But I suspect a mind like yours is more interested in deeper matters than this season's fashions."

Dr Maxwell is about the same age as Robert, but he has never married. There were rumours of a broken engagement with a supposed contessa many years ago, and I have heard hints of *affaires d'amour*, but there has never been any public scandal. I rather like him. We reach the corner of Bell's Wynd. "Well, my messages are done," I say, "and home I must go."

"I'll walk with you, if I may. I was on my way to the university library." He taps his forehead. "Must keep the knowledge fresh in this old head of mine."

"I suppose there are hundreds of books in the library?" I ask as we make our way down the wynd.

"Hundreds? No, thousands I would say."

I try to imagine so many books. Hutchison's shop would be as nothing compared to it. "But it is only for students, and people like yourself?"

"Aye, students, graduates, clergymen and the odd visiting scholar." He glances at me quizzically. "Why do you ask?"

"I suppose no woman has ever darkened its door."

"There's an old charwoman dusts the shelves and sweeps the floor." He must notice the irritation on my face, for he says, "But now I see I have offended you."

"I just think it is a shame that the library is not open to any who would make use of it."

"But then every apprentice scrivener in the town would be there trying to improve his prospects and there would be no room for the likes of myself."

We reach the Cowgate and cross to the head of College Wynd. Hutchison's shop looks as quiet as it was earlier. "I think we have reached the parting of our ways," Dr Maxwell says. He bows, gallant as ever, and heads off through the wynd towards the library. I turn for home, my almost-empty basket knocking against my skirts as I walk.

Mungo

All men are a mixture of good and evil, virtue and vice, kind-ness and malice. It is often only as a friendship grows that we perceive the darker side of one whom we first thought possessed of nothing but light. So it is with Thomas. What I at first took to be high spirits and genius I have gradually come to see as a dangerous discontent. I am endeavour-ing to disentangle myself from his acquaintance, but he is proving unwilling to be cast off. The Lord has seen fit to grant me a memorable appearance, and so I find it near impossible to evade Thomas by blending into the crowd at our lectures. I make haste to be the first to leave when they end, sometimes being compelled to hide in a doorway or anteroom until I am sure he has gone. One day, though, he catches me, and insists on accompanying me back to my lodgings.

"I scarcely see you these days," he complains. "Why is that?"

I make some excuse about the demands of my studies and my scant budget.

"Katharine asks after you," he continues. "I believe she had hoped you would be a good influence on me. And you have missed several invitations to visit Dr and Mistress Carruth."

"Patrick didn't say anything."

Thomas shrugs. "Oh I didn't bother taking him along. He's dull company, don't you think?"

"So you went alone?"

"Why not? The company is pleasant, the conversation stimulating and the refreshments better than I'm used to. I am quite the favourite there."

"With Dr Carruth?" I struggle to keep the disbelief from my voice.

Thomas smiles and shakes his head. "Hardly. But with Mistress Carruth, and the children too. They are quite charming. Sometimes I contrive to be there when the good doctor is at home, although I fear I don't please him much."

I think of the one occasion I was at the house on the Pleasance. It is true that Mistress Carruth provides a good dinner, but the mood in that family is like a musical instrument whose strings had been overtightened. Thomas seemed oblivious to it, plucking blithely at the tension between the doctor and his wife.

We arrive at my lodgings and try to go in by the shop door, but find it locked.

"That's odd," say I. It is a foolish thing to say, for it piques Thomas's curiosity, and any hopes I might have had of ridding myself of his company are undone. He follows me down the wynd to the yard door, and we come into the house through the back kitchen. The white dog is standing in the doorway between the kitchen and the shop, growling softly, the hackles on the back of her neck raised. Her pup is at her heels, imitating his dam.

Thomas glances over at me questioningly, but when he finds no answer in my face he lifts the curtain in the doorway aside and strides into the shop. "Good day, gentlemen," I hear him say in his boldest voice. "You have us quite mystified. Mungo!" he calls, "Come through and see this."

Most reluctantly I do as he asks. There are three strangers in the shop, two of them lifting books off the shelves and out of cupboards. As each book is lifted and examined the title and author are read out loud, and the third stranger makes notes in a pocketbook. Hutchison stands in the midst of them, paler than usual and picking at the fraying cuff of his jacket.

The man with the pocketbook looks Thomas and me over. "And who might these be?" There is something cold in the way he appraises us. I feel like a child standing before the most merciless of schoolmasters.

"My tenant, Mungo Craig," says Hutchison, "and his friend, Thomas Aikenhead."

I long to say that he is not my friend, but good manners compel me to stay silent.

"What's going on? says Thomas. "Are you having an inventory taken, Hutchison? Thinking of selling up?"

"These gentlemen have been sent by the Privy Council," Hutchison says, "who very wisely are taking stock of all the booksellers in the burgh, to ensure there are no... unsuitable books for sale."

"Unsuitable?" Thomas says. There is a bright, hectic gleam in his eye. "What do you mean by unsuitable?"

The man with the pocketbook stops writing. "We are rooting out works likely to encourage freethinking, atheism, deism and blasphemy. I regret to say we have found two such books in this establishment." He gestures towards two books set apart from the others.

"I see," says Thomas, his voice rising. "So you mean to... castrate the bookshops in the same way you've already done the university library?"

I am anxious to remove myself from the situation as soon as I can, and begin backing towards the door into the kitchen. "I must go," I say. "I have a great deal of studying to do." None of them responds, so I make my way quickly to my room. I sit on my bed, silently praying that Thomas will not follow me up. After a time I hear the back door bang and breathe a sigh of relief. An hour or so later the shop door scrapes open. I guess that our visitors must be gone, and go back downstairs.

Hutchison is still in the shop, putting the books to rights. "What will they do?" I say.

He shrugs. "Nothing much. They confiscated the ones they didn't like the look of. I'd already got rid of the worst of them."

"You knew they were coming?"

Hutchison gives me a wan smile. "I have a friend or two in the Privy Council."

I am reading by Hutchison's kitchen window, with the dog and her pup for companions. It is a week since the shop was raided. The glass is thick with frost but I've rubbed it away to let in a wee bit more light. My toes are warm, at least. I am close enough to the hearth to stretch out my legs and feel the benefit. The fire is the one reason I am here, and not upstairs in the peace of my bedroom. Hutchison is working in the shop, but he has a tendency to wander in and out of the back room. I long for solitude – dear Lord how I long for it! My mind is jumping and itching as if it were flea-ridden. I am badly behind with my studies.

The shop door scrapes open. That noise sets my teeth on edge. A familiar voice. Thomas. The white bitch and her pup raise their heads in unison. The pup leaps up and scurries out into the shop, setting the curtain that hangs in the doorway between the kitchen and shop billowing. The creature gives a volley of excited yelps. Thomas laughs. "Good day, my little friend," he says, in that daft voice people save for pets and bairns. I stay very still, afraid to move in case a floorboard creaks and betrays me.

"I suppose you've come to call upon your big friend," I hear Hutchison say.

"Aye. I couldn't find him at the library."

"I've a notion he might have gone out." Hutchison swishes past the curtain and looks at me with an eyebrow raised. I shake my head. No. He turns towards the stairs and shouts, "Mr Craig! Are you there? Mungo!" He holds his hand up to me, the index finger pointing heavenward, as if to say, *keep silence*. He walks back into the shop. "Not a sign of him, Mr Aikenhead. I scarcely see him, these days."

"That makes two of us, Mr Hutchison."

"Does he owe you money?"

Thomas laughs. "No," he says. "Not that."

Sunday. The Lord's day. As is my custom I go early to the kirk to ensure a seat at the front. I bring a pencil and notebook so that I may take note of the chapter and verse of the readings. The congregation has not long been seated when the doors are thrown open. "Make ready the penitent's stool!" someone cries out from the back of the kirk.

I am doubly glad of my seat at the front, for it means that when the tottering stool is brought out I am only a few paces away from it. An unkempt man dressed in a sackcloth tunic is led forward by a group of burly men. The sinner clambers up on to the stool. He is trembling, naked and barefoot under his rough penitential attire.

"That's Frazer," the elderly man next to me whispers.

"Who?"

"The blasphemer."

I look more closely at Frazer. He is younger than I first thought, his hair and face grey from the ashes that have been heaped on him. Is he conscious of so many eyes staring at him? He gives no sign of it. His own eyes are downcast, and he grips the edges of the stool as if he is afraid of falling.

"What exactly did he do?" I ask my neighbour quietly.

The old man sucks his teeth and shakes his head. "I heard tell he read some of them bad books, and tried to bring the people he lodged with to his way of thinking. They were wiser than that, thanks be to God." He glances at my notebook and pencil. "You young ones should take heed. There's only one book we should be reading."

I could argue with him the virtues of many fine volumes of exegesis, but this is not the time or the place. Frazer shifts on the stool and I look up at him. For a moment our eyes meet. His expression is unfathomable, and I am glad when he looks away.

After kirk I walk to Leith, for it is a fine crisp day, and I have not visited my mother for some weeks. The road is quiet, with it being the Sabbath, free from the weekday clatter of carts and carriages to and from the port. I hurry past the

Gallowlee, where the mortal remains of some poor miscre-
ant hang in chains. Now that I am beyond the huddle of
Edinburgh I can see the sea at the end of the Leith road,
blue as a jewel in the sunshine.

When I reach Talbot's Close I find the house empty.
Mother must still be at kirk. The minister in Leith is a fine
preacher, and the Spirit moves him mightily and at great
length. Mother keeps the little house spick and span. The
hearth is cold and clear of ashes. There are two covered
dishes on the table – one containing a handful of shrivelled
blaeberries, the other two pieces of tattie scone. Mother's
settle bed is neatly made up in its nook.

I climb the narrow stairs to my own bedroom, and the
boards creak under my weight. The little room is just as I
left it, the narrow bed against one wall, and a small, rough-
hewn desk under the skylight. There was a time when I
could stand upright in this room, but since the age of twelve
or thirteen I have had to stoop or risk dashing my brains out
on the ceiling. I sit at the desk and bend to smell the wood.
There's still the faintest trace of cinnamon and pepper. The
desk was a gift from the dockmen, after my father died and
I won my place at Heriot's school. They made it themselves
from a broken packing case that had carried spices from the
Indies.

I hear my mother return. "Is it yourself?" she calls.
Somehow she always knows when I am here.

"Aye," I reply, and come down the stairs.

"Well, well," she says, "sit down till I get you a cup of
water. Will you take a tattie scone?"

"Water will suffice."

She limps over to the shelf and lifts a cup down. "A
big laddie like you needs more than a drop of water." In
spite of my protests she pushes the two dishes towards me.
"Eat what you want, son. I'll take your leavings later." She
stands over me until I have eaten one of the scones and
a few of the blaeberries. They are bracingly sour. I recall

my childhood days, and late summer ventures up the hill where the blaeberries grew. I would return with hands and mouth stained with their juice. Some of the local children must have shared their harvest with my mother.

"Is that the last of the berries?"

"Aye. There was a poor enough show this year."

"No wonder with the weather we've had."

We sit in silence. Mother takes repeated quick glances at me. I notice the basket of neatly folded mending in the corner of the room. "You're keeping busy enough?" I say.

"Aye, there's always someone will pay for a needle-woman." She goes over to her bed and reaches into the mattress.

"I wasn't after money," I say quickly. "I was just... conversing."

She ignores me and extracts two coins from their hiding place in the mattress. "It's no' much."

I take the money. "When I become a minister, Mother, we shall live in a fine manse and you can stay with me and keep house."

"Aye." The expression on her face is a mixture of pride and wonderment. I try to imagine her in a house like the Carruths'. She would be baffled by its capaciousness and comfort. For myself, though... How at ease I would feel in the world if I had a feather bed to sleep in, and hot meals served to me every day at a polished table. I determine to apply myself more diligently to my studies. I will go nowhere but the lecture hall, eat nothing but penny loaves, and eke out the money Mother has given me.

Patrick brings news of the arrest, blattering in through the shop door and shouting the news up the stairs to me at such a volume that half the neighbourhood must hear him. I am lying in bed under the blankets in the hope of getting warm, and he puts me in such a panic that I run downstairs in my stocking soles.

"We were just coming out of Dalton's," he says, still gasping for breath. "A man approached, with a warrant in his hands, and two of the watch behind him to take hold of Thomas."

Hutchison comes in from the shop as Patrick speaks. "What's the charge?" he says.

Patrick looks wildly at Hutchison then back at me. "Blasphemy."

Isobel

The keyman of the Tolbooth prison has a peculiar walk, tilting from side to side as he moves along the corridor so that his coattail swings like a hussy's skirt. The bunch of keys chime with each step he takes. We pass a number of closed doors with several names chalked on the bare wood. At length we stop. This door is different from the others, in that there is an oblong of slate attached to it by means of a frame. The name "Aikenhead" is scratched on the slate. "Have you a wee handkerchief, missus?" he says. "The ladies sometimes like to cover their noses, ye ken? Although it's no' sae bad being as it's winter."

I have no fears of being overcome by the noxious stench of a gaol cell. However, I know what is expected of me in my role as gentlewoman-visitor to the Tolbooth. "I have a handkerchief, thank you, and it's well scented with lavender oil."

"The young lad is sharing a cell with a coarse piece o' work by the name of Black Archie. If he gives you any bother just rap on the door and I'll fetch you out." With these unsettling words he opens the door and ushers me in. "Here's a lady to see you, Mr Aikenhead."

Thomas springs up from his pallet bed and advances with a broad smile, as if he is welcoming me to a soirée. "Mistress Carruth! You are very kind to visit me."

I take in my surroundings. The cell is neither as dark nor as dank as I had feared, though it is very small. There's a high window that lets in sufficient light to see by, although it would hardly do for reading. A grizzled man with a dense beard and the dazed eyes of a habitual drunkard reclines on another pallet. The air is not good – I suspect the bucket in the corner is an overfull chamber pot – and I would be glad enough to make use of my lavender-scented hankerchief, but I do not want to appear too delicate. "Thomas, my dear," I say, "what terrible pickle is this you find yourself in?"

"I would offer you a seat, but you can see there is none to be had."

I sit down on the pallet and motion for him to sit beside me. "So," I say. "What is to be done? Have you engaged an advocate?"

"Archie here is my unofficial advisor."

The bearded man grunts in amusement but says nothing.

"Seriously, Thomas. You need an advocate." I pause, and say – as delicately as I can – "If it's a question of money."

Even in the poor light of the cell I can see his face colour. "It's always a question of money, Mistress Carruth."

"Then I shall speak to my husband, and ask him to engage an advocate on your behalf."

He shakes his head. "The trouble is, I do not know how I can be defended."

"Well, your advocate will study the charges against you, and then refute them."

"But what if the charges are true?"

"I don't understand."

He hesitates for a moment before speaking again, his voice so soft and urgent I can barely make him out. "In the beginning was the Word, but the Word was a lie. Aye, the very first time He spoke to Adam, God told a lie. 'Dinnae eat from yon tree,' He said. 'If you eat frae it you'll die.' The Bible puts it better, mind. More poetical. 'But of the tree of the knowledge of good and evil, thou shalt not eat of it: for in the day thou eatest thereof thou shalt surely die.' But Adam ate the fruit, him and his wife too. And did they die? They did not. Well, not right away. According to that same old book, Adam lived to be nine hundred and thirty years of age. That's a quare stay of execution, eh?"

For a moment I am too stunned to reply. "You cannot," I say, "call God a..." – I hardly dare say the word – "a liar."

"I can call Him whatever I like, since I don't believe He exists at all."

Black Archie stirs on his bed and struggles upright with many sighs and groans. "He's his own worst enemy, missus," he says. "There's a time tae speak out and a time tae howl yer wheesht."

Thomas ignores him and continues talking, his eyes as bright and fervent as any fanatic Covenanter. "The thing about questions is, once you've asked one you cannot stop asking. You may learn sense enough not to ask them out loud – it doesn't take too many hammerings from the schoolmaster to teach you that – but the questions keep coming, crackling across your mind like lightning until you daren't open your mouth for fear that sparks will shoot out."

I wonder if he is ill. The Tolbooth is notorious for the epidemics that sweep through its noisome cells. Gaol fever may have turned his head. Could I persuade Robert to tend to him? I doubt it. Perhaps Dr Maxwell would be more adventurous.

"I telt him, missus," says Archie, "he needs an advocate, and him up against Wily Jamie."

"Wily Jamie?"

"Sir James Stewart, Lord Advocate of Scotland," Thomas explains.

"I've never heard him called Wily Jamie."

"He's known as Trimming Jimmy to some, on account of his ability to turn with the tide, to step nimbly from a sinking ship to one in full sail. Whichever party is in the ascendant, Trimming Jimmy will be among their number. Archie here calls him Wily Jamie, for he's rarely outwitted."

"Aye," Archie confirms. "What's worse is, he's a godly man. He keeps a strict Sabbath." He eyes my basket. "Have you anything in there worth eating, missus?"

"Manners, Archie!" Thomas says.

"I wasn't sure what would be most appreciated." I take the cloth off my basket and lift out bread, cheese and several thick slices of pressed tongue wrapped in waxed paper. "I should have thought to bring more."

Archie reaches out a grubby hand and takes a slice of tongue. "Aye, well, ye'll ken better next time, eh?"

I catch Thomas's eye and notice his amusement. "Oh please don't look so severe, Mistress Carruth," he says. "I must take my entertainment where I find it."

"It will not be so diverting when you are paraded round the town in sackcloth and ashes. What will the university think of that?"

Thomas jumps up and paces across the small distance to the cell door and back again. "But what can I do, Mistress Carruth? Lie and grovel to gain my freedom? Recant like some poor soul before the Inquisition?"

"Sometimes – and I know this is hard for a young person of brilliance to hear – a lie can be in our best interests."

"She's right," says Archie, who has now moved on to the cheese. "My arse has warmed more penitent's stools than I can count on the fingers of my two hands" – at this point I notice that he has fewer fingers than is usual – "but it would have warmed a deal more if I always told the truth." He sees me staring at his hands, and smiles. "A wee misunderstanding, missus, with a fish-gutter in a Leith tavern."

I leave the Tolbooth determined to engage an advocate for Thomas, whether he wills it or no. The prospect of raising the matter with Robert does not fill me with delight, but I hope I can persuade him. He still carries a lingering sense of guilt over James Aikenhead's downfall. For all Robert's faults, his conscience does not slumber. And if I cannot convince him, I have a little money of my own put by.

Robert is in his study. I decide against disturbing him just now. When we have dined and said family prayers I will have a better notion of his mood. Timing is all. I adjourn to my own little parlour and prepare to record today's visit to the Tolbooth in my journal, but before I have even put ink in the inkwell I am surprised by Robert's knock on the door. He comes in bearing a letter in his hand and a grave expression on his face.

"Is anything the matter?" I say.

Robert pulls up a chair and sits close to me. "Dr Leitch has written to me from Lauder."

"My mother's physician?" I feel suddenly chilled.

"Your mother had a fall. Her leg is broken."

"Dear God! When did this happen?"

"Just yesterday, and Leitch wrote to me directly."

I suppress a flicker of annoyance that Dr Leitch wrote to Robert rather than to me, as if I were incapable of hearing such news without my husband as intermediary. "I suppose I must go to Lauder then, or poor Hetty will be worn out attending to her."

Robert does not immediately respond, but rather stares down at the letter. "There's something more," he says at last.

"Tell me."

"When Hetty helped your mother to undress she found a deep sore, on the breast."

"I don't understand." For a moment I see the resemblance to Henry on Robert's face – the way both father and son flinch at the prospect of causing distress.

"It is a cancer, Isobel. According to Leitch she must have been suffering it for some time."

"But – she has mentioned nothing in her letters. Only her usual complaining–" I stop, ashamed of my disloyalty. "Is there anything can be done?"

Robert shakes his head. "Leitch says it is far gone. When a cancer takes root it weakens the bones."

"So the broken leg…?"

"Likely she was more fragile as a consequence of the cancer."

174

I try to order my thoughts, but they feel frozen. My desk sits before me, all as it was five minutes ago. The ink bottle, the open journal, the pen in its stand. If I could undo time I would. "Does Dr Leitch say if she is in dreadful pain?" It is a foolish question. A child's question. I can see Robert weigh up in his mind whether or not to tell me the truth.

"I believe she suffers greatly." He reaches over and takes my hand in his. "We can go within the hour. I will bring opium. Leitch will not object to my intervention, I hope."

"But the children? And your patients?"

"Agnes and Alison can take charge of the children. My patients are not in peril – they will do very well without me for as long as is needed."

Mungo

We visit Thomas in prison, of course. "I know what they want," he says, looking across the cell to make sure the other miserable wretch detained there is listening to his boasts. "Another penitent to parade around the kirks in sackcloth and ashes. Well they won't get it, not from me."

There is no persuading him. Patrick tries but the more he urges Thomas to a show of repentance, the more stubbornly he resists.

As we are leaving he lets Patrick go on ahead and holds me back. "You should make up one of your rhymes about this, Mungo," he says. "Have it printed and sold and use the funds to pay for an advocate. What do you say?"

"This is no time for jokes, Thomas. You are in a perilous situation. We all are."

My cautionary words only embolden him. "All the better reason to take full advantage. We'll never again be the makers of news." His eyes glow with passion, like an overexcited child's. "I'll wager the whole town is agog to know more about me, and you're the very man to supply their need. Come, Mungo, say you'll do it. Ask Hutchison to have it printed up." And as it was in the first days of our friendship I find myself unable to refuse him. I venture a last, practical obstruction. "But how am I to pay for it? Hutchison's credit is not good. Any printer will want his money in advance."

He falls back, hesistant for a moment. "Leave that with me, my dear Mungo." He glances over at his cellmate – a fierce, ill-favoured ruffian with a black beard that seems to sprout near enough all the way up to his eyes. The villain grins at us, and Thomas smiles back at him. "I will consult with my mentor here. He's an ingenious chap." He slaps me heartily on the back. "Press ahead, Mungo. Put your pen to work, and turn my woes to gold."

"How was he?" Hutchison says when we are back at our lodgings.

"Poor Thomas," says Patrick. "They have him in a mean, dark cell with a very disreputable fellow."

Hutchison touches the shiny pink skin where his canker used to be before Thomas cured it. "That will knock the spark out of him."

"I wouldn't be so sure," I say. "He seems to be revelling in it."

"Shame on you, Mungo," says Patrick, blinking like a broken-hearted calf. "He's full of fear."

"He'll enjoy the trial," I say. "Centre of attention."

"When is it to be?" says Hutchison.

"Before Christmas."

"And none to speak for him?"

Patrick crouches down in front of the fire to pet the white bitch and her pup, which is now near the size of its mother. She snarls at him, and he withdraws his hand. "I thought Dr Carruth might know how to advise us, but when I called at his house I found half the household removed. Mistress Carruth's mother is three-quarter's way through death's door, according to the servant. They're away to Lanarkshire to be with her until she steps over the threshold entirely."

"You didn't tell me you were going to call at the Pleasance," I say.

He looks up at me. "Did I not?"

"No, you didn't." I am embarrassed by the petulance in my voice.

Hutchison asks the question I dare not pose. "I wonder what made them light on Thomas." He glances at us both in turn.

There is a long silence.

Hutchison speaks again. "You lads shouldn't be rushing back to visit him," he says. "Guilt by association, and all that."

"We'd be poor friends if we turned our backs on him now," says Patrick stoutly.

Neither Hutchison nor I respond immediately. "Thomas had the idea of me writing a pamphlet about the case," I say. "He seems to think there'd be many a one who would pay to read about it.

"Did he now?" Hutchison has the same expression on his face when he is totting his accounts. "He might be right."

"But how would we pay for it to be made?" asks Patrick.

Hutchison thinks for a moment. "Ways and means, young Middleton, ways and means. Leave that to me."

How was I to know that the story would change in the writing? It was as if my pen, once charged with ink, could not be contained. The rhymes tumbled forth, and the firm iambic beat battered in time with my heart. Thomas was merely the spark that lit the fire of my invention.

Hutchison reads the manuscript for my pamphlet, squinting at my handwriting. The white bitch and her pup sprawl by the hearth. A fire is burning there, but it does little to warm the room. He turns to the last page, reads through it, looks up at me. "Are you sure about this?"

"Thomas told me to do it. It was his suggestion."

"I doubt he expected you to confirm his guilt." Hutchison leafs through the pages. "The poem seems overlong to me, but then my taste doesn't run to versifying." The pup stands and stretches. It pads over to the back door and scratches at the floor. Hutchison hands the manuscript back to me and lets the dog out into the close. He comes back to me and takes the pages once more. "Very well then."

"How much will it cost? How much will it make?"

"I've a printer will run off a hundred at tuppence a piece. We'll need to sell them for sixpence."

"So, four pounds profit?"

Hutchison twists his mouth into a smile. "You're assuming they'll all be sold."

"Won't they?"

"Likely not."

"But anyway, we'll make some profit?"

Hutchison nods. "And split it two ways."

"But it's my work!"

"And my efforts to bring it to print. Do you think it was easy persuading the printer to take the job without payment in advance?" His mouth twists again. "You're quite free to go elsewhere, Mr Craig. Don't feel obliged to deal with me simply because I am your landlord."

Two days later. My words, made real by a printing press. My name, on the cover. Thomas's too, of course. But he is not the author. He is merely the subject, not the progenitor.

"Well?" says Hutchison. "Are you happy now?"

The men who come for me stand out in the throng of students. They stop one of the porters, and he points in my direction. I watch as they walk towards me. No men of the watch in their company – that's something, then. My guts clench. Their faces look sharp-edged and clear, as if I am studying them through eyeglasses.

"Mungo Craig?" asks the chief amongst them. I nod to confirm. He reaches into his coat, and I expect him to draw out a warrant for my arrest. Instead he brings forth a copy of my pamphlet. "We should like to ask you some questions, Mr Craig," he says amiably, "about your friend Thomas Aikenhead."

Isobel

Hetty has worn herself out sitting up every night with my mother. "There was no choice, Miss Isobel," she says. "She wrestles around on the bed and I am afeard she will hurt herself worse if she falls out."

Mother is asleep now. I had feared I would find her sadly changed, but her complexion is unexpectedly fresh. Watching her in repose, mercifully numbed by opium, I can almost convince myself there is nothing the matter with her, and this has all been a terrible mistake. The bedclothes are held clear of her broken leg by a wooden frame brought by Dr Leitch. He seems a practical man, young and brisk and well used to tending to the injuries common to a rural practice. A fire blazes in the hearth. The air is heavy – the clensing herbs Hetty has tied about the bed mingle with stale sweat, and the floral sweetness of opium does battle with the stench of the sore on Mother's breast. Robert cleaned the wound as best he could, but the process caused so much distress with such doubtful benefits that he and Dr Leitch are agreed it should only be repeated every other day. "Go and get some rest, Hetty. And later we must discuss bringing in some help. There must be women or girls hereabouts who could be employed to cook and clean while we care for my mother?"

Hetty nods. That tells me how exhausted she must be. She has always taken an austere pride in running the house single-handed. As she makes her way from the bedroom I notice how stiffly she walks. I have known her all my life, always thought of her as fixed at some indeterminate age, but now I realise she's an old woman.

I sit by the bed. Mother's breaths come deep and slow. Sometimes there is such a gap between them that I think the end has come. I freeze, half hoping, half fearing that it is over. Robert has warned me that her suffering could continue for some time yet. The room is dark, the windows shuttered and curtains drawn, so that even the sparse hours of winter daylight are denied me. I close my eyes and doze for a moment, then wake with a start. Thomas! In all the turmoil of these last days I had completely forgotten him. I must speak to Robert, prevail upon him – it is not difficult to have a letter carried to Edinburgh.

Around noon Robert comes into the room. Mother has started to stir, but her eyes are still closed and she does not appear to be in great pain. "You should eat," Robert says to me. "Hetty has left out a plate for you."

"I hope she is not working in the kitchen? I told her to rest."

"She would not be satisfied until she had gathered a meal together for us. But she's gone to bed now. And she's sent word to some of her kinfolk to come and help for the next while."

I vacate my seat so that he can sit down. "I meant to speak to you," I say, "about young Thomas Aikenhead." I ignore the dark look on Robert's face and continue, "You know he has been arrested?"

"I had heard something of that, but really, have we not more important things to be concerning ourselves with? You more than me."

"He has no money for an advocate, and he seems blithely unaware of how serious a situation he is in."

"How do you know this?"

I feel my face colour. "I went to see him in prison. Just before we had the news about Mother." As if in response to my voice, Mother murmurs something and tries to scrab at her nightgown as if she would tear it off. I make soothing noises and take her hands gently in mine until she settles.

"Go and have something to eat," Robert says.

181

I long to reply, *And what about Thomas?* But the look on his face keeps me silent.

When I return to Mother's bedroom I find her awake. She looks dazed, and winces every now and again as a spasm of pain runs through her. "Does she need more opium?" I ask Robert.

"We should try to hold off a little while longer. She needs to be persuaded to take some sustenance, and she cannot do that if she is asleep. Leitch will be calling later. I don't want him to think that I'm treading on his toes." He rises to leave. "Your mother has been talking – wandering in her mind, I think. She asked where you father was."

"How did you reply?"

"I said he'd gone hunting." He lowers his voice. "It's kinder."

I take his place beside the bed. He closes the door softly on his way out. Mother's eyes are closed again, and I think she has fallen asleep, but she begins to mutter Hetty's name.

"No, Mother," I say, taking her hand. "It is Isobel."

She opens her eyes and looks at me in puzzlement. "Are you my daughter?"

"Yes, yes I am."

I am rewarded with a weak smile and she rests back on to the pillow. "Hetty is a good servant. A good and faithful servant."

"She is."

"I found you a servant once."

"That's right. Agnes, Hetty's neice."

"Not Agnes, no. The Irish one. What was her name?"

I am about to correct her. That other girl – I can't remember her name now – turned up out of the blue. It wasn't mother's doing. Then I remember what Robert said. Mother is confused, and there is nothing to be gained from contradicting her. "I don't recall her name."

"She did well enough. Did what I asked of her."

This must be what the memory does as life draws to a close. Every fragment, every hidden recollection, is tumbled like autumn leaves on a windy day. I try to call up some remembrance of that servant girl. Dark hair. From the north of Ireland, I think. The pain of those early weeks of my marriage is still with me, even after so many years and other, greater sorrows.

"If I sinned I pray God forgives me," Mother says.

Hetty taps on the door and comes in bearing an old spouted cup that I recall from my childhood. "Now, mistress," she says, "here's a warm caudle I've made for you, to give you strength." Together we help my mother to sit up, and I support her while Hetty persuades her to sip from the cup. She has little appetite, and soon turns her head away, like an infant refusing the breast. We make her comfortable, but before long she is in clear discomfort. She twists on the bed and with each movement lets out a sob of pain.

"I will get Robert," I say, and go swiftly from the room. Downstairs I hear voices from the parlour. I hesitate in the doorway – Robert and Dr Leitch are in deep conference. They both look towards me at the same time, for all the world like two schoolboys caught at some mischief by the schoolmaster. "Mother's pain is growing stronger by the minute," I say. "She has taken a little of Hetty's posset, but I do not think she can be persuaded to take more."

"Your husband has been advising me on the latest thinking on pain relief," Dr Leitch says, with the slightest hint of resentment in his voice. "You can be sure I will follow his instructions when he returns to Edinburgh."

Robert looks embarrassed. "I had not yet discussed my intentions with my wife."

Dr Leitch glances from me to Robert and back again. "Ah, well… Perhaps I should go above and see to my patient."

When he is out of the room I turn to Robert. "I thought we were both staying here until… until the end."

He cannot meet my eye. "It is hard to tell in these cases how long it might take. My assessment is that it may be weeks rather than days or hours. I have my work to think about, Isobel. Patients who may go elsewhere if I am too long absent."

"When will you leave?"

"Leitch says he can arrange a horse for me tomorrow morning." He pauses. "I am sorry you had to find out in this manner."

I blink back tears – why is it that my anger must manifest itself in such a show of weakness? – and steady my voice. "The children will be pleased to see you home. I will write to them this evening and you can carry my letters to them."

"Of course."

"You might also find time to assist Thomas."

Robert's hangdog expression is replaced by one of exasperation. "If Thomas Aikenhead has got himself into trouble through his own foolishness then it is not my responsibility to rescue him."

Whatever protective instinct I usually feel towards my husband is quite absent. My heart is frighteningly hard. "Remember his father, Robert. How a trial ruined him. Ruined his life and that of his family."

"Yes, but–"

"You had a role in that. Will you stand by while his son goes down the same path, with no one to take his part?"

Robert looks tormented. Trapped. "I will see what I can do. Pay for an advocate. Will that satisfy you?"

"Yes. And write to me. Let me know how things go on."

He nods, looks pensive for a moment. "Shall we go up to your mother?" Almost at the moment he speaks there's a terrible cry from Mother's room. Robert grabs his doctor's bag and runs upstairs. I follow as quickly as I can, hampered by my skirts; conscious that it was on these unforgiving stone steps that Mother fell.

When we get to the bedroom Mother's agony has subsided, it seems. She is whimpering, pitiful as a wounded animal. Her eyes find mine and seem to beg for mercy, but I have nothing to offer except soothing words. Robert and Dr Leitch confer briefly over the opium bottle and prepare a draft that Dr Leitch helps Mother to drink, while Robert watches attentively. When she has taken it Dr Leitch looks up to Robert and receives an approving nod. "That's just the way," Robert says. We wait until Mother's breathing eases and her eyes close.

"Thank the Lord for opium," I say.

"Amen," responds Hetty, who has been standing a little distance away from the bed, her hands clasped together as if in prayer.

"Indeed," Robert replies. He and Dr Leitch exchange a glance. "But it is not a panacea, Isobel," he continues. "The body grows accustomed to it. The dose that numbs your mother's pain today may not be sufficient in a week's time. This is why I am so frugal in my use of it."

"Do you mean it may stop working... before the end comes?"

Robert looks grave. "That is my fear. For all the damage her illness has done, your mother has a sound heart and lungs. In most instances that is a blessing – a robust constitution can better withstand the assaults of disease and injury – but in this case rather the reverse. The body is at battle with itself, and although death will be the victor, the war may be long drawn out."

"Be assured, Mistress Carruth," Dr Leitch says, "I will be prudent in my use of the drug."

And with that both men leave the room. Hetty must read something in my face I did not know was there, for she says, "Never mind them, Miss Isobel. Coming into the world and going out of it – it's the women have all the labour. We shall tend your poor mother ourselves–" She stops abruptly, and when I look over to her I see that tears are coursing down her cheeks. I go over to embrace her, and find that I am crying myself. And so we weep together, while Mother rests easy for a while in her opium sleep.

Mungo

Those of us who must bear witness against Thomas are quarantined in a cramped chamber near the courtroom, seated on two hard benches, facing each other at close quarters. Myself and Patrick. Some others from around the university or Hutchison's shop. I recognise John Neilson and Adam Mitchell, but cannot put a name to the other fellow. "They call this the Judas room," John Neilson says. He's clerk to an advocate, and fancies he understands the law. One of his eyelids is puffy and red. A gobbet of yellow mucus sits in the corner of his eye like teardrop that will not fall.

We can hear the hubbub outside the door as the crowd passes on the way to the courtroom. It sounds as if half Edinburgh is here – the murmur of men's voices is interspersed with cries from the officers urging them to move faster or slower, to make haste or have patience. At length the tumult subsides, and I hear a smaller group tramp past. "That'll be the jury and judges, being brought in," says John Neilson. "Thomas will be brought directly from the Tolbooth. There's a tunnel between it and the courtroom."

Patrick springs up. "I cannae do it. I won't speak against him." He tries the door but finds it locked, and he looks around wildly. "When they bring me in I'll refuse to say a word."

"Aye, and then you'll be joining him in the Tolbooth," Adam Mitchell says. He looks to John Neilson for confirmation.

"That would depend on the judge," Neilson says, "but you'd do Thomas no good. They have your sworn statement." He gives a bleak smile. "You've already spoken against him. It's too late now."

"So if they have our statement," I say, "why must we appear in court?"

"To confirm what you have already testified. You'll be asked to read out your affidavit, and answer any challenge from Thomas's advocate."

"He has no advocate," Patrick says.

John Neilson looks grave. "That's bad."

"They say he refused one," says Adam Mitchell.

We sit in silence for a few moments. There is little sound now from outside our chamber. "They'll be swearing in the jury, and then the indictment will be read out," John Neilson says. After more, interminable waiting we hear footsteps approaching and the door is unlocked and a dour clerk peeks in.

"Adam Mitchell," he says. Mitchell rises and leaves the room.

The boy whose name I don't know pulls a surprisingly clean hankerchief from his sleeve and wipes his face. "I feel poorly," he says, looking at each of us in the expectation of compassion. "Do you think they would let me go away without speaking?"

"You'd need to faint down dead to have any hope of it," Neilson says, "and even then they'd probably throw a bucket of water round your head in hopes of reviving you."

"What did you all say about Thomas?" Patrick asks.

The nameless youth says, "I was that afeard when they questioned me I cannot remember what I told them."

"I heard Thomas say that Jesus was no more than a magician, and his miracles mere tricks that only the foolish would believe," says Neilson, "and that he deliberately chose as his followers ignorant men, who would believe his sleight of hand."

"He told me that Moses was a trickster too, but a better politician than Jesus, in that he had the wit not to be executed." Patrick slaps his hand over his mouth, as if that might pull the words back in.

I add my tuppence worth. "I heard him say that Moses never existed, and that the Holy Scriptures are stuffed full of contradictions, and that Christianity will end before another hundred years have passed." I am surprised by the tremor of righteous anger in my voice.

The door opens again and John Neilson is summoned forth. It is just three of us now. Patrick, myself and the other lad. "How do you know Thomas?" Patrick asks the boy.

"I have lodgings in the same tenement," he says. "When I started at my studies Thomas would walk with me to lectures. Said he'd be my guide to the ways of the university."

"Young men should be prudent in their choice of mentor," I say.

Patrick looks over at me with a strange expression on his face. "You sound like an auld preacher," he says. "And you're neither."

I'm taken aback by his reproof. When this is over I will, perhaps, try to distance myself from him. He is weak, soft-hearted, and I must avoid weakness. I should take my own advice, and find a wise consellor. Reverend Crawford at the Tron Kirk, for example. He might advise me on how to find a congregation to take me on when I have my degree.

Patrick is deep in thought, his brows knotted with worry. "Did Thomas ever say to you that the book of Revelation is a book of alchemy, where the wise man will find a recipe for making the philosopher's stone?"

I shake my head. "He declared that the blessed Trinity is a contradiction, like a man-goat, or a circular triangle." I pause. "A dreadful blasphemy."

The boy says, "He told me he had the means to make himself immortal, and to transport himself to the moon." He looks from me to Patrick and back again. "I thought he was speaking in jest. He must have been, mustn't he?"

Then it is Patrick's turn. He walks from the chamber with only the briefest, inscrutable glance at me. I close my eyes and utter some incoherent prayers. *Lord defend me. Lord guide me.* I must settle my mind, silence it, and wait for the voice of God. The boy shuffles where he sits, blowing his nose, fidgeting. I try to block out the sound. *Lord defend me. Lord guide me.*

A hand on my shoulder startles me back to the present. The boy is nowhere to be seen. He must have been taken to give his testimony while I was deep in prayer. The clerk looks down at me with an implacable expression on his face. "Your time, Mungo Craig," he says, and leads me to the courtroom.

After the confinement of the little chamber where I have sat this past hour or more the courtroom is overwhelming in its dimensions, and packed with people. I see the judges at one end, seated behind a long table on a raised platform. The clerk leads me to a lower table piled with papers. There is no stool or seat, so I remain standing. I look around to see where Thomas is, and find that he is staring hard at me from his place on the other side of the room. He has at least been allowed to sit down. There are two burly men who I assume to be guards, each one standing on either side of him.

A man in advocate's robes addresses me. "Confirm your name."

I swallow. My mouth is dry, and my stomach cramps with hunger. "My name is Mungo Craig." A mutter travels from person to person through the courtroom. *Mungo Craig, you say? Was he the informer? Who knows? These days it could be any one of us…*

"Your sworn statement is before you on the table. Be so good as to read it out."

Before I can say a word Thomas springs to his feet. "I object!" he declares. There's laughter from the crowd. The guards pull Thomas down, but he goes on shouting. "This man, my so-called friend Mungo Craig, has told lies about me." There's no laughter now. They don't want to miss a thing.

"You are accused of blasphemy," the advocate says, "and this court shall try if those accusations have a firm foundation."

"And you think Mungo Craig is a reliable witness?" says Thomas, his eyes blazing. "When he's making money out of this even as we speak?"

The advocate's voice is flint-hard. "I hope you do not imply that Mungo Craig is in the pay of the court?"

Thomas sits back, calculating, as if such a thought had not occurred to him before. For once he appears to think before he speaks. "Indeed not. I refer to this pamphlet" – and here he pulls a crumpled copy of my pamphlet from his jacket, smoothes it flat, holds it up for all to see – "wherein Mungo Craig denounces me, and reviles me, and urges the court to vengeance. All for sixpence a copy. How can such a witness be judged impartial?"

The advocate regards Thomas gravely. "Mungo Craig will give his testimony under oath. No man would lie under oath, for fear of the wrath of the Almighty." He turns to me. "If you would, Mr Craig."

The clerk pushes a paper in front of me; I pick it up and glance over the words. I can barely remember saying them, but sure enough, there is my signature at the bottom of the page. "I, Mungo Craig," I begin, "student, in Edinburgh, aged twenty-one years, unmarried, purged of malice, prejudice and partial counsel, and solemnly sworn, do attest that I heard Thomas Aikenhead deny the existence of God, and say that he cursed those who took him for baptism, declaring that it was a pretty trick to play on an innocent babe, to make promises on his behalf when he knew no better. And that by these means the ministers of religion captured the minds of the young with their snares and shackles. And that he hoped most fervently to see Christianity destroyed, and that were he banished for his freethinking he would take up the pen against religion, and make Christianity tremble."

The judges and jury sit up, alert. I can sense a quiver of excitement rippling through the room. "You may defend yourself now, Mr Aikenhead," says one of the judges.

Thomas gets to his feet. "I can explain," he says. I risk a glance at him. He is calm now, his anger transformed to swagger. "I may have said those things, but the words were not my own." He turns to the judges and jury. "Surely you educated men understand the concept of quotation?" The educated men look grave. "I have read some books," he continues, "that many might consider atheistical." He pauses, and bows to acknowledge the disapproving noises from the crowd. "What I say is, if these books are so wicked, then why were they in the university library, eh?" He seems unaware of the penitential mood in the room. The lightning is crackling across his brain and the sparks are flying. "And anyway," he says, waving a casual hand at me, "this man here, who denounces me for what I said, read these books with me, on the same day, at the same library table!" I feel sick, light-headed. He stares hard at me, points his finger and imitates the distinctive tones of the Reverend Crawford as he says, "Swear you didn't if you dare, my friend, but remember that you are still under oath. Beware the wrath of the Almighty!" The room is in uproar – some laughing, some shouting him down – and Thomas himself seems delighted, taking his seat and favouring me with a triumphant smile.

It seems I was the last witness. I take my place among the others, sitting beside the boy whose name I still don't know. The judges mutter briefly together, in consultation with the advocate, who then steps forward. "Before the jury retires to consider its verdict, I ask them to consider this," he says.

"That's James Stewart," the boy whispers to me. "Wily Jamie."

"We are a covenanted people," James Stewart continues. "Day and night we wrestle with our sinfulness, and while – with the Lord's help – we can quell the iniquities of our own corrupt human nature, we see all around us the admonitory hand of the Almighty. Crops have failed, pestilence has thrived, fires have destroyed whole rows of tenements and strange, dead beasts of the sea have been washed up on the shores of Leith. And why is the Lord displeased?" The crowd in the courtroom is absolutely silent. "The one thing that has changed in this most devout of lands is a new infection, lately arrived from foreign parts, carried within the pages of certain books. Its names are legion. Some call it freethinking, others deism, still others atheism. Whatever the name, a remedy must be found. The diseased parts must be cut out, for the salvation of the whole." He nods towards the jury. "Consider your verdict prayerfully, gentlemen. Prayerfully and in fear of the Lord."

The session is adjourned while the jury and judges confer. Thomas is led away, back to the Tolbooth until a verdict has been reached. The courtroom is cleared, to the protests of those who would prefer not to brave the bitter December cold outside. I am glad enough to be out in the air. Patrick finds me and we make our way to the head of a wynd, simply to be out of the crush of passers-by and loiterers. A crowd gathers outside the Tolbooth. The prison squats like a giant mastiff in the middle of the high street, so that the road must split into two narrow tracks on either side of it, hemmed in on all sides by tall buildings black with soot.

"Which floor is Thomas's cell on?" Patrick asks. "We did not go up many flights of stairs when we visited."

I scan the dark flank of the Tolbooth, and count the rows of small windows – eight rows in total. "Perhaps the second?" There are shouts and cheers from the crowd. "You showed them, Tam." "To hell with the kirk." "Can a man no' think what he wills?" "Bonnie Thomas, marry me." The voices echo through the canyon of the street. I'm sure Thomas must be able to hear them. How he will preen.

"They are on his side," says Patrick. "That must be good, don't you think?"

"We should go." The mood in the street thrums with energy, like the air before a thunderstorm.

"But we must wait for the verdict." He gives me an accusatory look. How many of those have I had from him this last number of days? As if he had not given evidence against Thomas as surely as I did.

"I'm not sure I could bear it." The words are out before I've thought them. Are they true? I hardly know.

"We must be strong for Thomas," Patrick says, though he is trembling. He grips my arm. "Look, people are going back into the courtroom."

"Have you reached a verdict?" asks one of the judges.

"We have," says the foreman of the jury.

"What is that verdict?"

"Guilty."

"And is that the verdict of you all?"

"It is."

I feel cold. Colder than I was outside. Cold in spite of the crush of people around me. I dare not look at Thomas.

The judges shuffle papers until they find what they are looking for. One of them lifts a page and begins to read. "The jury having unanimously found the accused, Thomas Aikenhead, guilty of railing against God the Father, and railing against God the Son, and denying the existence of God the Holy Ghost, thereby impugning all three persons of the Trinity, and denying that our Blessed Saviour Jesus Christ was the son of God, and scoffing at the Holy Scriptures – we, the Commissioners of Justice adjudge that the said Thomas Aikenhead be taken to the Gallowlee betwixt Leith and Edinburgh, upon Friday the eighth day of January next to come, betwixt two and four o'clock in the afternoon, and there to be hanged on a gibbet till he be dead, and his body to be interred at the foot of the said gallows, and ordain all his moveable goods and gear to be confiscated and inbrought to His Majesty's use, which is pronounced for doom."

The room is in uproar, the few cheers swamped by boos. I cannot see Patrick – he has been swallowed up in the jostle of bodies – and I push my way towards the door, desparate to be as far away as is possible to be. My size and height give me the advantage, and those who turn to remonstrate take note of my dimensions and content themselves with scowling. I have almost escaped when – in spite of all – a surge of men from another part of the room spins me so that I am facing the way I have come. For a moment, through the crowd, I see Thomas being walked from his place to the prisoners' entrance that will take him back to the Tolbooth. The two guards have him lifted nearly off his feet. He looks as tiny as a child between them. I look away from him, and force my way to the door with renewed urgency, elbowing aside any who impede me.

Isobel

"Heavenly Father, for mercy's sake, I beg you, let her die."
Kneeling beside the bed where I slept away the nights of
my childhood, I utter the prayer I dare not say out loud in
the sickroom. There Hetty and I choose our words more
carefully. *Release thy servant, we implore thee, Lord.* But the
meaning is the same. My mother's existence has become a
nightmare of suffering. She roars and howls like an animal.
We have had to tie her to the bed, otherwise she would
throw herself on the floor. Dr Leitch's wooden frame to keep
the blankets from her broken leg has been set aside, for it
was doing her more injury as she tossed around the bed.
The opium that he administers pacifies her somewhat – at
least, it quietens her cries. I fear it does not ease her bodily
agony one jot.

I cannot tell if it is day or night. At this low ebb of the
year it seems to be dark every time I look out the window.
It is days since I ventured outside. Hetty has organised
a brigade of womenfolk from the village to help about
the house and take turns sitting with my mother. She
sends me to lie down when she sees I am near exhaus-
tion, just as she did when I was a little girl, and I obey
her more meekly than I ever did as a child. Sometimes I
sleep for an hour or two. More often I lie staring at the
darkness, my mind like a river in torrent. And I pray. I
do not question God – who am I to demand an explanation from Him? – but I beg that he will bring this horror
to an end.

I hear the sound of horse's hooves approaching the house.
It must be Dr Leitch. He has been calling twice a day, bearing the jar of opium as reverently as a miraculous cure. I
must speak to him, and then I will try to rest.

I intercept him on the stairs before he gets to the sick-room. The sound of my mother's sobbing is audible even from here. "Any change?" says Dr Leitch.

I shake my head. Mother screams and Dr Leitch flinches. "The opium," I say, "it doesn't seem to give her as much relief as it did."

"Your husband tells me that patients develop a tolerance for it."

"Should you not then increase the dose?"

A shadow of annoyance passes over his face. "Opium is a dangerous drug, Mistress Carruth. Too much can put patients into such a deep sleep that they might not ever wake." He stares hard at me. "I will do what I can to ease your mother's suffering, but I will not force the hand of God."

"I was not suggesting you do," I say, frightened now of the thoughts that are racing through my head, "but surely you could increase the dose a little?"

"If you are dissatisfied with my care, Mistress Carruth, I suggest you write to your husband and ask him to take over the case." With that he stalks on towards the sickroom. I follow him, fearful that he will somehow take out his anger on my mother. But once he is at her bedside he seems more himself, and administers the opium dutifully. When she has calmed a little he touches her hands, and then goes to the end of the bed and carefully examines her feet. Hetty is in the room, and we stand side by side watching him.

"Is the time near, Doctor?" says Hetty.

"I believe so. Perhaps a day or two more." He pauses, as if he is about to make some significant pronouncement, but instead merely says, "I will call again later today." And with that he takes his leave. Hetty makes no move to show him out, and I give her no instruction to do so. Let him find his own way to the front door.

I write to Robert, imploring him to come. Not that I think he will do anything differently to Dr Leitch – Robert is the very opposite of reckless – but I long for his companionship, for the warmth of his body beside me when I lie down. One of the womenfolk is returning to the village and takes the letter for me. I try to pray again, but I can find no words. The last time I was beyond prayer was when my first child miscarried. I remember how I envied papist women, who could pray to Mary the mother of Jesus. What comfort there must be in prayerful conversation with Mary, a suffering woman who knew what it was to bear – and lose – a child.

Mother continues much the same for the next day. Almost imperceptibly she is losing strength, and no longer tosses around on the bed. Hetty and I agree to untie her bindings. There is no danger of her falling out of the bed now. Her breathing is more laboured, and she can only whimper when the pain overwhelms her. The other women retreat from the sickroom. Now that the end is approaching they occupy themselves in the kitchen. The minister – my father's successor at the kirk – visits and prays with us. After a time his presence and voice begin to grate on me and I ask him to leave.

Hetty and I sit on either side of the bed, each holding one of Mother's hands. "She is so cold," I say.

"That's how the doctor knew the end was coming," Hetty says. "The hands and feet get cold. It's a sign that life is retreating." She draws her knowledge from decades of deaths.

The room is very still. I study my mother's face. Her eyes are closed, and her chest rises and falls, each breath like a sigh. Hetty leans down to speak in her ear, murmuring endearments. I wish she would stop.

Mother exhales. There is a long gap before she breathes in again. Hetty falls quiet and we wait. Another breath out. Something changes in Mother's face – something so imperceptible, and yet so definite. As if the light in the room has altered. I look over at Hetty and she nods. The silence in the room feels dense with sanctity. Hetty folds Mother's hands together over her chest and goes to the window. When she twitches the curtain aside I see that it is daylight. She opens the window just a little, and the cold air rushes in. "I know it's fierce cold, Miss Isobel, but we must let her soul be on its way." She comes back to the foot of the bed and looks down at my mother. "My poor mistress," she says simply, and starts to cry. I go to her and embrace her. Why am I not crying too?

When we leave the room I find two women seated outside, one in her middle years, the other very much younger. Hetty nods at them, and directs them into the room.

"Who are they?" I ask.

"Lizzie Reid and her daughter," she says. "They have the laying out of the dead in the village." She pauses. "I'll go in to help them, Miss Isobel. I'd like to do this last thing for your mother."

"Of course. Thank you." I wonder if I am expected to do the same, and am relieved when Hetty instructs me to rest in my room.

Remarkably, I sleep. When I awake I find that Robert has arrived and is in the parlour, reading through some papers. He puts his arms around me. "I'm sorry I arrived too late. But I can be of more use now, with arrangements. I've written to Alison and asked her to tell the children." I feel a pang of longing to see Henry and Margaret. These past days I have nearly forgotten I am a mother.

"How are they?"

"Very well. Margaret had a little head cold, but she made no complaint." Robert looks pleased at the thought of our stoical daughter. He looks down at the papers. "There will be a lot to attend to."

"What other news from Edinburgh?"

The expression on Robert's face alarms me, but at this very moment the minister is announced. We sit and discuss the funeral arrangements. He addresses all his questions and comments to Robert. This is my punishment, I suppose, for dismissing him from the deathbed. It is agreed that the burial will take place tomorrow.

When he has gone I turn back to Robert. "Have you news of Thomas?"

He nods. "He was found guilty, Isobel."

"And the penalty?" His look gives me my answer. The room seems to lurch and I clutch the sides of my chair.

"I did as you asked me, and offered to pay for an advocate. He wrote to me that he was not a beggar and would not take charity,"

"Stubborn boy."

"He changed his mind once the sentence was passed. Charity was not so distasteful to him then. The advocate petitioned for mercy, on grounds of his youth and good character, and when that was rejected he pleaded for a stay of execution, in order that Thomas might better prepare himself to meet God."

"Surely they could not deny him that?"

Robert shakes his head. "They could and they did."

"So when does he…" I cannot bring myself to say the word.

Robert looks down, not meeting my eye. "Tomorrow."

Mungo

It is after noon, but I am curled up on my bed, heels to the wall, knees hanging over the edge. Fully dressed. A great weight of blankets piled on top of me. I cannot get warm. My skin is prickled with goose pimples that will not subside.

A window in my mind cracks open and I see – just for a moment – Thomas, being led from his cell, out of the Tolbooth, along the Leith road as far as the Gallowlee. I echo each blink of his eye with my own. Am borne along by the steady drum of our heartbeats. Swallow, though there is nothing to swallow in the sour dryness of our mouths.

I throw the blankets off and struggle to my feet. Only movement will keep that fearful empathy at bay. One stride takes me to my window. I put my eye to the gap in the shutters. The street seems empty. I open one shutter and unlatch the window. This is something different from Sunday silence. The air crackles with it. *They mean to take him from the Tolbooth after noon.* Patrick's words. *You'd be wise to flit.* Hutchison's words. No. I'm going nowhere. I have done nothing wrong. Anyway, where would I go? My mother's house? I think not.

Will I know when it is finished? My mind is stretched tight as a drum-skin. I yearn for relief, as the hunted deer pants for sanctuary. Surely I will feel it in the depths of my soul? The Lord will stop the tongue of the unrighteous. The boil will be lanced. Blessed be the name of the Lord.

Be near me, Lion of Judah. Strengthen and guide me. The path of righteousness is a dark one. I stumble, and lose my way.

Inspiration comes to me like a bright light illuminating my mind, and I know it must be from the Almighty. I will write the story down. This ordeal is God's gift to me, to test me in the fire and find if I am made of gold or base metal. I must keep a record of it while it is fresh in my memory. Then, some years hence, I will take out my notes again and compose a memoir, or set of spiritual exercises, for the encouragement and comfort of others. The wisdom of hindsight will allow me to discern the hand of the Almighty in my current travails. I have pen, ink, paper and light enough to write by. Thomas's ending will see the beginning of my work. Such is the wondrous pattern of the Lord's plan.

The Memoir of Mungo Craig, recounting the Strange and Troubling Occurrences leading to the Execution of Thomas Aikenhead for Apostasy, 8th January 1697

I first met with Thomas Aikenhead on 30th April 1696. The first day of the summer term. Easter was past and Christ our Saviour was risen. The Lion of Judah walked beside me on the road from my mother's house in Leith into town. You, reader, may wonder at this, so I must explain that I often imagine the Lord to be with me in the form of the Lion of Judah, and take great comfort and reassurance from his presence. I suspect I am unusual in this notion, for I have never heard anyone else describe it. But to return to my companion, the Lion of Judah. The rough stones did not trouble Him, for He was wise as a cat, strong as a horse, choosing where to set each footstep so that He came to no harm. He was with me when I left my bag at my lodgings. He was with me when I walked into the lecture hall. Because of Him I did not fear the buzz of clever words from the swarming wits of Edinburgh. They elbowed past me, talked around me as if I were not there, but the Lion of Judah was with me, and I did not shrink from battle.

When the lecture was done we all pushed out of the hall, hungry for air. A sweat-sweet crush, elbows digging in ribs, boots treading on toes. My shoulders were a match for any of them. Dockman's shoulders, the only legacy passed on to me by my father. I muscled my way to the door and out into the street.

A cough behind me. A "pardon me" cough. A quizzical cough. Wry cough. Dry cough.

I turned. There stood a slender lad, smiling, footering with his collar, looking as if he hadn't quite made up his mind about something. "You," he said to me, "must be Mungo Craig."

"Yes." The heat flared in my face and spread up and down and around until I felt as if my very scalp must be blushing. I wanted to say who are you and how do you know me and why are you talking to me? But I didn't. I couldn't say a word.

"Have you any money?" he said.

"No."

"Ah well," he said. "Shall we go to Dalton's?"

"But we've no means to pay." My belly gurgled. I slipped my hand in my pocket and touched the slice of bread I'd palmed off my mother's table before I left Leith that morning.

His smile grew wider. "But I, my dear fellow, have credit." He ambled onward. I hung back. Was I included? Really? He must have realised I wasn't following him, because he stopped and looked back. "Come along then, man. What are you waiting for?"

I was squeezed in a corner of Dalton's for the first time in my life, sipping my first coffee (bitter, black, thirst-making stuff, I concluded), watching him scan the room in the same way he had already skim-read the copies of the Edinburgh Courant and the Protestant Mercury that lay on the table. This much I now knew: he was acquainted with my fellow lodger, Patrick Middleton; he had heard I was an uncommonly clever fellow; he liked that I was not spindly and wan, as most students are; he admired my name, thinking it had a certain air.

"Middleton tells me you can turn out a verse in next to no time."

"It's a diversion," I said. "A reward after a day's studying. It'll hardly earn me my keep."

202

"What are you meant for?" he said. "Medicine or the kirk?"

"The kirk."

He slapped the table, earning a frown from the gentlemen sitting around it. "Well then, you can enliven your sermons with a bit of versifying." He pulled over one of the newspapers and studied it. "It says here that a goldsmith and a laird are lately imprisoned in the castle for denouncing the King. Can you turn that to rhyme?"

I thought for a moment, rifling through the words in my mind, trying them out side by side, counting the beats, hearing the tune of them. "For wise men know that treason hides itself, beneath the gaudy silks and trims of wealth. Disloyalty, a sin despised of old, can not be gilded o'er with gleaming gold."

His smile came slowly, and he seemed to grow with it. "By the Lord," he said, and gathered some more frowns from our neighbours, "that's splendid, Craig, splendid." He reached forward, grasped my arm. "Say you'll be my friend, Craig. Mungo. May I call you Mungo? Every man should have at least one friend who is a genius, and none of my sorry circle comes even close. So will you? Will you? I should like it very much if you would."

"Yes," I said. "I will."

What other answer could I give?

The day has darkened. There is a candle by my bedside, but no kindling to light it. I stand and stretch as best I can in the narrow room. My feet are numb with the cold. Outside there are sounds of life in the street – two men arguing; a dog barking; the slow clop of hoof beats from a solitary horse. I take the candle and go downstairs to the back kitchen. The dog is sleeping in her usual corner, the white of her coat tinted red by the faint glow of the fire. She opens one eye to look at me, then goes back to sleep. As I light the candle from the fire I hear the key turn in the front door of the shop and the scrape of wood against the stone floor. Hutchison keeps promising to mend the door. The winter damp has warped it worse than ever it was. The sound of it makes my flesh crawl.

Hutchison and Patrick come through to the kitchen. They carry with them the smell of smoke and liquor. The dog raises her head this time. Her stump of a tail wags, slapping against the flagstones.

"Well?" I say, not knowing how to phrase the questions I have.

"Very well, I thank you," says Hutchison. He walks over to his chair, bumping against the table as he passes. "You might have tended the fire better," he says, settling himself down.

I look over to Patrick. He meets my gaze for a second, then bends to stir up the fire with the poker. "Shall I put more coal on?" he asks.

"It's no' worth it, at this hour," says Hutchison, twisting his accent so that he sounds like a common man.

Patrick pulls up a stool and sits close to the fire, his back to me.

"It's over then?" I say. Neither of them speaks. "How... how did it go?"

"They hanged him. That's how it usually goes." Patrick's voice has an uncustomary edge.

"Did he say anything?"

Patrick turns and looks up at me. "What do you mean?"

"He died like a true Christian," says Hutchison. "By which I mean he had a Bible in his hand – whether by his own wish or not I cannot tell – and the praying of the clergy was so loud that no one could hear a word he said."

"He had a speech written and prepared," Patrick says. "He tried to read it, but he lost heart."

"And there was no trouble?"

Patrick shakes his head. "I kept thinking the reprieve must come, even today. And then, when it was done, I half expected to see a messenger gallop up bearing mercy from the King. That would have meant something, even when it was too late."

"What are they saying in the town?"

Hutchison stretches out his legs until his boots are near enough in the hearth. "Some say this will be the end of it. The Kirk has had its blood sacrifice. Others say it's only the beginning."

Isobel

Thomas Aikenhead is already two days dead by the time I return to Edinburgh. Robert and I bring Hetty with us. My mother's house is shut up. As we left, locking the door behind us, it felt to me as if the building itself was dead.

My spirits lift a little as we draw near to the Pleasance. Henry runs down the stairs and throws himself into my arms. He seems taller than when I left, though that is hardly possible. "Are you sad, Mama?" he says, looking up at me with a tenderness that melts my heart.

"Of course I am, my darling," I say, "but I am happy to be home again."

Margaret has paused halfway down the stairs. Alison is hovering behind her. "Go and greet your mother," she says, nudging Margaret forward. My daughter comes down the stairs and stands in front of me. She raises her face towards me and I bend down to kiss her. Then she steps back and regards me coolly.

Once we are settled I declare I have need of a solitary walk while it is still daylight and leave the house. I follow the gradual downhill slope of the Leith road out as far as Gallowlee, for the judges had ordered that his body be left hanging in chains on the gibbet. It is a raw day, and the air is hard and clear as the finest glass. The cold makes the tears start in my eyes.

There are no more than a dozen people at the Gallowlee. It is likely the chill keeps the curious away, or perhaps the destruction of Thomas is old news. One common-looking fellow sits on a stool at the foot of the gibbet. The gallows guard, no doubt. I avoid looking at the gibbet itself, but am conscious of it at the edge of my field of vision, nudging for my attention like a bad thought. As to the rest of the people gathered, there is only one other woman. She looks no more than five and twenty, and something in her narrow features reminds me of Thomas. There are two gentlemen of middling quality, and the others – including a gaggle of children – the lower type. They all watch me walk up the path to the hanging place. The older of the gentlemen raises his hat, his companion then taking the hint and doing likewise.

I make myself glance over at the gallows. Thomas's body has been placed in a man-shaped metal cage and hung from the gibbet, like an obscene birdcage. One of the mercies of a winter hanging is that there are no flies to use the dead man's flesh as a hatching feast for their young, but the cold doesn't keep the corbies away. They'll seek their food in any weather. A pair of them flap and squabble around the gibbet as I draw closer. One of the children lobs a stone towards them, striking Thomas on the chest so that the cage sways from side to side, like a pendulum. The birds retreat for a moment or two, then return, bolder than before. One clings on to the metal strut closest to Thomas's face. I force myself to look up.

In my first confusion I think the bitterness of the season has blackened and disfigured his face. It seems scarcely human – dark and distorted, like an ancient carving that has been dirtied and worn down by time. I look away, and catch the eye of the gallows guard, still perched on his stool. His expression is as blank as a gambler at the card table. If my unease moves him in any way – to pity, or contempt – he does not show it. I make myself look at Thomas again. Trussed as he is in the cage, he could pass for one of the effigies the students burn when they are full of fervour and devilment at Christmas. His stockings are stained, and one shoe has come loose so that it hangs half on, half off. When I look at his hands I see that they too are black and unnatural in appearance.

"Why are his face and hands so strange-looking?" I ask the gallows guard.

"We tarred them afore we put the corpse in the cage," the man says. "It saves him frae the weather. When we tarred his face we pulled the hood back down, to spare the distress o' the likes o' yourself. You wudnae want to gaze at him if the corbies had dined on his eyes, eh?"

"When will you bury him? It seems unchristian to keep him from his grave."

The man shrugs. I reach for my purse and fumble for a coin. My fingers are numb with the cold, in spite of my gloves. He watches me, but no spark of avarice flashes in his eyes. Nonetheless, when I offer him the money he takes it readily enough. "The order was tae leave him dangling a day or two more. Have you some interest in seeing him planted sooner?"

I glance over at the young woman. She is standing apart from the other spectators, a black cloak pulled tightly around her thin figure. "His friends would rest easier if they knew he was past this indignity," I say. "There's money to smooth the way, if that's what is needed."

He doesn't respond, and chews absently at his nails. I turn and begin walking away. "Hold there," he calls after me. I stop and look back, but make no move to return to him. When he stands up and comes towards me I know I have him snared. He doesn't speak again until he is close enough that he will not be overheard. "My lad and I can do the job for you after sunset, for ten shillings."

"I'll pay you five shillings now, and five when I know the job is done."

"Ha! You may cheat me."

"You can come calling at my door for the balance, and if I try to renege on our arrangement you can shame me in front of my neighbours."

He thinks about that, eyeing me. I am chilled to the marrow, and I tense every sinew to stop myself shivering.

"For that I'd need to know where you bide, and what your name is," he says.

"Come to the Pleasance, and ask for me at Dr Carruth's house. I am the doctor's wife. I am Isobel Carruth."

I walk over to the young woman. "Forgive me for intruding," I say, "but are you kin of Thomas's?"

She studies my face, as if she is appraising me. "Aye. I'm his sister, Katharine. Did you know him?"

"A little. He and his friends dined with us now and again. My husband is a doctor, you see, so Thomas…"

"Your husband is Dr Carruth?" she says sharply.

"Yes." There is something in her tone that makes me afraid to inquire further. "If there is anything we can do to assist you, please come to us. We're at the Pleasance."

"I hope I can manage very well without your help, or anyone else's," she says, straightening up and thrusting her chin out. Just like her brother. Proud and obstinate, when provoked.

"Will you walk with me back into town?"

She shakes her head. "I'll bide here a while longer."

So I walk home alone, past the scrubland that borders both sides of the Leith road. The soil is too ungenerous to put forth anything more fruitful than whin and rough grass. There are a few dwellings, but none of any substance. The hard ground is inimical to firm foundations. Although the landscape is as desolate as my spirits I am glad of its bleakness. In my oppressed state of mind I welcome the emptiness of the scene.

Returning now from the Gallowlee my dearest wish is to retreat to my desk, but first I am compelled to attend to the kitchen and my children. I find Hetty working listlessly at helping Agnes to prepare the evening meal. Her eyes are still red with weeping for her old mistress. I offer my help, which she declines, saying, "I'm better keeping occupied,

Miss Isobel." As I walk away from the kitchen along the passage I hear the steady tap-tap of her knife as she cuts through a parsnip at the kitchen table. Robert is out, calling on that small group of esteemed lady patients who are never content unless he can discover some malady in them. He had considered placing a notice in the *Protestant Mercury* to advertise that he was returned from his melancholy duties in Berwickshire, but I advised that there was no need. These particular patients of his are consummate spreaders of news. By noon tomorrow every lady in the city will know that he is once again available for consultation.

Upstairs in the nursery Henry and Margaret are sitting side by side on the window seat with their Bible open across their laps. They are both reading silently, Margaret tracing her finger under the passage she is studying to keep her place. Their faces are parchment-pale in the fading winter light. Tomorrow I will insist they both go for a walk, to stir some colour into their cheeks. "What story are you reading?" I ask.

"Joshua and the walls of Jericho," says Margaret.

"Very good," I murmur.

"I think it's ill-hearted," Henry says without raising his eyes from the book. His frank, open face is darkened with a frown. The nursery-maid, Alison, who has been sitting quietly by the fire darning a stocking, looks up and stiffens.

I sit down on the window seat beside the children. "Why do you not like it, darling?"

"Why did Joshua have to kill everyone in Jericho?"

Margaret sighs. "Because they were heathens, you gaupie."

This does not satisfy Henry. "But it was wicked of him to kill the women and children and animals too."

"Well," I say slowly, aware of Alison's eyes on me, "Joshua was only doing what God told him to do, and perhaps God had some very good reason to want them all killed."

"Even the animals?"

210

"God's ways are not our ways, Master Henry," Alison says, her darning forgotten in her hands. "We should not question the ways of the Lord."

Henry looks up at me for confirmation of Alison's words. My mouth feels dry. Should I clip the wings of his fledgling curiosity, or leave it free to thrive and fly? I touch his hair – deep brown, like Robert's – and think of Thomas. How would he have answered Henry? His mind fizzed with intelligence and questions, and it had brought him to the gallows. "Alison is correct, Henry," I say, the words like ashes in my mouth. "We must not question God."

Henry's eyes fill with tears, and he rubs at them desperately.

"Henry is a crybaby," Margaret says, her mouth turned in a sly smile. "He cries more than me, and I am a girl."

"Perhaps he has a warmer heart than you," I reply sharply. I recall Margaret's dry-eyed acceptance of her grandmother's death.

She shifts away from us both along the window seat, and her movement nearly causes the Bible to tumble down on to the floor, but Henry catches it. I wish I could like my daughter better.

Henry closes the Bible and twists round to look out the window. "Will Thomas visit us, now that we are come back?"

"Not for a while," I say weakly. "I believe he has gone away."

Henry looks up at me, frowning. "Where has he gone?"

"I'm not sure." I cannot bear to tell him. The idea of breaking his heart with yet another death is too much to endure.

Alison follows me out of the nursery. "Pardon me, mistress," she says, with an expression on her face that is a mixture of determination and boldness. "Do you not think it is your duty to lay before the children what befell that young man Thomas Aikenhead? His death was intended to put a stop to this raging spirit of atheism that has the country in uproar. His blood will go to waste if word of it is not spread among the young." Her eyes sparkle with passion.

"I will tell them in my own time, Alison."

"I'd urge you not to mourn him. He was lost, you ken? Lost to the ways of the Lord."

"We are all sinners, Alison. Let he who is without sin..." I don't finish my quotation. Her breed of Christian has little appetite for mercy.

She reaches into her apron pocket and pulls out a pamphlet. "You won't have seen this. It was circulated after you and the master had gone off to your home place to tend your poor mother. Read it, mistress. You'll find a full account of his wickedness there."

I carry the pamphlet to the landing window, the better to study it. A *Satyr against Atheistical Deism*. Below is a subtitle: *An account of Mr AIKENHEAD's NOTIONS Who is now in Prison for the same Damnable APOSTACY*. And below that, the name of the author. Mungo Craig. "But Mungo was his friend!" I say in shock.

Alison blinks at me. "Aye, from the pen of his closest companion. It's all there, mistress. Of course, he doesn't repeat the blasphemies themselves. They were too dreadful to place in print." She shudders, but her mouth twitches into a smile, as if her horror gives her pleasure.

I struggle to understand what I am seeing. Robert told me Mungo had testified against Thomas – several in his circle of friends had done so – but to publish a pamphlet defaming him was something quite different. "When did this appear?" I say.

Alison frowns as she tries to remember. "You and Dr Carruth went to the country at the start of December, and this was all around the town by the middle of the month."

So Mungo wrote and published this before Thomas's trial. That had begun on the 23rd of December. Sentence was passed on Christmas Eve, and then the fine, godly men who condemned him retired to their homes to ignore the season as good Presbyterians must. "May I keep this, Alison?" I say.

"By all means, mistress. Keep it, and read it, and thank God you were not infected with his poisonous notions."

I leave the nursery and walk downstairs to my parlour. When I first heard that Mungo had given evidence against Thomas I supposed he was coerced. All it would have taken was a hint that if he did not cooperate with the Privy Council then they might next direct their attentions to his soul. This pamphlet is evidence of something much worse, but I will not know its full extent until I read it. Anger and melancholy crush on my heart like weights. These past days I have met death and deceit at every turn. My mother's cruel decline drained has the very life from me. Thomas is dead, and Mungo is his betrayer. And how or when am I to tell the children about Thomas? Margaret will likely regard the episode with heartless curiosity, but as for Henry... he adored Thomas, and longed for his visits. However, I must at all costs protect Henry from the dangers of freethinking. A sudden thought chills me. What if it is too late? Thomas himself once told me that he had been no more than ten years of age when the first doubts crept into his head. Perhaps, had his parents still been living at that time, they would have counselled him into conformity. I determine to watch Henry carefully, and take every opportunity to guide him to safety. Someday, when he is older, he can think what he pleases. I hope he will have the wisdom to keep those thoughts to himself. As I do.

At last I am at my desk. I light the lamp and sit for a moment with one hand over my eyes, as if that might shield me from my thoughts. All through these last weeks of Thomas's arrest and trial I never believed it could have come to this. Perhaps if I had not been compelled to remove from Edinburgh due to my mother's final illness I might have achieved more. I could have written letters on his behalf – reasoned, lucid letters. Visited him. Given comfort, guidance... The notion torments me. That I was not here in town during Thomas's last days increases my sense of dislocation. The sensation puts me in mind of when our infant daughter – my last-born, two years after Margaret – died after one day of life. I was too ill to see her in her winding sheet, to bid her farewell, and somehow that made it seem as if she was not really dead. Even to this day I have a fancy that she is somewhere in the house – being rocked in her cradle by Alison, perhaps – eternally locked in babyhood, always a newborn child. But the cradle stands motionless in a dark corner of the nursery, its only occupant an old dolly of Margaret's. I was not able to kiss my little lost one goodbye, and I think that is why she haunts my thoughts.

The last time I saw Thomas in his cell at the Tolbooth his eyes were bright with defiance. Neither of us had any notion that his life might be in peril. I cannot tally that boy with the tarred mannequin I saw dangling in its cage at the Gallowlee, and yet it was him. Him and not him. I try to blink away the memory, but it lingers in my mind. And then come the other images from these last days. My mother's face in the moments after her death – how was it that it could change so suddenly, and yet so subtly? The intense, sacred silence of the death chamber. My shameful relief when Hetty and the local wise women ushered me out of the room so that they might wash the body.

I turn to Mungo's pamphlet. The publisher, I see, is Robert Hutchison of College Wynd. Mungo's landlord. Did they hatch this pamphlet between them? Perhaps he saw in Mungo's connection to Thomas an opportunity for profit. I can happily condemn Hutchison's character – I thought little of him when I met him – but I cannot conceive that Mungo would have been so moved by money-lust. It does not sit well with the young man I am acquainted with. Then again, I know him only slightly. He seemed quiet, diffident. Further than that I cannot tell.

I flick the pamphlet open. The first page lists the inventions Thomas promised to bring to the world – all nonsensical fancies, of course. *A sovereign antidote against all external and internal causes of death; a new engine whereby we may have easy commerce with the moon; an infallible and cheap way of making the philosopher's stone, in four hours, and for four Scots pounds.* I can imagine Thomas, face flushed with delight at being the centre of attention, making such claims to entertain his companions. Had Mungo not understood that they were merely jokes? What was the purpose of listing them here? It occurs to me that perhaps Mungo's true purpose had been to help Thomas – to convince his readers that here was a frothy and crackbrained lad who posed no threat to the good order of the state. However, Mungo's final description of Thomas's views on Christianity chills my benevolence: *A complete aggregate of all the blasphemies that ever were vented by the atheistical Ministers of Satan in all ages.* How could he say such a thing, with Thomas about to face trial? He concludes the first page with the promise that Robert Hutchison can produce witnesses to support his claims.

The next number of pages contain a lengthy poetic diatribe against the irreligious: couplet after couplet of blood and thunder. I skim through it. He vents his rage against the *proud ungodly scum*, the *sluttish minds* of the freethinkers. There is an energy to his work, no doubt of that, and now and again he seems to capture something of Thomas's essence: *Such are the blazing comets that attract th'amazement of the novel-catching pack.* Yes, that was Thomas. A bright star in our dark lives, and Mungo was drawn to his light as irresistibly as any of us. There is nothing here that might damn Thomas directly. I begin to think that Mungo and Plooky Robert Hutchison played a sleekit hand, using Thomas's name and notoriety to gull their customers into buying a pamphlet filled with nothing more than wasted ink and effort. But as I read on the tone becomes more pointed. *Will Scotland nourish such Apostacy? A covenanted people!* These are words chosen to inflame the Godly men of the jury. *Atone with blood th'affronts of heav'n's offended throne*, Mungo urges. *Atone with blood.*

Robert is in an unfathomable mood at the dinner table. He begins to recount some tittle-tattle he's acquired from one of his lady patients, then halts abruptly and assumes a mourning face. After a few kind-toned but offhand platitudes he falls into deep thought. I want to tell him about Mungo's pamphlet, but dare not raise the matter while the children are here, as it will certainly lead them to ask questions about Thomas.

I wonder how best to open the subject. There has been no further discussion between us on the subject of Thomas's trial and execution since the day my mother died. I wonder how he will respond to the news of Mungo's perfidy. Robert always seemed more comfortable with Mungo than with Thomas – perhaps there was something in Mungo's humble background that chimed with him.

After the meal is done, the lamps lit and the children gone upstairs, I bring out the pamphlet for him to study.

"So this is Mungo's infamous publication," he says.

"You know about it?"

"It was mentioned at a number of my visits. The good ladies of the Burgh have rather taken against our young friend Mungo."

"Do they mean to make Thomas the hero of a romance now that their husbands have killed him?"

Robert looks up sharply. "Bitter words, Isobel."

I say nothing, but look down at my hands while he scans the pamphlet. I count the pages as he turns them.

"You see how he's dressed up his qualifications?" Robert indicates the list of letters Mungo has placed after his name. "Has he even received his degree yet?"

Trust Robert to quibble over such niceties. "Perhaps he thought it gave him more *gravitas*."

"Along with some lines from Juvenal." He points to the Latin quotation on the front of the pamphlet. "Shall I translate?"

"My brain is not so rusted that I cannot attempt it." In spite of the dreary circumstances, I cannot resist the challenge, and take the pamphlet back from him. "*Semper ego auditor tantum?* That is straightforward enough. 'Must I always be the listener?'" Robert nods in approval, and I continue. "*Numquamque reponam vexatus toties?*" These are the opening lines of Juvenal's first satire. I had known them by heart as a girl. "'Am I never to get a word in?'"

Robert peers at the words and agrees. He taps his forefinger against his lips. "Young Mungo seems determined to show his learning."

"Typical of his type." I repent the words as soon as I say them, more so when I detect the flicker of disapproval on Robert's face.

"What do you mean by that?"

I feel my face colouring. "Well, he was a charity scholar, wasn't he?"

"Some of our most promising young men have been educated by the charity of the town."

I bow my head again, accepting his reprimand. "That was ungracious of me. He cannot help his origins."

Agnes's approaching footsteps halt our conversation. She taps on the door, and Robert calls for her to enter. The door opens a little, and her face appears around it. She seems more rosy-cheeked than usual. "There's someone at the back door for you, mistress."

Robert frowns. "Who would call at this hour? And to the back door?"

I am equally perplexed for a moment, until I remember. The gallows guard. He had quite slipped my mind. I turn to Robert. "Ah, I recall now," I lie, "I promised charity to a poor family – they have some connection to an old labourer of my father's." I rise and hasten first up to my parlour to fetch some money, then back down to the kitchen, followed by Agnes. I do not quite know why I lied to Robert.

Agnes has closed the door against the gallows guard, and left him standing in the yard. "I didn't like to let him in, mistress, and leave Hetty alone with him," she whispers, unbarring the door and opening it. Hetty herself is seated by the hearth, staring into it as if she has no interest in these goings-on. Apart from the fire the only light in the room comes from a small lamp on the kitchen table.

I motion for the man to come in. He steps forward cautiously, peering into the dark corners of the kitchen as if he suspects an ambush.

"I did as you asked," he says. "He's down and buried at the gallows' foot."

"How can I be sure of you?"

"Aye, I kenned you'd want proof. When me and my boy cut him down, we had a root through his pockets."

"And what did you find there?"

"A coin for me, as is customary. You maybe don't know it, missus, but should you ever come tae the gallows you must mind tae tip the executioner, and leave money in your pocket for those who are obliged tae gather you up afterwards." It is clear that he takes a certain enjoyment in informing me of these niceties. There are certain men – and not only among the lower orders – who thrill at distressing women with unpleasant truths. I am determined not to betray any sign of disturbance.

"I take it you must have found some other thing?"

He nods. "Aye. There was a letter."

"To whom was it addressed?"

"I couldnae tell you." He reaches into his jacket pocket and pulls out a sheaf of folded papers that are sealed with a coarse lump of wax.

I take the bundle from him and study the front of it. "'Turn thee unto me, and have mercy upon me; for I am desolate and afflicted,'" I read out loud. "I wonder who it was meant for?"

"You'd know that better than me, eh missus?"

I slip the papers into the folds of my sleeve and say, "I must pay you what you're owed." I begin to count the five shillings out into his hand.

"Tae tell you the truth, missus, I was sorry tae see him hanged. If we strung up every young lad who had daft notions in his head there wudnae be too many of them left, eh?"

I hear a movement behind me, and turn to see Robert in the kitchen doorway. Something in his stance makes me nervous. I can sense his eyes on me, even though his face is in shadow. Agnes too stands looking on, like judgement personified. My hand shakes as I place the last shilling in the gallows guard's outstretched palm. The skin of his hand has a yellowish tinge in the lamplight, and the coins look like five dark tar-drops against it.

He pockets his fee, glances over my shoulder at Robert, hesitates for a moment and then nods his thanks and retreats back out the door into the unlit backyard.

I take a deep breath to compose myself. "You may bar the door, Agnes," I say. "We'll hardly have more callers tonight."

Robert waits for me in the hallway. "He didn't sound like a countryman," he says.

"I don't understand you." I brush past him and walk towards the dining room. "Shall we go back to our translation?"

"What was his connection with your family? Exactly?" He follows me as he speaks, like a dog on the scent of its prey.

"Och for goodness sake. My father knew half the poor folk of Lanarkshire, and many a one had kin in Edinburgh.

Do you expect me to keep a ledger of all his patronage?" I stop at the dining room door. "Will we continue with our study of Mungo's pamphlet?"

Robert holds back. "You are capable of interpreting it by yourself. It seems you prefer to conduct your affairs without my assistance." He turns and goes back down the hallway and into his consulting room.

I consider pursuing him, doing what a good wife should and calming the troubled waters of his temper. But I have Thomas's papers, and I am determined to read them tonight. I ask Agnes to light me a candle, and thus equipped I go upstairs to my parlour and open the bundle. The outer sheet is a letter, addressed to no one in particular.

Tolbooth prison, 6ʰ January 1697

Being now wearing near the last moment of my time of living in this vain world, I have by the enclosed under my own hand, now, when I am stepping into eternity, given a true relation of the original rise, matter and manner of my doubtings, for which I am to die. I carry this in the hope that it will be delivered to my dear and worthy friends, in order that they may convey it to the world in general. I hope I shall be forgiven, by the mercy of God, and that these papers will give satisfaction to you in particular, and after I am gone produce more charity that hath been my fortune to be trusted hitherto with, and remove the apprehensions, which I hear are various and many about my case, being the last words of a dying person, and proceeding from the sincerity of my heart.

Sic subcribitur
Thomas Aikenhead

I can hear his voice in the words of his letter. What bravery, to compose such fine phrases in the very anteroom of death. What thoughtfulness – and common sense – not to

220

name the intended recipient. I suppose it was meant for Katharine, for I can think of no one else whom Thomas might have deemed a friend. I will have to find out where she stays, and pass these pages on to her, although I quail at the prospect of meeting with her again. It was clear from her manner today that she is not well disposed towards our household.

I glance at the rest of the papers. The writing is so cramped that it is near impossible to read by candlelight, particularly as my eyes are half blinded with tears, but I force myself on. It seems to be a treatise – or a speech perhaps – explaining the spiritual road he had travelled. Certain phrases leap out at me: *It is a principle natural to every man to have an insatiable inclination to truth, and to seek for it as for hidden treasure … the more I thought thereon, the further I was from finding the verity I desired … I cannot have such certainty either in natural or supernatural things as I would have.* The words chime true inside my own soul. These past weeks, watching my mother's agonies and finding myself utterly uncomforted by both private prayer and the words of clergymen, I too have been seeking for truth. The Bible promises that those who ask will not be turned away hungry, but I have been. Doubt gnaws at me like the pangs of starvation.

I scan forward to the final paragraphs, my eye caught by Mungo's name. Thomas writes: *I must vindicate my innocence of those abominable aspersions made in a printed satire of Mr Mungo Craig, whom I leave to reckon with God and his own conscience if he was not as deeply concerned in those hellish notions for which I am sentenced as ever I was.* Is Mungo an atheist too? I recall Thomas once joking about Mungo's freethinking tendencies. It cannot have been true. Mungo has ambitions to become a kirk minister. But if it is not true, why would Thomas have written it? Was it a malicious dart thrown from the grave, revenge for Mungo's pamphlet? I can understand such an impulse, but would Thomas have wanted his last words to be a lie?

Mungo

Classes resume today at the university. I prepare my pens, ink and copybook, and pack them into my bag. When I go downstairs I find the kitchen empty. There's a bustle of commerce sounding in the shop – Hutchison's voice, and a customer responding. On the table in front of me sits a heel of bread and two plates smeared with butter and crumbs. I go back to the foot of the stairs and call up to Patrick, but get no reply. He must have gone on ahead without me.

I go out through the back door and into the wynd, then up the steep way to the university. It is scarcely daylight. This is the first day I've stepped across the threshold in over a week, and the cold air makes my head ache. I feel as if every eye is upon me, but I know that cannot be so. Few would recognise me outside my own small circle. Fewer still would know me by name.

There's an odd atmosphere about the town. I find it hard to determine what it reminds me of. Like the morning after a storm, perhaps. Yes, I remember a great tempest when I was a child in Leith, and how we all – men, women and children – were drawn out to the shore the next day to see what harm had been done to the boats. But the mood today is something different from that. There's a sense of aftermath, yes, but more than that too. Is it shame?

As I get closer to the university my chest tightens. I pray silently, calling upon the Lion of Judah to walk by my side. The Faculty of Divinity is housed in a ramshackle building that was once a merchant's house, until he died and bequeathed it to the college. Some say he did it as much to spite his family as to glorify God. The courtyard in front of it is crowded with students and here I cannot pretend that I am not being remarked upon. I see nudges, pointing fingers, heads leaning together to share whispered words. In the hope of blocking them out, I pray. *Lion of Judah, Lion of Judah...*

I reach the sanctuary of the faculty. The hallway is blessedly empty, although I can hear a murmur of conversation from the common room. My fellow scholars will be gathered around the fire, warming themselves before facing the chill of the lecture hall. I hesitate at the door for a moment, and before I can lay my fingers on the handle it is pulled open and John Row, the regent, barges into me. We both leap back, I uttering an apology, although our collision was not my fault. He glares at me.

"Listening at keyholes, Mr Craig?" he says.

"No!" I exclaim. I can see the other students standing in the room, staring out at me. "I was just about to come in."

Row says nothing in reply, but goes past me and up the stairs to prepare for the morning's lecture. I walk into the common room. The others neither obstruct me nor shrink away from me, but as if on a signal they begin to leave the room, one after the other, until I am left standing alone before the fire.

I stop writing, aware suddenly of someone standing over me. It's one of the old men who works as a college messenger. I don't know his name.

"Mr Row asks tae see you," he says. I will face a reprimand, no doubt, for choosing to absent myself from this morning's lecture. It was not through cowardice, for while I do not claim to have any personal bravery I am confident the Lion of Judah would have strengthened my failing spirits. No, the reason I have spent the morning here in the library rather than in the lecture room is that this memoir of mine – this narrative of the soul – has got such a grip on me that I am only at peace when I am writing it.

I gather up my papers and go in search of John Row, weighing up whether or not I should tell him about this manuscript I am working on. Many fine men of the Kirk have produced such works. He should not disapprove. It occurs to me then that he may instead wish to address the scandal caused by Thomas's execution. While I am blameless, it could be that the university authorities have taken offence at my association with Thomas. That would account for the silence with which my peers greeted me this morning.

The faculty is empty now, my fellow scholars dispersed in search of food and drink before the afternoon session. I go through to John Row's office at the back of the building and knock on his door. I enter at his command.

"Mr Craig," he says, without raising his eyes from the ledger in front of him.

"Yes, Mr Row." I wait, my tongue itching with explanations.

He runs one finger across a line on the ledger. "It has been brought to my attention," he says, "that your library fee from last year is still outstanding." He glances up at me.

For a moment I am speechless. This was not what I expected. I feel my face heat with humiliation. "I beg your pardon, sir," I say. "I had quite forgot." And I had. In all the turmoil of last summer, as my friendship with Thomas grew ripe and then spoiled, I had neglected the diligent attention to administration in which I usually took such pride. "I can pay the fee now," I say, "by which I mean, not this moment, but in a day or two. I would need to draw out some of my bursary."

"That's all very well, Mr Craig," says Row, "but you have breached one of the university's regulations. We have been too lax about such matters this last while, and the result has been clear to see."

"What must I do?" I ask.

"Pay what you owe, of course, and that as soon as possible. There must be a penalty however."

I wait to hear what it is, calculating what inroads a fine might make on my scant funds.

"You are suspended from the university for a period of one month from the date the fee is paid," he says.

The injustice of it overwhelms me. "This is harsh, sir. It will stand against me when I look for a kirk congregation to appoint me minister."

Row fixes his appraising eye on me. "You should have thought of that when you defaulted on your fees." He leans back in his seat and favours me with a milder look. "This is a season of scapegoats, Mr Craig. You have fared better than some."

Isobel

I sleep badly in the days after the gallows guard's visit. Sometimes it is the memories of my mother's last days that keep me from my rest, but – to my shame – more often it is thoughts of Thomas that consume me. The words in his letter run round my mind. It is what he said about Mungo that troubles me most. At some point in the depth of the night I resolve that I will seek Mungo out, and hear from his own lips how he responds to Thomas's accusation.

And so I make my way into town in search of enlightenment. I equip myself with my basket and set off. There is no need to offer any explanation to Robert or the rest of the household. After all, an Edinburgh lady is provided with many good reasons to make her way about the more respectable parts of the town. It is assumed she has an insatiable hunger for bonnets, ribbons and gossip. It is expected that she must ever be replenishing her supplies of needles, pins and thread. She may even – if she is particularly virtuous – take it upon herself to visit the worthy poor. A superannuated maidservant, perhaps, or the widow of her husband's groom.

Once again I find myself outside Robert Hutchison's place of business. Mungo has his lodgings somewhere in the tall, narrow house above the shop. The lie of the street, and the height of all its buildings, mean the building dwells in a perpetual twilight.

When I go in I find that the room is almost bare. The bookshelves are empty and the trestle tables unpopulated. A pair of young men stands in conversation, although they stop speaking as I walk in, and both now stare at me. I look more closely around the shop. The back wall is fitted with a cupboard. Perhaps that is where Hutchison keeps his goods now. A length of sacking is tacked over a doorway that I guess leads to the private part of the house. "Attention here," I call out. My voice sounds shrill in the quiet room, and the two young men appear to flinch.

There is a muddle of sounds from the back of the house. A chair pushed back, a cough, the yelp of a dog, a muttering voice and footsteps. Robert Hutchison appears in the doorway. "Ah!" he says, "Mistress... I fear you must remind me, madam."

"Carruth."

"Mistress Carruth. Of course. I trust your last purchase gave satisfaction? As you can see my stocks are sadly diminished – so many publications are deemed unacceptable these days – but I hope..."

"I'm afraid I am not here to buy," I say, in what I hope is a pleasant tone. "I am come in search of one of your lodgers, Mr Mungo Craig."

The two young men leave, pulling the door behind them with a scraping sound that makes my skin prickle into gooseflesh.

Hutchison scratches the sore on his lip. I can hear the rasp of his nails on the scab. He makes no reply to my enquiry.

"Is Mungo here?" I say.

"He's gone, alas. Moved elsewhere."

"Where does he bide now?"

"That I wouldn't know."

I can't tell if he is lying. I have no skill at sniffing out untruths. "You must feel the lack of his rent," I say, reaching into my basket and pulling out my coin purse. Perhaps the clink of money will clear his mind.

Hutchison looks greedily enough at my purse, but says, "There's always someone looking for decent lodgings. His bed won't lie empty for long."

I feel a sudden surge of dislike towards Robert Hutchison. "I suppose the sales you made of his pamphlet will cushion you from any loss," I blurt out. "Did the two of you split the earnings? Or did you take the greater share, having the expense of printing and stitching it?"

Hutchison looks thoughtful, then turns and saunters to the doorway into the back of the premises. There he pulls aside the sacking, purses his lips, and gives two or three sharp whistles. A dog barks in the back room and comes padding out, its claws clicking on the bare boards. Its coat is dirty white and its dark eyes narrow as it looks first at Hutchison, then at me. As if at some unseen signal it begins to growl so quietly I can barely hear it. Hutchison murmurs something to it, and in response it advances towards me across the shop, snarling. "One word from me and she'll go for you, madam. Go for your face, I would think. She may mistake you for a rat."

Both man and dog fill me with fear, but I stand my ground. "I'll bring a charge against you. I'd wager you could do without a fine from the Privy Council in these hard times."

He shakes his head, as if he is disappointed at such a paltry threat. "I have friends aplenty in the Privy Council, madam. You cannae frighten me with them." He scratches the sore on his lip again. "Mistress Carruth. Wife to Dr Carruth, as I recall. I suppose he's fond of books?"

"Yes," I reply, puzzled by this new turn in our conversation.

"But not a customer of mine."

"Indeed not." I cannot resist a supercilious glance around Hutchison's paltry shop. "He orders his books from London, as a rule."

"I trust his library would bear the scrutiny of the Privy Council? They're on the scent of the freethinkers now, you know. Half the books in the town have been put to the flame. They'll be turning their attention to private libraries soon enough."

"We are a Christian household," I say, trying to conceal a tremor of fear. "The contents of my husband's library are beyond reproach."

He leans against the doorframe and folds his arms. "Are you sure? There's many a gentleman has volumes hidden in his library that his wife kens nothing about." He leers at me for a fraction of a second, and then assumes a sombre expression. "Imagine the shame of it, if your Christian household should be discovered to contain the same books that launched young Aikenhead on his voyage to the gallows."

The trap snaps shut. I know that Robert is only interested in books concerned with medical matters, and his faith is of the most robust and orthodox type. Even so, if our home were to be searched by the Privy Council it would tarnish his reputation, and diminish his standing.

"Be on your way, madam," Hutchison says. "You'll get no intelligence from me, and if you trouble my place of business again I may be reminded to point our friends in the Privy Council towards your family." He stares at me in silence then whistles to the dog. The two of them return to the back of the house, leaving me alone to wrench open the warped door of the shop.

My anger hastens my steps as I walk home, but my heavy skirts impede my stride, and I curse the layers of silk and linen that tangle around my legs and slow my progress. A memory flashes through my mind of running across the fields at Lauder when I was a child, the wet grass soaking my shoes and my heart pounding as fast as my feet. I must have been very young – too young for full skirts and petticoats and stays. Now I must moderate my step, which makes me brood more deeply on my encounter with Hutchison. His reaction to my questions bespeaks guilt, and if he is guilty it is a mere step of logic to conclude that so too is Mungo. It seems a final injustice that Mungo's words of condemnation are preserved forever in his wretched pamphlet, while Thomas's voice is silenced.

I formulate a plan as I walk home. It is so simple I wonder why I did not think of it before. I will make copies of Thomas's speech, and circulate them around the town. It may not cause the sensation a printed pamphlet would, but my handwritten efforts will serve. I know enough of Edinburgh's appetite for gossip to be confident that the key parts of its contents will soon be common knowledge.

Once back in the Pleasance I acquit myself of my household duties as swiftly as I decently can, and adjourn to my desk. I am a quick scribe, although not as neat as I might be, and before an hour passes I have progressed to my third copy of Thomas's letter and speech. My right hand aches, and my fingers are spotted with ink. I am so absorbed in my task that I do not notice Agnes until she is standing by my side.

"Dr Maxwell is here to call on you, miss," she says, peeping over my shoulder at the papers in front of me. I must stare at her dumbly, for she goes on, "To offer his condolences, I expect."

"Yes. Of course. Show him up. " I sand the page I have been writing on and put it aside. There is no hiding my ink-stained hands however.

I rise to meet Dr Maxwell as he enters the parlour. He is taller than Robert and moves with great assurance. There is nothing remarkable in his features – he is neither strikingly handsome nor repugnantly coarse – but there is something in his appearance that attracts the gaze. His eyes, perhaps, which have a sleepy look whatever time of day it is. However, the sharp bite of the January air does not agree with his complexion. When he takes my hand and kisses it, his lips feel chapped. I look him in the face and see that his skin is dry and rough.

"I was sorry to hear of your loss, Mistress Carruth. How are you bearing up?"

"Well enough, thank you," I say, motioning for him to sit. "I have plenty to keep me busy, which is a blessing."

"I suppose Carruth is out consorting with his lady patients, instead of attending to you?" he says, with the merest hint of a twinkle in his eye.

I feel a tiny spasm of unease that Dr Maxwell had chosen to call when there is a good chance of Robert being away from home. "Stop trying to make mischief," I chide. My voice sounds brittle and false. Robert left in a sour mood this morning. He is still brooding about my visit from the gallows guard.

Dr Maxwell shrugs. "If it falls to me to console you, I suppose I must thole it."

I am suddenly disgusted with him. In his eyes my bereavement is nothing more than an opportunity for flirtation. I hope this visit will be brief. He must sense my change in mood, because his face becomes serious, and he says, "Forgive me. That was ill-judged. You must be suffering greatly."

Am I suffering? I do not think so. The only feeling I am aware of is a kind of lightheadedness, as if there is a pane of glass between the rest of humanity and myself. "On the contrary, I am… a blank. I feel nothing. I'm afraid I am quite unnatural."

"No, no. It is the shock."

"Am I not cold-blooded?"

Dr Maxwell lifts my hand again and gently presses each of my fingertips in turn with his thumb. "There is no such thing as a cold-blooded woman."

For a moment I am hypnotised by his voice and the sensation of his skin against mine. At last I rouse myself from his spell and ease my hand out of his.

We sit in awkward silence until he speaks again, his voice still softer than usual. "Your mother… what was it took her? Forgive a physician's curiosity."

This is safer ground, but no easier to tread. "She had a fall at her house in Lauder, on the stairs down to the kitchen – they are stone, and quite uneven – and her leg was broken."

"A fracture can be a serious matter."

"That was not all." I take a deep breath before I go on. "When Hetty went to undress her, she found a deep wound."

"On her leg?"

"No." I hold my hand over my left breast, to show where the sore had been. "The flesh within was quite rotten."

"And she was in great pain?"

"From head to toe."

He nods, a grim expression on his face. "A cancer, then. The broken leg was but a sign that the weakness had seeped into her bones. What did Carruth do for her?"

"He brought opium with him. It gave her some relief at first, thank God, but at the end not so much." I try to blink away the images that are burned on my memory. "We prayed for it to be over."

"My poor girl."

At any other time I might have smiled at his words. It is many years since I have been a girl. I make an effort to pull myself together. "You are very kind, Dr Maxwell, to listen to me." He bows in acknowledgement. Over the years I have heard many rumours about Dr Maxwell but at this moment he has every appearance of being the most sincere gentleman in the kingdom.

He reaches out and takes my hand again, examining the ink stains on my fingers. "You have been hard at work with your pen, I see. I hope I'm not keeping you from your correspondence?"

I stand, walk to my desk, and lift one of the copies of Thomas's letter and speech. The decision to confide in Dr Maxwell is taken almost before I know it. "I would value your thoughts on these pages," I say, handing them to him.

He takes the manuscript and reads. I sit and wait, watching the expression on his face. He gives little of his opinion away, only raising an eyebrow once or twice. At length he finishes and looks over at me. "How did you come by this?"

"I went to the Gallowlee when I returned to Edinburgh, to arrange for Thomas's burying. The gallows guard found the papers in Thomas's pocket."

He sits back in his seat, and regards me with a serious expression in his eyes. "Was Carruth with you?" When I shake my head he says, "You did not go alone, I hope?"

"Yes, quite alone. I saw Katharine Aikenhead there."

"The sister?" He leans towards me with a grave expression on his face. "If you care to take the advice of an old friend, do not ally yourself with the likes of Katharine Aikenhead."

"There is no danger of that. I offered what help I could, but she spurned it. She seemed angry with me. It is the grief, I suppose."

"They were always a trouble-prone family." He glances at my desk. "Do I conclude you have been making copies of these papers? To what purpose?"

"To let Thomas have his reply against his accusers, against Mungo Craig…"

"Ah yes. Young Mungo. The Judas of our tale."

I turn to him. "Are you certain?"

"The talk is it was he who informed on Thomas. There's no evidence."

"I welcomed him to this house. He ate food at my table."

"You nursed a viper. Be thankful it was not you who felt his sting."

"He was Thomas's friend."

Maxwell shrugs. "Who else has more means to betray us than our friends? Or more cause."

Is it safe to criticise the authorities to Dr Maxwell? Safe or not, I carry on. "We both know that Mungo's testimony would have meant little on its own. The judges were fixed on hanging Thomas from the outset."

"Yes."

"What are we to do, when our leaders can murder a boy on a whim? What kind of country are we?"

He sighs, and looks at the papers again. "You have not explained to me why you are making these copies."

"I will distribute them – discreetly – around the town. In coffee shops and the like." How foolish the idea sounds, now

233

that it is spoken out loud! The expression on Dr Maxwell's face seems to echo my own doubts.

"I do not understand why you feel so compelled to act. You realise in doing so you may draw the attention of the Privy Council down on your own head? Thomas cannot be resurrected no matter what you do, so why take such a risk?"

"It seems an injustice to me that Thomas has had no right to reply to Mungo's accusations. I know that what's been done cannot be undone, but I can at least give him his voice. And my conscience is troubling me: had I been here in Edinburgh for the trial I might have helped him more. I could have written to the judeges. Robert has one or two acquaintances on the Privy Council who could have been spoken to, if I had been able to persuade him."

He takes my hand in his again. "Your mother was dying. Your place was by her side. You have a tender heart, and are stricken with guilt, but – believe me – there's nothing to be gained from such thoughts."

I allow my hand to lie still under his. "Perhaps we can learn from what befell Thomas. If we examine the signs that led to his undoing, we can be on our guard against their recurrence. My children have bright, enquiring minds, and I must protect them."

"You will not protect them by putting yourself in harm's way."

At once I am irritated with Dr Maxwell. His jaded charm, his pragmatic dismissal of Thomas's death, his prac-tised way of finding excuses to touch my hand. I stand and walk to the window, looking out into the street in the hope of calming myself. Reckless thoughts tumble through my head, and I must not speak them. Outside the day carries on like any other. The heavy cloud of yesterday has gone, and the air is bright with chilly sunlight. Maids sweep their masters' front steps; respectable wives and daughters step out with their baskets on their arms, in search of shopping and conversation; a gentleman on a dapple grey gelding clip-clops his way along the length of the street. I hear Dr Maxwell rise and walk towards me. "You were fond of the boy," he says. His voice is uncharacteristically frank.

"I was," I say, still staring out the window. There is a tremor in my voice. "I think Robert rather resented it. He was more in sympathy with Mungo."

"I take it Carruth knows nothing of your plans to distribute Thomas's papers?"

I notice the faintest change in Dr Maxwell's expression. There is a hint of something predatory. "He would disapprove," I say, realising as I speak that my words will be like bait to him.

"Perhaps you would permit me to be your helpmeet in the task," he says. "Let me take one of your copies. I know a poor clerk who will reproduce it as many times as needed, and in such a strange hand that no one will trace it back to him."

"And would you be able to circulate it?"

"Of course."

"You said a moment ago that it was a risky enterprise. Is the danger not as great for you as it is for me?"

He smiles. "I have more experience in covering my tracks than you have – which is quite as it should be."

The door to the room opens, and Margaret slips in. She stops when she sees Dr Maxwell, and regards him coolly.

"Are you playing hide-and-seek, my darling?" I say, conscious of the heat in my face. I hope I am not blushing, but fear I am.

"Not hide-and-seek, no. I'm hiding from Alison."

"Is she cross with you?"

"Of course not. She only ever chides Henry, not me."

Dr Maxwell interjects, "So why hide from her then?"

Margaret tilts her head to one side in a way that looks affected, but I know is not. "She is very pleasant, but sometimes her company grows tedious."

Dr Maxwell laughs out loud. He glances in my direction. "You are correct, Mistress Carruth, about the cleverness of your children. But now I must go. May I take a set of the papers?"

"Of course." I retrieve the necessary pages from my desk and hand them to him.

He offers me a knowing smile, kisses my hand yet again, and leaves, bidding me to give his regards to Robert.

Margaret runs to the window and looks out, watching him descend the house steps and walk on his way up the Pleasance. "Who is that man?" she says.

"He is Doctor Maxwell, an acquaintance of your father's."

"And he thinks I am clever?"

"Yes."

She ponders this for a moment. "Alison thinks I am clever," she says at last, "and Alison is a fool."

Another Sabbath day tightens its grasp on Edinburgh. The weekday jostle of commerce is stilled, and an observer looking up and down the high street might fancy this a city whose citizens have fled. Of course there can be no such observer, for every decent man is in kirk, like as not on his knees, imploring the Lord for forgiveness. Robert and I are among that number, with Henry and Margaret alongside us, and the servants in their own places towards the back.

We have barely settled in our seats when a murmur of conversation begins at the rear of the kirk, moving through the congregation like a wave on the sea. I turn to see what the cause of it is. A group of plainly dressed elders are processing up the nave, and in their midst is a wretched-looking youth, dirty and lean. He is clad in a roughly made sackcloth robe, and his naked arms look indecent in such a setting. One of the elders bustles on ahead, and lifts the penitent's stool from a corner, placing it in the centre of the kirk. The unfortunate sinner clambers up on to it and sits, his head bowed. I see now that his legs are bare and shoe-less. His feet are filthy with dirt and blood.

"Who is it?" I whisper to Robert.

"It must be that fellow Frazer. The other blasphemer. He's obliged to do penance in all the kirks of the city."

Reverend Crawford pronounces the absolution, leads us through the Lord's Prayer, and announces that day's psalm. The congregation rise to their feet, and the air is filled with the rustle of silk as the ladies smooth their skirts. I glance down at Margaret to make sure her dress is not crumpled, but she is already shaking out the creases. She must sense me looking at her, for she glances up with a hint of challenge on her face. I lean over and adjust her shawl. If we were any-where else she would pull away, but here, under the eye of Reverend Crawford, she endures my interference. She takes advantage of the moment to stare at Frazer, still perched on his stool. I too find my gaze drawn towards him. His story was the subject of much debate the summer before. He dared to question God's word in a private conversation that was passed on to the Privy Council, and he has lain in the Tolbooth ever since. Each Sunday he is brought out to be paraded for the correction of all our souls – and as a warning to other young men who might be of the same mind. This punishment is regarded as mercy. I suppose it is, compared with the vengeance that swallowed up Thomas.

Henry, meanwhile, is oblivious to this, gazing up into the rafters. I wonder what has enchanted him – a sparrow per-haps, hiding from the cold – but I do not dare follow his example. Ten-year-old boys might be allowed to let their thoughts wander from Divine Service, but their mothers are not granted the same dispensation.

The thought of the day ahead weighs down on me. There will be nothing to fill it but piety and despair. Our Sabbath will wend its penitential way to evening, and as darkness closes in the whole household will gather in the parlour for more prayers. Robert will read from the Bible. We are still working our way through Isaiah. That strange, pro-phetic book disturbs me. It flits from implacable vengeance to compassion expressed with such tender poetry that it brings tears to my eyes. The only mercy is that January days are short. I can retire to my bed not long after nightfall. In the dark of the bedchamber there is no stern presbyter to overlook me, no watchful acquaintances to scrutinise my every word. In the other world behind my closed eyelids I can say and do as I please – and dream away the time until Monday and freedom, of sorts.

At last the Reverend Crawford steps up into the pulpit to begin his sermon. This marks the middle ground of the service. His sermons are notoriously long, but I con-sole myself that when this part is done we will be well past the halfway point. Reverend Crawford's sermons are not much admired by the congregation. He is a learned man, and it seems sometimes that his knowledge has turned his mind into a thing of great complexity but little practical use. Even Robert, conventional as he is, complains that he understands less of God's intentions at the end of one of Crawford's sermons than he did at its beginning. Still, his voice is musical, and I view the sermon as an opportunity for my own contemplations. I bow my head decorously. It will be assumed by any who care to look that my mind is turned on holy matters.

"In the Gospel of Luke," Reverend Crawford begins, "in the twenty-second chapter, starting at the twenty-first verse, it is written: 'But, behold, the hand of him that betrayeth me is with me on the table. And truly the Son of man goeth, as it was determined: but woe unto that man by whom he is betrayed! And they began to enquire among themselves, which of them it was that should do this thing.'" His words make me raise my head. Reverend Crawford peers over the pulpit. For a moment it seems that he is looking straight at me. "We know, of course, who the traitor was."

"Judas," Margaret whispers, just loudly enough for me to hear.

"Judas Iscariot," Reverend Crawford says, as if echoing Margaret. "An untrue friend. A faithless disciple. We condemn him, do we not? To betray the Son of God for thirty pieces of silver! What sort of man could do such a thing? Not you or I. We would be steadfast, would we not? True on to death!" He glares round the congregation, and keeps silent so long that people begin to shift in their seats. When he speaks again his voice is softer. "Look into your hearts," he says. "Have you ever let a friend down to spare yourself some trouble? Have you ever told a lie that would advantage you? I know I have." He points down at Frazer, who sits as he has all through the service. "Look at this poor wretch here, clothed in the sackcloth and ashes of the repentant sinner. He has done great wrong, admitted and acknowledged. But what think we of the man who betrayed him? A good Christian? How much better would it have been if that man – instead of skulking off to his betters – had admonished this sinner to acknowledge his wrongdoing. Had prayed with him and for him. Had engaged the offices of a minister of religion. The Good Shepherd rejoices at the safe return of the lost sheep. He does not demand its destruction."

My heart is battering inside my ribcage as if I had just climbed the steepest wynd in the city. What has got into Reverend Crawford? It seems he is not simply condemning Judas, the betrayer of the Son of God, but every faithless creature who gives up their friend to the cruelty of the law. Is this his covert way of condemning those who betrayed Thomas? According to Dr Maxwell the whole city thinks it was Mungo. Is he Reverend Crawford's target? The idea of Mungo hounded and reviled thrills me in a way I am sure is not Christian. Perhaps this is how Thomas's persecutors felt as they closed in on him. I begin to understand how intoxicating such a pursuit might be.

At last the service ends. Frazer is led through the kirk and out, back to his prison cell. We remain in our seats as the first surge of people pushes towards the door. Henry kicks his toes absent-mindedly against the pew in front of us until Robert leans over, taps him on the knee and shakes his head sternly at him. When the crush subsides somewhat we stand and made our own way out. A lady who is our neighbour in the Pleasance takes my hand and offers her condolences. For a moment I do not understand her, and then remember that I am a woman mourning her mother. Other people of our acquaintance follow the neighbour's lead, and murmur appropriate words.

I glimpse Dr Maxwell through the crowd. He nods over in my direction, his eyes meeting mine for a fraction longer than is usual.

Mungo

To Mr John Row, Regent of the Faculty of Divinity, University of Edinburgh

13th January 1697

Dear Sir,

As I hope you will now be cognisant of, the debt mentioned in our conversation of two days ago has been discharged. I apologise most humbly for the oversight on my part that led to this embarrassment, and trust that you will forgive it with that same spirit of justice and mercy you have so often displayed in your care towards we who are fortunate enough to be shepherded through our studies by you.

On the matter of my suspension from the university, I acknowledge that this punishment is fully merited. I do not plea for clemency on grounds of my own superiority, or with any suggestion that the penalty is unjust. However, I do implore you to readmit me to my studies at the earliest opportunity, out of compassion for my aged mother. You will know that I am the fatherless only child of a poor family, and every week of delay in my being ready to seek Godly employment in the world is another week that my poor mother must scrape by on the few pence she is capable of earning. She is afflicted by a tremor, and her hands are greatly twisted and painful, which makes such occupations as a woman of her station might typically hold, viz washerwoman, seamstress & co, almost impossible.

I stop writing. This grovelling sits badly with me. I know it is pride that causes me to stumble, and that pride is a sin. It is also a luxury that I cannot afford.

I step away from my desk and lift my New Testament

from the bookshelf, flicking the pages forward until I find the book of Revelation.

And I went unto the angel, and said unto him, Give me the little book. And he said unto me, Take it, and eat it up; and it shall make thy belly bitter, but it shall be in thy mouth sweet as honey. It is no good. Not even the strange alluring terror of John's visions can brace my mind. Down in the kitchen Hutchison embarks on a bout of coughing. It has been getting worse these past few days. Thomas might have made a tincture to relieve it. He had his father's talent for compounding cures. Thomas again. Always Thomas. I must continue to write him down, to turn him from memory to pen scratches on white paper. That might contain him.

Patrick clumps up the stairs. He stops on the landing. The boards creak as he waits there. At last he knocks on my bedroom door and walks in. He looks earnestly at me, and then at my desk. "Are you working?" he says. I notice he has a scrolled piece of paper in his hand.

"In a manner of speaking, yes," I say. "No matter."

He chews his lip.

"Is there any news around the town?" I say.

"You should see this." He hands me the paper.

I unroll it, note that it is written in a neat secretary hand, and read the title: *The Last Speech of Thomas Aikenhead, written by Him the Night before his Execution at the Gallowlee, 8th January 1697, and Entrusted to the Care of his Closest Friends.* "How did you come by this?" I say.

"It was in Dalton's, among the newspapers." He sits down carefully on the edge of my bed. "Read the last part, Mungo. The paragraph but one before the end."

I do as he bids me. Thomas denies my assertions – must he get the last word, even now? But worse, much worse. That I am as guilty as he. In my memory I hear the *hiss, hiss, hiss* as we push that damned book to and fro across the library table. A sick shudder runs through my body like a sudden ague. "Did you see anyone else read this?" I say.

Patrick doesn't meet my eye. "There was more than one copy in Dalton's. And I heard a fellow say he'd already come upon it at the library."

"And what are people saying about it? They surely don't believe him, do they?"

Patrick makes no response, but the reddening of his face gives me my answer. I set the paper aside and look down at my day's work. The latest instalment of my spiritual memoir. The unfinished letter to John Row. All futile, utterly futile. My efforts are entirely undone. But before I fall completely into despair I feel the first pulse of anger. Thomas means to carry me after him. The rising nausea of fear. Will there be action taken? "Has anyone spoken to you about me?" I say to Patrick. "Asked questions?"

"People have talked of little else."

"No, I mean—" I fetch a handkerchief from my pocket and wipe my face. "The authorities. Have you—?"

"No. None of that sort has approached me. Not yet." He offers no promises. That time is past.

This is calumny. No less. I will wash mine hands in innocency. For I am innocent. What was it Plautus said? "One who has done no wrong ought to be bold, yes, and self-confident and forward in his own defence." Let the lying lips be put to silence. But they are silent. They were. They ought to be. Silenced by his great swollen tongue. I saw a hanged man once. The tongue black. Long as a cow's. No. Push that thought away. His mouth filled with earth at the gallows' foot. Better. Almost poetry. Ten beats. What rhyme for foot? Boot? Root? Soot? No. Stop it. Calumny, remember?

What was that line from Horace… "If anyone pursues me with a poisonous tooth, shall I, unavenged, weep like a child?" No. No. I will not. What's that? Hutchison shouting from downstairs, and Patrick joining in. Arms around me – dear Lord, they are come for me already, they mean to take me and hang me! I lash out with all my strength and am free. I lunge for the door, but Hutchison is there, blocking my way, the white dog at his heel, her teeth bared in a snarl.

"For God's sake, calm yourself," he says. I stand gasping, slowing my breath, feeling the storm-surge of my rage ebb away, until all that remains of it is a strong, steady current of resentment. I turn and see Patrick spreadeagled on the floor. He struggles to his feet.

"I was only trying to save you from harming yourself," he says, a hurt expression on his face. Did I hit the wall in my rage? My knuckles are ringing as if I've been boxing.

"Are you done, Mr Craig?" Hutchison says. "Can we leave you without fear that you'll pull the house down around our ears?"

I nod, afraid to open my mouth in case the fury is only slumbering. Patrick backs out of the room and then he and Hutchison tramp down the stairs. The dog stays for a moment, staring at me, until Hutchison calls her and she too goes.

Steady now. Here's pen. Here's ink. Here's paper. Stretch out my fingers. Nothing broken. A vindication. Yes. That's what is needed. A vindication of Mr Mungo Craig. From a calumny cast upon him by T.A. Set it out properly. Section 1. Yes. Containing the Introduction, the Calumny, and some General Observations. That's the way. Calm. Thoughtful. Measured. Where's my Bible? I need to read it. Take succour from it. And quotations. *Whom the Lord loveth he chasteneth, and scourgeth every son he receiveth.* I must prove myself a Christian.

Does Thomas think I dare not speak ill of the dead? He thinks wrong.

Isobel

If I thought that distributing Thomas's speech might quell my discontent, I prove myself mistaken. Yes, I feel a certain pride that I am the means of letting his voice be heard, although I must admit to myself that my satisfaction is laced through with vanity. How many other women of my station can say they have presided over such a sharing of truth?

Beneath these feelings, though, is the tremor of fear. Even as I sleep I am aware of it stirring, and I wake in the morning with it fluttering in my breast. I try to reason it away. Dr Maxwell is the only one who knows of my role, and I am sure he will not betray me. He enjoys secrets. And after all, what wrong have I done? No law has been broken. Still, there is some part of me that regrets unleashing Thomas's speech on the town.

I spend the first part of the morning with the children. Alison is catechising them, and invites me to observe their progress. Margaret has hers almost by heart. Each time she stumbles she pauses for a moment and closes her eyes, her face a mask of resolve, before starting again from the very beginning. Henry shuffles on his chair, impatient for his turn. When at last Alison turns to him he is rushed and careless, mixing up his answers.

"Dear me, Master Henry," Alison says severely. "You must do better than that. Here's your sister knows it back to front, and her two years younger than you."

Henry glances over at me for a brief, imploring moment and tries again. "My duty towards God is to believe in him, to fear him, and to love him with all my heart, with all my mind, with all my soul, and with all my strength..." He frowns in puzzlement. I can imagine the questions he has.

How can I love Him who I must fear? How can I love Him with all my mind if I may not question his ways? But perhaps these are my questions, not his.

There's a knock on the nursery door, and Agnes comes in. "Pardon me, Mistress, but the master asks if you'll join him in the consulting room."

I am glad to be released from the strictures of Alison's domain, but feel a niggle of anxiety as I descend the stairs. Robert and I have been tiptoeing around each other since the night the gallows guard called at the house.

Robert's consulting room is a place I rarely enter, and only ever at his invitation. It is his space, just as my little parlour is mine. The walls of the consulting room are lined with medical books – some few inherited from his father, but the bulk steadily acquired by Robert himself, from his student days onwards. He is behind his desk when I go in, but has placed a chair close to his so that I can sit alongside him. A letter and some other papers are spread out on the desk. "I thought you were out," I say.

He smiles weakly. "My lady patients are enjoying good health today. I had few house calls." He studies my face. "And what about you, Isobel? How are your spirits?"

His solicitude is unexpected and gratifying. "I feel a little numb. That will pass, I suppose. I'm not sure I want it to, for then I will feel my loss."

"Do you feel able to discuss... practicalities?" He glances at the papers in front of him. "I have a letter from your mother's advocate, with a copy of her will."

"Oh, of course. What does the advocate say?"

"It's straightforward enough. There are a number of small bequests – to the servants, the children and so on. And your mother's jewels and gowns to you, naturally. The house and land at Lauder are ours now. We must only decide what we wish to do with them."

How delicate he is in his choice of words. The house and land are *ours*, he says. *We* must decide. The law sees things a little differently. Everything that belongs to me is his, to do with as he pleases, but in all our years of marriage he has never behaved as if that were the case. Flawed as he is, he always shows me that respect. The frost of the last few days begins to thaw.

We discuss our options. The idea of removing to Lauder appeals to me – I yearn for the countryside; miss the greens and duns of its fields and ditches. There is something in the constant scrutiny of Edinburgh society that oppresses me greatly, but Robert's work is in town, as Henry's schooling soon will be. I know any notions of retreating to my childhood home must be deferred. Robert accepts that the property will not be sold – his own father scrimped to become a householder, and he understands well that land and buildings signify more than mere financial worth. We agree to retain the agent who managed the land for my mother during her years of widowhood, and seek a tenant for the house. Robert is preparing to write to the advocate when there is rap at the consulting room door and Agnes comes in.

"There's a Miss Aikenhead come to see you, mistress," she says.

Robert frowns at the name. "Why is she calling with you?" he says.

The fear that has stilled over the last half hour begins to flutter again. "I don't know," I say. My first thought is to speak to her privately in my parlour, but I recall the trust Robert has shown me this morning and ask Agnes to bring her into the consulting room. I stand up and smooth my skirts. Robert is looking at me quizzically, unsatisfied by my response. "Now that I think of it, I wrote to her offering my assistance," I lie. "Perhaps she needs help. Or money. It must be difficult for her, don't you think?"

"Be careful, Isobel. You know what that family is like."

Agnes shows Katharine into the room a moment after Robert finishes speaking. I cannot tell from her face if she heard his final words. She refuses a seat, so we both stand awkwardly.

"How are you, Miss Aikenhead?" I ask. "This is my husband, Dr Carruth."

She looks Robert over, but makes no direct response to my question. "I declared I needed no help from you, and I meant it, but beggars can't be choosers, as the saying goes." She gives a short, humourless laugh.

"We will assist you in whatever way we can." As I speak, I sense Robert shift uneasily. "What is it that you need?"

"Thomas's sentence deprived him of his property as well as his life, and I have been working these last days to overturn that part of his punishment at least."

"If you need an advocate I'm sure my husband can recommend one." I turn to Robert for confirmation, and he nods grudgingly.

Katharine gives that strange laugh again. "Oh, I've got an advocate. You forget, Mistress Carruth, that my family has a long association with the law."

"Well then…"

"Matters were proceeding steadily enough," she interrupts, "and then copies of this began appearing around the town." She takes a folded sheet of paper from her skirt pocket and hands it to me.

I know before unfolding it what it is. Thomas's speech. I make a show of scanning it before handing it to Robert. "Have you seen this?" I ask, working to keep the tremor from my voice.

"Yes," he says curtly. I think of the original document, still hidden in my little desk upstairs like a secret sin.

"I wanted to know," Katharine goes on, "who are the friends who claim to have been entrusted with this speech?"

"Perhaps," says Robert, "some of those he knew at the university?"

"Those same who queued up to give evidence against him? I think not."

My mouth is dry and I moisten my lips with my tongue before I speak. "Are you not glad that Thomas's voice has been heard?"

Katharine stares at me as if I am deranged. "Glad? I wish he had never been so rash as to open his mouth in the first place. All he had to do was stick to his studies, and become a doctor. We'd have been secure then. I could have kept house for him instead of trailing out to work behind the counter of a shop every day. And now this!" She points an accusatory finger at the paper. "It has roused up the coffee house gossips all over again. My advocate advises me to delay now, until things have settled. I expect the Privy Council's bailiffs at my door any day, for our home is in Thomas's name. What am I to do then?"

I turn to Robert. He looks ill at ease, but he says, "If it comes to that you must ask us for assistance until the matter is settled. A confiscation order can be overturned, even if it has been executed..." He stops, flustered by his unfortunate choice of word.

Katharine makes a dismissive movement with her hand, but does not reject Robert's offer outright. "You do not know then, who is responsible for circulating this speech of Thomas's?" she says, looking from me to Robert and back again. We both shake our heads. She gives me a final hard stare. "In that case I will be on my way. But if you do happen to discover who it was, you can tell them from me that they have done me a disservice." And with that she turns and leaves, not waiting to be shown out.

"Poor Miss Aikenhead," I say into the silence that stretches between Robert and me.

"She left Thomas's speech behind," he says, picking it up. "Do you want to keep it?"

I take the paper from him. "Why did you not tell me that you knew this was circulating?"

"I thought it would distress you. You have enough grief of your own to contend with."

I consider how I would respond to this if I were guiltless, and try to match my actions to that other, innocent Isobel. "You are thoughtful, Robert, but you must not shield me from the world. I am not a child."

"I know that."

I fold the paper into a tight square. My own words remind me that I have not yet told Henry and Margaret the truth about Thomas's absence. I persuade myself it is the prospect of that conversation that makes my heart heavy with dread.

Mungo

Though the tempest rage and the mouth of the seas would devour me, the word of the Lord holds me fast. My spirit is strong – with the Lion of Judah's help – but my mortal body is full of fears, and I have felt compelled to take refuge beyond the town, back where I began, in my mother's house. These four walls embrace me like the love of God. The stairs creaks. I hear the rattle of crockery on the tray as Mother bears my meal up to me. I stand, open the door, let her shuffle across the small distance to my desk. She sets the tray down on top of my papers.

"Well?" I say.

"Nothing tae report," she says. She meets my eye for a moment. Long enough for me to see how she scrutinises me. *Was it for this he was reared?* her eyes say. *Is this my reward for his schooling?* And the most fearful question of all. *What now? What next?* I cannot explain to her – she would not understand – that I will prevail. It is a sign of my strength that I did not let Thomas's speech deflect me overlong. I made my rebuttal, and at this moment dear, faithful Patrick is having it set to print. I will have the last word.

She goes, and the little house creaks its familiar tune as she descends. I clear my plate in a matter of minutes, and still my belly tightens and gurgles, demanding more.

I hear the first knock on Mother's front door since I've been here. A murmur of conversation. I stay in my room. I don't want to be seen.

Mother's slow, uneven step on the stairs. Her tentative tap on the doorframe, there being no door in it, only a curtain. "Come on ahead," I say.

She shuffles in. "There's a laddie here says he's your friend. Mr Middleton."

"Send him up, then."

She looks around the room, eyes flitting from the thread-bare bedcover to the black mould on the ceiling. "I've no' emptied your chamber pot the day," she says, wrinkling her nose, then glancing at me like an anxious servant in front of her master.

I sigh and stand up. Why is she always this way? It's as if she's paralysed by shame. "Very well then, I'll see him downstairs." She lets me go first, knowing I haven't the patience to follow her limping descent.

Patrick is standing by the fire, his face pinched with the cold. He has a package in his hands.

"You have them, then?" I say.

"Aye. You'd best unwrap them. My hands are too numb to undo the knot."

I set the package on the table and unwrap it. The front page of my new pamphlet stares up at me: *A Lye is no Scandal, Or a Vindication of Mr Mungo Craig From a Ridiculous Calumny cast upon him by T.A. who was Executed for Apostacy At Edinburgh, the 8th of January 1697.*

"Will it do?" Patrick asks. "The quality of the print is not as good as the last one."

"A rush job, I suppose. How much did you have to pay?"

"Thruppence a copy."

"That's dearer than before, and for fewer pages."

"The printer said it was because we only wanted fifty copies. The more you print the less it costs per pamphlet." He shifts from foot to foot. "When do you think you might be able to repay me, Mungo? I don't mean to press you…"

"Keep every penny you make from selling them until you have your money back. Is that fair?"

"Aye, I suppose so." He looks unhappy. Patrick is not the world's most natural hawker of pamphlets. Thomas would have been better fitted for the job.

Isobel

"Henry, my darling, I have something I must tell you about Thomas. It is something very sad, and you must try to be brave."

He looks up at me, his eyes sombre. "Is he dead?"

His stark question throws me for a moment, but it deserves a frank reply. "Yes," I say simply.

Henry turns away, staring out of the parlour window. "What did he die of?"

I silently run over the words I have rehearsed. The truth, but a version of it fit for a sweet-natured boy. "I'm afraid that Thomas got into trouble with the law, and he was hanged for it."

"Did he do something very bad?"

"He said that he did not believe in God."

Henry looks back at me, frowning in puzzlement. "But that's silly. How could he not believe in God?"

For a moment I feel giddy with relief. "I know, my darling. It was very foolish of him to think it, still less to say so." I feel the tiniest pang, quickly suppressed, that Henry has accepted the teachings of the Kirk without question. He is safe, that is what matters. Untainted by doubt.

"Poor Thomas," he says. Then, "May I go now, Mother?"

"Yes, of course." For some odd reason I am disappointed. I expected tears, even prostration, had prepared myself to soothe his broken heart with kisses and caresses. "I have not told Margaret this news," I say to him.

"Why not?"

"Because you are the eldest, and a boy, and so you had to be told first."

He absorbs this idea, and appears pleased by it. "Shall I send her down to you now?"

"Not yet, my love. There'll be time enough to tell her later." I savour this private triumph over my daughter, and wonder at what sort of mother I am to enjoy it so.

I walk along the Grassmarket in such a state of preoccupation that I do not see Dr Maxwell until I almost collide with him. He steadies me by taking hold of my arm. "Well, well, Isobel," he says, scrutinising my face with a smile on his. "Is your head turned by the stir your handiwork has caused?"

"I hardly think our few copies of Thomas's speech have caused a great commotion in the town," I say. I make no mention of Katharine or her angry reaction.

Dr Maxwell regards me steadily. "So you haven't seen Mungo's response then?" When I shake my head he continues. "He has published another pamphlet."

"What does he say? Do you have a copy?"

"I do. It is tucked away in my consulting room. Here, my house is only a step away."

As he leads me to his home – one of the better old houses on the Grassmarket – I belatedly realise that this is the first time he has called me by my Christian name. Until now only three people in the world have called me Isobel, just Isobel. My mother, my father, and my husband. Those three have some claim to ownership of me: my father sired me; my mother grew me in her womb; and my husband is the sole possessor of my body. And now Dr Maxwell has claimed that same intimacy. Perhaps he thinks it is his right, after the favour he has done me in disseminating Thomas's speech. I should be offended by his presumption but I am not.

Dr Maxwell's housekeeper appears almost the moment that we enter the house. "Ah, Missus Copeland," Dr Maxwell says, "here's Dr Carruth's wife has taken a dizzy turn. Let's help her into my consulting room." The lie glides from his lips with ease.

The old woman tucks her hand under my elbow and guides me in through the first doorway we come to. The room is no larger than Robert's consulting room, but the furnishings are older and more distinguished. Missus Copeland settles me in an upholstered chair. "Shall I make you a posset, madam?" she asks me.

"I believe a glass of Rumney wine might be more the thing," Dr Maxwell says, before I have the chance to reply. "And do you have any sweet thing hidden in the pantry?"

"There's a nice bit of boiled cake, sir."

"That will do very well."

When she leaves us, Dr Maxwell goes to his desk and leafs through a sheaf of papers until he finds what he is looking for. He pulls up a seat close to mine and hands me the pamphlet. "Take your time," he says. "The print is badly smudged in places."

"It must have been a rushed job," I reply and begin reading. The housekeeper returns with a decanter of wine and a plate of cake. I accept a glass from Dr Maxwell as I read on. At first I feel angry with Mungo, and irritated by his pompous way of arguing his defence, but as I read on I am troubled by a growing sense of unease. He utterly rejects Thomas's accusation against him with every appearance of sincerity. He cannot comprehend how Thomas could die with a lie on his lips, and what distresses him more is that so many in the town believe it. For the first time I wonder if Thomas's words had been lies. When I look up from the pamphlet I see that Dr Maxwell is regarding me with interest.

"You have the most intriguing face," he says. "Watching you just now I could see how your thoughts brightened and darkened, and yet I would not hazard a guess as to what those thoughts might be."

"What do you make of the pamphlet?" I say, ignoring his gallantry.

He turns away with a slight smile, like a gambler accepting a loss with good grace. "I think he's frightened."

"Is it possible he's innocent?"

"Innocent of informing against Thomas? I cannot say. But innocent of freethinking? Yes, that would be my guess."

"If that is true then I have done him an injustice."

He takes the pamphlet back from me and returns it to his desk. "Young Mr Craig seems well able to defend himself."

"I'm not sure that he is. Yes, of course, he has responded through his pamphlet, but he has no connections, no wealth to secure him if the Privy Council come seeking another scapegoat."

Dr Maxwell looks as if he is wearying of the subject. "There's nothing to be done now."

I stand up, infected by Dr Maxwell's restiveness. "If I could speak to him, ask him directly, I would be better able to judge whether or not I have done him wrong."

"Is he still in Edinburgh?"

"His landlord said not, but I could not tell if he was lying. I should go and enquire again." I remember Hutchison's reaction to me on my last visit. "Dr Maxwell," I say, "would you be kind enough to accompany me to Mungo's lodgings? His landlord is an uncouth fellow, and was most uncivil to me when I called there before."

"Was he now?" says Dr Maxwell. "Then of course you must permit me to be your knight." His words are as empty as his smile. I sense that he is tired of this – how fickle he is! – and only his sense of courtesy compels him to accede to my request.

Once again I stand in Robert Hutchison's shop, in spite of the threats he'd made at my last visit. He takes a moment to recognise me, and when he does he says, "Ah, it's you, is it?"

Dr Maxwell is by my side, and I am aware of how much stronger a lady's argument is when she is accompanied by a gentleman – any gentleman. "I imagine you can guess what brings me here?" I say.

There is one elderly customer stooped over a volume bound in red calfskin. He turns a page with much licking of his fingers and riffling of paper. Hutchison walks over to him and tucks a hand under the old man's arm. "I have some business to attend to, sir, and must ask for privacy," he says. "Would you like me to hold this book over for you?" The customer appears not to hear this offer, and Hutchison is obliged to repeat it several times, at ever increasing volume. Eventually the old man is persuaded from the shop. Hutchison locks the door and turns to face us. "I suppose you think I had Mungo's latest pamphlet printed?"

"Did you not?"

Hutchison doesn't reply for a moment, and then says, "You may come through to the back. It's warmer there."

I wonder at his sudden concern for my comfort.

He holds the curtain aside to let Dr Maxwell and me walk through an ill-lit corridor that leads to a small back room. A decent fire burns in the grate, and the white dog lies sprawled in front of it. I see now that she is in pup, her teats congested and her belly swollen. She looks up sleepily to see who is in her domain, and although her eyes shift from face to face she gives neither sign nor sound of menace.

Hutchison gestures for me to sit in the chair, and pulls up a stool for Dr Maxwell. He perches himself on a crate that serves as a table of sorts. "Young Aikenhead wasn't a bad young gulpin," he says, staring into the fire. "Used to make me poultices for my sores." He scratches at his face, although it is free of chancres for the moment. "Heated them in that very grate." For a moment I imagine I can smell the acrid after-scent of a mercury poultice. Hutchison looks over at Dr Maxwell. "They say a hot poultice is the best thing for drawing the badness out of a sore, don't they?"

Dr Maxwell nods his assent, and glances over at me with a glint in his eye. Hutchison must assume that Dr Maxwell is my husband.

"So," I say, "am I to take it that Mungo Craig did not come to you with his latest enterprise?"

"No." Hutchison's face darkens. "Did you note how shoddy this new pamphlet is? Sure the numbers are all out of kilter. It's badly done, and half the town think it's me who's behind it. This will damage me, so it will, and times are hard enough."

"When last we spoke I was angry. With Mungo and with you." I pause. "Since reading this second pamphlet of his I am less certain of my view."

"Not so confident that your indignation is righteous?" Hutchison says with a sly look.

I nod. "I would like to speak to Mungo and make a proper judgement. If he has suffered from a calumny I must help make amends."

"If I knew where he was, I'd tell you as readily as may be."

My heart sinks at this. "So you truly don't know where he's staying?"

Hutchison shakes his head. "I mind him saying as how his old mother lives out in Leith. He could be lying low there."

I catch Dr Maxwell's eye. He speaks for the first time. "Tell me, Mr Hutchison," he says in the casual tone I have come to recognise, "do you print many pamphlets?"

"Just the odd one."

"But you don't have a press here?"

"No, I contract the work out." Hutchison sounds guarded. He is not fooled by Dr Maxwell's smoothness. Perhaps he is wiser than I'd suspected. The dog begins to growl very softly although she still lies basking in front of the fire. I look down at her and see her belly distend as one of her unborn pups stirs inside her.

"I suppose you must have paid a Scots pound or two to have Mungo's first pamphlet printed?"

"I've yet to meet a printer who'll work for nothing."

"Aye, indeed. Which printer did you use? It was a pretty enough piece, one any printer would be proud to put his name to, unlike this latest issue." When Hutchison says nothing Dr Maxwell smiles over at me. "Shall we go, my dear? I'm sure Mr Hutchison wants to be attending to his business."

We all stand and Hutchison escorts us out through the shop. Dr Maxwell hesitates at the door. "Did you fund the printing yourself, Mr Hutchison?"

Once again Hutchison does not reply. His face is set like a mask. He pulls open the door – still warped and scraping along the floor – and waits for us to leave without giving an answer.

We walk far enough away from the head of College Wynd to be out of Hutchison's view, and stop to face each other. "What was the purpose of your questions?" I ask.

Dr Maxwell looks thoughtful. "Who do you conclude was the inciting genius behind Mungo's first pamphlet?"

"I had not given it much thought. Mungo, I assumed. Must it not have been Mungo's idea? Fanned on by Hutchison, who guessed there would be an appetite for it."

"I don't know. Hutchison doesn't strike me as a man overafflicted with enterprise. Give him a commission and he'll carry it out, but that's about the height of his talents. And it's clear from his silence that he didn't put up the money to have the pamphlet printed."

"Mungo has nothing, I suppose. He depends on a charitable bursary, I believe."

Dr Maxwell raises his eyebrows at this. "Is that so? In which case, who paid the costs of the printing? And why?"

I understand him now. "You think some other party put him up to it?"

"It seems likely, don't you think? If you could find out who funded the pamphlet you would know who bears the heaviest responsibility for Thomas's death."

"The only person who might tell us who paid for the pamphlet is Mungo himself."

"We could make a trip to Leith to continue our investigation some fine day." He smiles. "Travel incognito in a hired coach. You swathed in black veils and me with my hat pulled down low and my muffler birled round my face."

This is no more than a game to him. "If I go to Leith I will go openly," I say. "I have nothing to hide."

"Your husband might wonder at it."

I consider this for a moment. What will Robert say if he hears of such a visit? I can honestly tell him of my concerns for Mungo, but not of my role in them. Surely his tolerance will not be infinite. "I must go now, Dr Maxwell. I have been away from home too long." I feel heavy with dread at the thought of returning there.

Dr Maxwell scrutinises my face. "If you took another dose of the head-staggers I'd have a respectable excuse to escort you to my consulting room again." A faint smile plays on his lips.

I shake my head. "I would like more than anything to avoid the companionship my own house offers me, but I cannot run away from it." I speak more frankly than I intend and am aware of a slight withdrawal in Dr Maxwell's manner. It is so infinitesimal as to be scarcely noticeable. I sense it rather than see it.

"I'll bid you good day then, Mistress Carruth," he says, bowing just as a gentleman should, before he turns and walks away from me up Peebles Wynd towards the high street with swift, determined strides.

I am near enough at Cowgate Port when I hear footsteps behind me, and hurry out towards the crossroads where there will be more people about. There is something about the Cowgate that makes my nerves jangle. The dark mouths of so many wynds open on to it. I cannot bear them, and never enter one if I see there is someone else in it. The narrowness of the way, and the great looming walls on either side nearly take the breath from my body, although I know they are often the fastest way to traverse the city. I turn to see who has come after me. It is Patrick Middleton, one of Thomas's circle. I have not seen him for over two months – not since before Thomas's arrest.

"Mistress Carruth," he says. He smooths his hair, conscious, perhaps, that he has come outside without a hat on his head.

"Were you in the house just now when I was talking to your landlord?" When he nods I continue, "I suppose you heard our conversation?"

"Enough to get the gist." He eyes me anxiously.

I realise that I do not harbour the same fury towards him as I do – as I once did – to Mungo. Instead I feel a kind of puzzled sadness. "What did Thomas ever do to you that made you all so eager to turn against him?"

Patrick sighs and leans against the wall. He looks terribly young, barely older than my Henry. Perhaps that partly explains why my ill feeling towards him is so much less. Mungo is as full-grown as any man in his prime, whereas Patrick still has the slight build of boyhood, as Thomas had. "We had no choice, Mistress Carruth. All those things we told of before the Privy Council, they were true sayings of Thomas. We all heard him speak them, so how could I say otherwise? I'd taken an oath to tell the truth. Should I have lied before God in order to save Thomas from trouble?"

"Tell me this, Patrick. How did the good men of the Privy Council come to know of Thomas's ill speaking in the first place? Did you tell them?"

He shakes his head vehemently. "Not I, Mistress Carruth."

"Who then? Mungo?"

"I asked him that myself. He denies it."

"So it was the birds in the trees went and sang it in the Lord Chancellor's ear?"

"At first I thought – you'll think my head's cracked – but I thought Thomas himself had passed the word to the Privy Council."

"Thomas? That's ridiculous."

"Aye, I know that, but Thomas liked nothing better than to be the centre of attention."

"Even to the extent of imperilling his life? I hardly think it. Does it not seem more probable that it was Hutchison? He's a sleekit sort of fellow, and he likely hoped to profit from Mungo's cursed pamphlet."

"I don't know."

"I should like to speak to Mungo. Do you know where he has gone?"

Patrick shakes his head. "I rose up one morning and found he had flitted."

"If you find out where he is, will you send me word?"

"I... I cannot say that I will." At this moment a group of countrymen jostle past us and Patrick flinches, backing into a doorway. It is harder to read his expression without the daylight on his face.

"Why ever not? What reason have you to deny me that?"

"Can you not just let things lie? It might be better for all of us."

"Is that why you came after me?"

He doesn't answer me at first, but steps backwards further into the shadows of the wynd. "We none of us can undo what's done, Mistress Carruth," he says, then turns and walks back up towards his lodgings.

Mungo

I write to anyone I am acquainted with who is in possession of respectability and good standing. They are sadly few. I have no influence. No connections. *Dear Dr Row.* No, he is ill-disposed towards me. *Dear Reverend Crawford.* Should he not help me? I sat often enough in his pews. *Dear Dr Carruth.* I detected something in him… a certain sympathy. I send the letters out, with a copy of my pamphlet enclosed, and receive no reply.

Patrick tells me the town is quiet. There have been no more arrests. In spite of his reassurance I am tortured by fear. Waking or sleeping it thrums through my body and mind. I think I must leave Scotland, if only to save my sanity. Here I sit, with scarce a bawbee to my name, living off my mother's meagre earnings. Hutchison has half my bursary in advance of rent prepaid until Whitsun, and refuses to refund me. Patrick says he has not yet recouped the cost of printing the pamphlet. I try to think of ways I might make a living.

I force myself to leave the house, for fear that if I do not I might never step over the door again. I walk to the Shore, where my father once earned his keep. The windmill is silent in the still, clear air, and there are a few boats moored, slumbering in the water. In these quiet hours, with no cries to be heard but those of seabirds, it is hard to imagine the bustle and turmoil when a boat docks. Then the whole port is black with men swarming in and out of the boat's hold, passing bales of linen, bushels of grain and all the other goods arriving from England and beyond to feed and clothe our citizens. Perhaps I would be better coming here at a busier time when I might be less conspicuous. The quay is almost deserted, save for a few dishevelled-looking fellows who seem to be loitering in hopes of employment. My coat is cheap, but its cut still marks me out as something more than a labouring man, and I am uncomfortable under their gaze as I pass them. I walk on to the end of the quay, determined that they will not deter me in my exercise. There is a small wooden building at the end of the quay, with the door lying open. I can see a figure moving about inside in the deliberate manner of a man with work to be done. As I draw closer he notices me, and steps into the doorway. He looks me up and down with a sharp eye.

"You're a bit late in the day to be looking for work," he says.

I feel affronted that he takes me for one such as the men I passed. I straighten my stance and adjust the buttons on my coat, to draw his attention to my respectable attire. "You mistake my purpose, sir. I am a student from the university, in search of nothing more than a breath of sea air."

He inspects me again. "Aye, right enough," he says. "You've a dockman's shoulders but a scholar's hands. No good to me."

"How is trade?" I ask, remembering this is a favoured subject for those who worked the Shore.

He shakes his head. "Poor enough. The only goods we send out into the world are wool and soldiers. There's always a market for soldiers, but little enough demand for good Scottish wool these days." He takes a pipe from his coat and pats his pockets in search – I presume – of tobacco. Finding none he replaces the pipe.

For a brief moment I entertain the idea of joining one of the regiments, but dismiss it at once. Without money or friends to secure me a commission I would have to be a common soldier, and I could not endure that. "When will these boats sail?" I ask, looking over at them.

"On the evening tide. The *Anne Maria* and the *Whiffler* are bound for Hull, and the *Minora* for Flanders. Are you after a passage?"

"No, no, I asked only to make conversation."

"Aye. If you'll take my advice, a young man such as yourself should set his sights on America. They've got towns as big as Edinburgh now."

I bid him goodbye and retrace my steps, past the ne'er-do-wells, past the boats whose names promised more beauty than their appearance merited. America. It is a madness of an idea, and utterly beyond my means, but just the idea of it disturbs me. A place far away, beyond the sea, with Edinburgh and all within it left far behind. A fresh start. My unsettled mind quickly darkens into despair at the impossibility of escape. I hurry home to seek peace in my writing, in hope that the scratch of pen on paper will calm me once more.

Isobel

Once again I find myself in the Tolbooth prison. The keyman unhooks the bunch of keys from his belt and unlocks the door. "Here's a visitor for you, Frazer," he calls in. "A lady." There is a sound of movement from within the cell, but the keyman stands in the doorway, blocking my view. He looks back over his shoulder at me, smirking. "Mister Frazer has a habit of falling to his knees when a visitor comes. He thinks it makes a good impression." With that he stands aside to let me in. "You may have ten minutes with him, if you can thole it that long."

The cell is better lit than the gloomy corridor, thanks to a fair-sized window set so high in the wall that it must be impossible for even the tallest man to see out of. Frazer stands beside a narrow pallet that I guess must serve as a bed by night as well as a seat by day. There's a blanket spread across it. His face has the pallor that comes with two seasons of incarceration and his eyes seem ill-focused, his gaze shifting from my face to my basket to the floor and then back again. It is as if he were afraid of looking at any one thing for more than a few seconds.

"My name is Isobel Carruth," I say. "I wonder if I might speak to you."

Frazer nods, then points towards the pallet. "Will you sit down, Mistress Carruth?" Neither pallet nor blanket look particularly clean, but I feel awkward standing, and my legs are weary after climbing the prison stairs. I sit at one end of the pallet, and motion for Frazer to sit also. He hesitates for a moment then sits down at the other end, as far away from me as he can manage without tumbling off.

"I have brought you some food," I say, taking the package Hetty had prepared from my basket. "There's half a loaf, and some cheese. A slice of dried tongue too."

"God bless you, Mistress Carruth," he says, his eyes fixed now on the package. He does not look too badly starved, but I imagine he'll be glad enough of something tastier than prison rations.

"I should explain why I am here."

He looks up at me, a wary expression on his face. "I assumed this was an act of Christian charity."

For some reason my face grows warm, and I know I must be blushing. "Of course. The book of Hebrews tells us to remember them that are in bonds. But I confess I have another reason. I had a young friend who is lately dead. Thomas Aikenhead."

Frazer becomes very still. "What of him?"

"I am trying to understand why it was he ended as he did. You survived, but he did not. Why were our judges so determined to destroy him?"

Frazer stands up and walks to the far corner of the cell. "When I was sentenced to do penance around the kirks of the town, it was meant to deter the likes of young Master Aikenhead from his freethinking. Would that it had. Did you ever see me paraded to the front of your kirk in my sackcloth and ashes?"

"Yes. Sunday just past."

Frazer nods. "What did you think of the spectacle?"

"I was... ashamed."

Frazer's expression softens, and for a moment I fear he might weep. "Don't show me kindness, Mistress Carruth. I do not think I could bear it." He rubs his nose on his sleeve and pulls himself together. "Every Sunday since last August I have been stripped of my clothes and dressed in sackcloth. The keyman and his friends bring in the ashes from their hearth and toss them over my head. They like to jest that they are powdering my wig. Then I am marched barefoot to whichever kirk is designated for that day's performance. Would such a display not be sufficient to encourage any young freethinker to discretion?"

"I don't know if Thomas ever saw you do penance."

"Maybe not, but his friend did."

I feel a chill in my heart, but force myself to ask, "Which friend?"

Frazer knots his brows together. "I do not think I can recall his name. A large-framed young fellow. Dark hair that was in need of a comb. He lectured me at length about repentance. That was *his* act of Christian charity."

Mungo, without a doubt. "When did he visit you?"

Frazer gives a hoarse laugh. "That I could not tell you. The weeks seem to run into each other. It may have been a long time ago."

"Before Thomas's trial? Or before his arrest, even?"

"I do not know."

I wonder if Thomas did ever see Frazer do public penance, and try to imagine how he would have responded. Knowing Thomas, the spectacle might have provoked rather than subdued him.

Frazer comes and sits down again, slumping against the wall as if he is exhausted.

"Have you no word of when you might be released?" I say.

He shakes his head. "I petitioned to be allowed out after Christmas in order to prepare my master's account books, but their lordships would not hear of it. I don't know how I can prove to them that my repentance is sincere."

"We live in a world where piety must be made a show of, as much as penance," I say.

Frazer looks at me intently. "But do you not think, Mistress Carruth, that the most sincere believer may be the one that bears his faith in the quiet depths of his heart?"

"The world seems to like evidence."

"I make my best efforts to provide that. Divine service as often as they will allow. The reading of worthy literature," – here he points at a small pile of books set on a low shelf – "to say nothing of loud prayer when I hear footsteps in the corridor." He leans forward and rests his head in his hands.

"And what about in the quiet depths of your heart?" I say softly. He looks up at me with anguish, and I know then that he is still tortured by doubt. The rigour of the law has quelled his outward acts, but it cannot silence the questions of his mind.

There is a sharp rap at the door and the keyman calls in some incomprehensible words, which I take to mean it is time for me to leave. I stand up, and take a few coins from my basket. "Will you accept this?" I say, reaching them to Frazer. "They may buy you some small comforts when the food is gone."

He steps forward and takes the money. "I wish with all my heart that the lad had learnt from my lesson."

"So do we all. I will pray that the Privy councillors release you soon."

He nods glumly at this. The door is opened, and the keyman leads me out, locking the door again behind him. "Well, missus," he says, as he escorts me along the corridor towards the outside world, "how did you find him?"

"Full of sincere repentance," I say, in as pious a voice as I can muster.

"God be praised for that," the keyman says casually.

"Yes indeed," I agree. "God be praised." As I say the words I know, absolutely, that I no longer believe them. The words in Thomas's paper – copied out again and again – have found an answering echo in my own mind. All my life I have prayed to, and praised, and implored this God. I read my Bible daily, and agonise over its arguments and instructions. And now I realise it has all been for nothing. My passions and hopes have been directed at a chimera. *The more I thought thereon*, Thomas wrote, *the further I was from finding the verity I desired.* I have found verity now.

I step out of the Tolbooth into the high street. After the gloom of the prison there is a Damascene brightness to the day. Yes, that makes sense. I have seen the light. But what to do when all those around me are still in darkness? And when the prisons and the gallows are at the disposal of those who will do anything to preserve it?

Robert's face is tight with anger. He tosses the paper – the original of Thomas's paper – down on the table in front of me. "What is the meaning of this, Isobel?"

"I do not understand you."

"It was in your desk, hidden away in a drawer. You cannot deny it. Am I to assume that you are behind those copies that have been circulated around the town?"

I take a deep breath to steady myself. "Have you taken to searching my desk, Robert?"

The question stalls him for a moment. He lowers his eyes, and his mouth works as if he is practising how to respond. "I would never do that," he says at last.

"But somehow it has come into your possession." I keep my voice calm, but my mind is in turmoil as I try to deduce who found it and passed it on to Robert. Hetty or Agnes? I think not. Surely not Alison? I quail at what she might do with such knowledge. "Margaret," I say out loud. The expression on Robert's face tells me I guess rightly. Yes, of course. She was in the room when Dr Maxwell called and saw me take the papers back to the desk. I feel as if a sliver of ice is piercing my heart. "To think how much I longed for a daughter," I say.

Robert stares at me as if he does not recognise me, then walks over to the window and looks out. I watch him – his straight back, and shoulders rather too narrow for a man. It is an insufficiency he disguises from the world with the assistance of his tailor. For a moment I am consumed with an almost unbearable pity for him. Even the fine wool fabric of his jacket makes me feel sad. What is it about our garments that seem so infused with grief?

At last he turns round to look at me. "What were you thinking of, Isobel? What was your object in this enterprise?"

"It was Thomas's wish that his words were circulated. He has no other friend than me to carry out his wishes."

Robert covers his eyes with his hand. "You have stirred up a nest of vipers."

"Is your head aching?"

He nods. "Of course."

"You are angry with me."

He says nothing, but returns from the window and sits down close to me. "If it became known that you were responsible for this, that would be a bad thing for us."

"Have I broken some law?"

"No, but…" He shifts impatiently in his chair. "You've made it clear where your loyalties lie."

"I have fulfilled the last wish of a dying man, and I cannot regret that, but –" I take a deep breath. "Mungo's second pamphlet has thrown my thoughts into disarray. He seems as sincere as Thomas. One of them has lied, and I do not know which."

Robert ponders this for a moment. "Who helped you?" he says, his voice hoarse with some new emotion. "I trust you did not traipse around the coffee houses of Edinburgh distributing these papers yourself?"

I feel a tremor of anxiety. "Dr Maxwell assisted me with the task," I say as lightly as I can.

Robert exhales with a hiss, and shakes his head. "That was… naïve of you."

"I think I can trust him to be discreet." Robert opens his mouth to object but I cut him off, saying, "I am as aware of his moral failings as you are, but tell me this: in all the years you have known him, has he ever revealed any secret to you?"

Robert stares at me, almost as if he is afraid of what I might say next. "He… hints at many things."

"Precisely. He hints. He teases. But he never tells, does he?"

Robert stands again. It seems he cannot stay still. "Isobel," he says, not looking at me, "I forbid you to do anything more in relation to Mungo Craig. All this…" he waves his hand at the paper, "must cease." He hesitates, and when he speaks again there is the slightest tremor in his voice. "I am not a tyrant, Isobel. I hope I have never behaved to you as if you were my subordinate, but in this matter I must ask... must demand that you obey me."

I bow my head. "Very well," I say.

Robert coughs, brushes at a smudge of powder on his coat, and begins to stalk towards the door. Before he opens it he turns back to me. "You think you know Maxwell," he says. "Believe me when I say, Isobel, you do not. He has one face in the company of women, and a very different one in the company of men."

But which is the true face? I think.

"I have asked you to desist from these current actions," Robert goes on. "Please know that it is not my intention to curtail your freedom. I will not... follow you... spy on you." A blotchy flush spreads across his face. "I trust you."

A sharp stab of guilt at these words brings tears to my eyes and I turn away to find a handkerchief. Robert walks quickly back across the room and embraces me with a tenderness that compounds my distress. I rest my head against his chest and weep, for I have already made up my mind that I will betray his trust.

The next day I busy myself with the children, and interfere too much in the running of the kitchen. Robert absents himself visiting his patients, and when he comes home remains ensconced in his consulting room. In this way we contrive to avoid spending more than a half hour in each other's company.

The following morning I venture out on some unnecessary errands. I have half a hope that I will encounter Mungo. Once I think I see him step into a close, but when I follow I am embarrassed to find it is not he, but only an older man with a similar build.

I arrive back at the house and find two sedan chairs,

complete with four bearers, waiting on the roadway outside our door. The bearers are all men of the same short, wiry build. Three are standing, but a fourth is lounging on the doorstep, and as he sees my approach he rises in a leisurely fashion and waves me up through the doorway as if he is the owner of the property.

Inside the hallway I note two gentlemen's cloaks and hats hanging from the coat stand. Evidently Robert has visitors – ones who are either too grand or too feeble to walk. It seems unlikely they are patients. Almost all of Robert's clientele is female, and those few gentlemen who do consult with him prefer to summon him to their homes rather than visit him here. There is no sound of conversation from his consulting room, so I assume these visitors are here on some other business. And indeed, as I make my way up to the nursery I see that the parlour door is closed. Robert and the gentlemen must be within.

Alison is dressing the children in their outdoor clothes. "I thought I would take them for a turn around the market gardens," she says, fastening the ties of Margaret's woollen bonnet. "I suppose it's braw enough outside?"

"Aye, cold but bright. Hold your head up, Margaret."

My daughter meets my eyes with a cool stare, but she tilts her chin upwards to let Alison finish her job.

Henry already has his coat and hat on. He kneels in the window seat looking down into the street. "Is it a very hard job, Mother, to work at carrying a sedan chair?"

"I'm sure it must be, but that type of man is very strong. They do not feel tiredness in the same way as a gentleman."

"How do you know?" Margaret asks.

I expect Alison to hush Margaret – she is usually averse to the children asking questions – but this time she says nothing. I sense she is holding back, with a certain eagerness to see how I will respond.

So how do I know that "that type of man" does not feel tiredness? It seems like one of those instances of instinctive wisdom. The labouring classes drudge from morning to night, yet still appear to have energy for all the fundamentals of existence – courting and marrying, drinking and dancing, praying and fighting. Margaret is looking up at me, waiting for my answer.

"That is an astute question, Margaret," I say, "for you have made me understand that I have no real basis for my observation."

"Young Margaret has a sharp mind," Alison says in an admiring tone. "She shines a light into dark places."

Margaret smiles up at her, and I feel a stab of jealousy. "'Out of the mouths of babes...'" I say, and instantly regret such a trite choice of biblical quotation. Alison glances over at me with a quizzical look on her face. I am sure she can tell that my attempt at acting the good Christian woman is no more than that – an act. It is a strange thing, but I realise it is only since my faith began to recede that I have taken to such public demonstrations of belief. In the past, when I really did believe, I was content to encounter my God and his Word in the quietness and privacy of my own mind.

Henry jumps down from his window seat. "Can we go now? I should like to see the sedan chairs close to, before they are carried away again."

Alison chivvies the children out on to the stairs, and I follow them. Henry thunders down, jumping two stairs at a time, ignoring Alison's admonitions.

We meet Hetty on the first-floor landing, bearing a tray with oatcakes and sherry towards the parlour. "Whisht now, wee man," she hisses. "Dinnae make such a rumpus when your father has fine visitors."

Henry giggles and continues down the stairs with exaggerated tiptoe steps, Margaret and Alison following after him.

"Who are our guests?" I whisper to Hetty.

"Let me take this in to them, Miss Isobel, and I'll come up to the nursery and tell you all."

A few moments later she taps on the nursery door and comes in, her eyes bright with agitation. "You'll never guess it, Miss Isobel," she says, twisting her apron in her hands. "It's two members of the Privy Council. Campbell, one gave his name as, and Hope the other."

Campbell and Hope. I know the names. Both were judges in Thomas's case. "But why are they here, Hetty? What do they want with my husband?"

"That I cannae tell you. They're sitting in there, with faces long as turf spades on them. I heard some mention of Thomas Aikenhead as I went in the door just now, but they stopped their talk as soon as they saw me." She bustles over to the window and looks out. "Those chair carriers are still there, loafing on our step as if it's a tavern."

She prattles on for a few minutes, until I bid her return to the kitchen and get on with preparing the dinner. When she is gone I sit on the old nursing chair, turning over in my mind the possible explanations for the Privy councillors' presence. I feel a strange compulsion to see these men who made the judgement against Thomas. The question is, how can I contrive to encounter them? It is unthinkable that they might be in my house and I not take advantage of the opportunity. At the same time, I have no wish to mortify Robert by any ill-advised conduct. I glance at the various toys and books scattered around the nursery, and my eye alights on the book I bought from Hutchison's shop, A *Token for Children*. I feel sure Campbell and Hope would approve of such an improving volume, with its accounts of the exemplary lives and joyful deaths of various invented Christian children. If I encounter the gentlemen on the landing, apparently on my way upstairs to return the book to the nursery, will not that seem like the most natural occurrence in the world? I stand up, take the book in my hand and, stepping as quietly as I can, creep down the stairs from the nursery on to the landing on the floor below.

I can hear the murmur of conversation beyond the door of the parlour – the familiar timbre of Robert's voice, with occasional low-pitched interjections from the two others. It is impossible to make out what they are saying, but it seems the visitors are asking questions, and Robert is answering. The sounds act on me like an enchantment, lulling me into a kind of dream. It is a state of mind I recognise from all those long hours in kirk on the Sabbath, and the many, many afternoons I have been compelled to waste in the dreary society of other respectable wives. I lose track of how long I stand on the landing. When the visitors do, at last, emerge from the receiving room I am nearly caught in my trance. The door is near enough opened before I come to my senses and assume my role of the busy mother attending to her children's education.

The first grand gentleman barely acknowledges me, but the second inclines his head in my direction. I am struck by the expressiveness of his face, so unlike the stony imperturbability of his companion's. Robert follows them on to the landing.

"Isobel," he says, his voice a little higher-pitched than usual, "I did not know you had returned." When the two guests pause he continues, "Gentlemen, may I introduce my wife, Isobel. Her father was the late Reverend Ogilvy of Lauder."

The first man sighs and murmurs his own name as if this social nicety is the dullest he has ever endured. The other gentleman takes my hand and bows properly this time. "Archibald Hope of Rankeillor, ma'am," he says.

"This is an honour, gentlemen," I say, doing my best to keep my voice light and modest. It must be too modest – there is clearly nothing in my manner to detain them – for they begin to move across the landing towards the stairs. How complacent they look, how untroubled by what they have done! "I am glad of this opportunity to speak with you," I say more boldly, ignoring Robert's look of alarm.

They stop and turn back towards me. "Mr Campbell," I say, addressing the grander man directly, "you have lately caused the full weight of the law to crush a young friend of our family's."

"I suppose you speak of Thomas Aikenhead," he says, and immediately fixes Robert with a glare like a schoolmaster's.

"My wife was moved by the lad's tender age and orphaned state," Robert stammers. "You know how women are swayed by such circumstances."

I am speechless at this betrayal. Never before in all our years of marriage has Robert belittled me in this way.

"Nonetheless," Campbell says, "she should not be so far swayed as to blink at atheism and blasphemy." He addresses his remarks to Robert as if I am not present.

Archibald Hope leans forward. "I am sure that was not Mistress Carruth's intention." He gives me a faint smile. "It is in a woman's disposition to show mercy and kindness – the Almighty has ordained it so, so that females are well fitted for the rearing of infants."

"Aye," says Campbell, with no hint that he agrees with Hope. "A little discretion is a useful attribute too. Don't you agree, Carruth?"

Robert nods mutely.

I am filled with rage against them all, and most especially against this God of theirs, who ordered the world in such a manner, and demands the sacrifice of any who oppose Him, and in return gives nothing, not one answered prayer. As the three of them clump down the stairs I remember how my mother screamed out to God for relief in her final days, and how I in turn prayed for her suffering to end. He was deaf to all our entreaties. She did not die until the disease had taken all it could of her. There was not one minute, not one second of her agony commuted by her merciless creator. My fury ebbs, and for a moment I am full of fear, awaiting some dreadful punishment for such thoughts. None comes.

By nightfall my anger has transformed into *froideur*. I retire before Robert, as is my custom, but I cannot sleep knowing that the time will eventually come for him to join me. There is no lonelier place than the marital bed when husband and wife are in disharmony. This I know better than most.

After the best part of an hour the candle has nearly burnt out, so I extinguish it. My dread is now superseded by anxiety. Why is he so late awake? Is he as angry with me as I am – as I had been – with him? It occurs to me that he might have taken it into his head to sleep apart from me. This has happened once or twice before in the course of our marriage, sometimes at my behest, sometimes by an unspoken mutual agreement. Never before has he withdrawn his company from me in quite this manner.

I must drop off at last, for I wake again some time later. In the January darkness it is impossible to tell how many hours have passed, or how close dawn might be. I reach out my arm to Robert's side of the bed, but it is unoccupied and cold. In an odd reversal of my earlier wish to avoid him, I now feel the need to have him by my side. I have not forgotten the manner in which he disparaged me in front of our exalted guests, but I know from old experience that this latest estrangement will only be resolved by companionship in sleep. Our bed is rarely a place of carnality, but it is often our field of refuge and reconciliation.

There is nothing for it but to seek him out, so I steel myself to the wintery cold beyond the bed curtains and slip out of bed. I grope in the dark for the shawl I'd tossed on top of the cabinet, and wrap it around my shoulders to stop me being foundered while I light the candle. I find my slippers, and leave the bedchamber.

Robert is in his study, seated at his desk. He has a sheet of paper before him, neatly ruled into columns and rows, with some words written along the first few rows. The fire has long since burned away, and I can see my breath in the chilly air. "Will you not come to bed?" I say. "You will over-tire yourself sitting up so late."

He consults his pocket watch. "Goodness… I had quite lost track of the time."

I pull a stool up close to his desk and sit down. "Is it your work that occupies you?"

He makes a dismissive gesture at his ruled paper. "No. Not that." He is silent.

"Is your… anxiety… in any way connected to our visitors today?"

"Yes. Yes, of course." He stands up and begins rearranging the papers on his desk. "They were curious as to our friendship with Thomas and his circle. Their questions were most pointed."

I feel my stomach tighten. "What information were they seeking?"

"They want to know who first introduced Thomas to the blasphemous ideas that undid him. All who were associated with him fall under suspicion. I reassured them that our acquaintance was slight."

"And then I blundered in with my defence of him." I bury my head in my hands.

Robert crouches down beside me. "Do you understand now why I had to belittle you in front of them? I am heartily ashamed of myself, but I was afraid of them."

I take his hand. "You have nothing to be afraid of, Robert. You are the pattern of a Christian gentleman. They may question all they like: they'll find nothing to reproach you with."

He nods, but the troubled expression remains on his face. "That may be true, but I'd prefer not to be the target of their attentions. We must be very careful from now on, Isobel. The Privy Council has sneaks on every corner."

We walk together out into the hallway, Robert carrying the candle high to light our way. A scrap of paper, folded and sealed, lies on the floor by the front door. I had not noticed it when I came downstairs earlier. Robert sees it too, and bends to pick it up. "It has your name on it," he says, handing it to me. In the flicker of the candlelight his face looks pale and fearful.

I break the seal and open it out. There is but one line of writing. *Talbot's Close, by the Cross Keys, Leith.* Mungo's address. It must be. I am conscious of Robert's eyes on me, and show the paper to him, as there is no possibility of concealment.

"What does it mean?" he says. "What business do you have in Leith?"

"None at all. I do not know why this has been delivered here," I say briskly, pushing the paper into his hand. "Here, you may do what you wish with this. Burn it, if you like." Who can have sent it? Patrick Middleton? Robert Hutchison? It scarcely matters.

"Isobel..."

"Please, Robert, no more. Let us go to bed. I am more weary than I can express." This is not true – my blood thrills with excitement at finding where Mungo is hiding, in spite of the dangers – but one more lie to Robert will make little difference now.

Mungo

I hear the carriage approach and stop near the house. It must be someone for me. No one else in Talbot's Close would have visitors who travel by carriage. The light, fearless knock on the front door. My mother rising from her seat and shuffling to open it. Her reply to whoever it is that stands there. "You've come tae see Mungo. I ken that well enough. You may come in then."

Nothing for it but to see who awaits me. I can't judge from my mother's tone who it might be. Officers of the Privy Council? Patrick, returned with more bad news? Perhaps – wild hope – a compassionate benefactor? I descend the stairs.

Mistress Carruth, dressed in mourning. Her sombre colours drain the light from the room. As she turns to look at me I hear the silk of her skirts rustle. No penitential worsted cloth for her garments, in spite of her bereavement.

"You'll no' be wanting me here," Mother says. She lifts her mending basket and retreats upstairs.

"What do you want with me?" I ask Mistress Carruth.

She looks around the room. "May I sit down?" she asks. There's no hint of hauteur in her voice, and I cringe at my uncouthness in not offering her a chair unprompted. I direct her to the best seat, and sit on the second best. She settles herself and runs her gloved hands over her skirts, smoothing them. I notice a light sheen of sweat on her brow.

"These last days must have been difficult for you," she says.

Her consideration is so unexpected that I feel tongue-tied, much as I did at that wretched dinner we attended at her house. I know I should offer some condolence for the loss of her mother, but the words do not come.

"I am confused, Mr Craig," she says. "I struggle to comprehend your part in Thomas's misadventure. I do not know whether to condemn you or pity you."

"Most people seem to have decided to condemn me."

She pauses, as if considering this. "I read your pamphlets," she says. "Both of them."

"Well?"

She stiffens slightly. Perhaps my tone was too abrupt. "I can understand your reasons for writing the second one…"

"Yes, I had to clear my name. He was accusing me of equal guilt with him. Every petition he submitted to the Privy Council tried to pass the blame to me. It was the talk of the coffee houses. I had to do something to defend myself."

She nods. "It's the first one that perplexes me, Mr Craig. Why did you do that to Thomas? I know you had no choice but to stand witness at the trial, but no one compelled you to publish his foolishness."

"Would you believe me if I told you that it was Thomas's suggestion?"

That stops her short. I can see her thinking, remembering how Thomas's mind would vault from one daring idea to the next. At length she shakes her head. "'Will Scotland nourish such apostacy?'" she says, quoting from the pamphlet. "'Atone with blood the affronts of heaven's offended throne.' Do you expect me to believe that Thomas asked you to write a pamphlet calling for his own death?"

I can think of nothing to say that will not condemn me more in her eyes. How to explain that once I had begun writing the pamphlet I was possessed – no, inspired – by a sort of divine rage? That I could not alter the direction the words took?

"It seems to me," she goes on, "that you were determined to settle a score with Thomas. 'Am I always to keep silent? Am I never to get a word in?'" The lines from Juvenal I had used on the front cover. "Those sound like the words of a bitter, jealous man."

I know it is wisest to keep silent, but some sense of right-eousness compels me to speak. "Thomas infuriated me. Always so full of himself. When he came into any room everyone turned to him. If he was in high spirits, then so were the rest of us. When he was sullen none of us dared smile."

"He was everything you were not," Mistress Carruth says. "Envy seems a petty reason to send a friend to the gallows." There's a sting in her voice.

Well I can sting too. "You had a part to play, Mistress Carruth."

That stops her. "How so?"

"Do you mind the time I came to dinner at your house?" She frowns, then nods her head ruefully. "But you barely noticed me. I was no more than one of Thomas's crowd, eh?"

"If I was in any way ungracious, I apologise."

I shrug and carry on. "I made some comment to you – an attempt at a witticism, I suppose. It must have been the only time I managed to interrupt Thomas. Perhaps I was hoping to impress you. That's what smart young men are meant to do, isn't it? Exchange badinage with their lovely hostess?"

"And what happened then?"

"Och, it fell flat, or course. I saw you and Thomas exchange a glance. It was clear enough what your mean-ing was. Not one of us. That was when I knew. It didn't matter how hard I strived. I would never belong with your class. You might say that was when it began. The seed was planted that flowered on Gallowlee."

She says nothing for a moment, and seems in deep thought. "You exacted a heavy price from Thomas for this slight."

"Do you think I intended matters to go so far?" My hands are shaking. "I wanted to scare him. Knock him off his perch."

"Thomas said that you read those cursed atheistical books as hungrily as he did. Is that true?"

"Reading is not the same as believing."

"So why did Thomas claim in his gallows speech that you were as much a freethinker as he was?"

"Because he was fixed on destroying my character from beyond the grave," I say. "All those things he claimed – that it was I who first showed him the damnable books that led him astray, that it was I who betrayed him to the Privy Council – all lies. But who will take my word against his? He's better thought of now that he's dead. It's a fancy trick he's played on me, and that's a fact. Who would believe that a lad on the brink of eternity would waste his last breath on uttering falsehoods? But that's what he did. I will swear on the Holy Bible, the things he said about me were untrue." I stop, exhausted. My shirt feels damp with sweat. I fear I may have been shouting. "You blame me for his death. I can see it in your face."

She shakes her head. "This did not begin with you. I hold our great men most particularly responsible. You were no more significant than the worm on the fisherman's hook." I cannot think how to respond. She exonerates me with an insult. After a moment of silence she says, "What will you do now?"

The impossibility of my situation closes in on me. Perhaps she will help me – she has the means, for certain, and I think she is not lacking in compassion. "I am excluded from the university, and afraid to return even when I am read-mitted. My mother is obliged to take in extra mending to make ends meet, and I have no means of earning a living."

She thinks for a moment. "You could teach. Find a wee school beyond Edinburgh in need of a dominie."

"No better than that? My greatest wish is to serve the Lord as a minister."

She looks at me sadly. "And why should you be granted your greatest wish when so many are denied theirs?"

I have no answer to give her. She stands and walks over to the window, stooping to peer out. "The day is clouding over. I had best be on my way before the rain comes on." She fastens her veil, so that her face is quite concealed.

I go to the door and hold it open for her. The carriage is sitting at the end of the close. She must have hired it, for I do not recall that her husband kept one. As she goes out she turns to me. "You are young, Mungo. There will be a future for you, no matter how bleak things look now. Be thankful for your good fortune."

"I thank God daily for His blessings."

She lowers her head prayerfully and murmurs, "Amen," then walks across the close towards the carriage. Before she has gone far she turns back and says, "Was it you who informed on Thomas?"

I swallow. "No," I say. "It was not."

Hidden as she is behind her veil I cannot attempt to read her expression, nor guess whether she believes me or not. "Well, well," she says, "I wonder who did?"

Isobel

The carriage lurches like a ship in a roiling sea as the driver turns it back towards the city. The windows are shuttered. I feel suffocated behind my veil and lift it away.

"Well?" says Dr Maxwell from the seat opposite. "Did young Mr Craig provide you with the answers you sought?"

"Some of them, but not all. There are many things I still do not know for certain. Who informed on Thomas. Whether or not it was Mungo who introduced him to those books. What Mungo really believes."

"Do these things really matter to you?"

"I think I would take comfort in the truth."

"'The more I thought thereon, the further I was from finding the verity I desired,'" Dr Maxwell says. In the half-light of the carriage interior it is hard to discern the expression on his face, but I think I see him smile sadly, and am touched that he remembers Thomas's words. "Can you be content without that verity?"

I look at the shuttered window, wishing I could fling it open. "I suppose the best I can do is recount the narrative in my own mind. There is no conclusion, no verdict. I must be satisfied with chronicling the events and nothing more."

We sit in silence as the carriage rattles along. It slows to a steadier pace on the long gradual slope of the road from Leith to Edinburgh. I wonder if we have yet passed the Gallowlee. Dr Maxwell is observing me. Nothing so bold as a stare, but I sense his gaze flicker towards me. In the close confines of the carriage we sit knee to knee, brushing closer to each other with every lurch, and then away again. If I think too long about what I have done in order to visit Mungo – this secretive journey, the excuses I gave Robert, the danger to my good name – the fear will overwhelm me.

And yet, this is the safest way. The carriage hire is in Dr Maxwell's name, and who will raise an eyebrow at a city physician wishing to make a trip to the coast? Had I insisted on making the journey alone, the risks were so much greater of someone taking notice.

After a time the carriage slows still further, swaying and creaking as it takes any number of turns. Eventually it stops. The driver thumps three times on the roof – some signal, I take it, agreed between himself and Dr Maxwell.

"Are we arrived?" I ask, reaching up to my veil.

Dr Maxwell leans forward and stays my hand. "Do not cover your face," he says. "It is the only part of you that is not swathed in garments." He keeps hold of my hand, quite gently, and lowers it on to my lap. "Will you take off a glove?" he says. When I do not reply he unfastens the wrist buttons and eases the glove off my left hand. His own hands are bare. The sensation of his fingers cradling mine disturbs me and compels me in equal measure. He bows his head and kisses the palm of my hand with such tenderness that I can barely stop myself from crying out.

Suddenly I am afraid, as if I have walked in my sleep and now awaken on the edge of a precipice. I pull my hand away from him. He sits back in his seat, studying me. "I suppose you will now tell me I have insulted you?" he says.

"No. I will not." I feel a flare of anger towards him, and disappointment too. "I am not a coquette – please do not think I am playing some amorous game." He begins to reply, but I speak over him. "I did understand, Dr Maxwell, that in accepting your help I might, in some way, be indebted to you. I was not so naïve as not to realise the manner in which you might wish to collect that debt."

"You speak as if we were merchants in the Cloth Market, trading bolts of wool and linen. Hardly the language of romance."

The driver gives another three thumps to the roof of the carriage. "Why does he keep doing that?" I snap.

Dr Maxwell laughs bitterly. "I am to reply to his signal," he says. "One knock of my cane on the roof means drive on to the back of St Giles, where I collected you earlier. Two knocks means take a turn out towards Arthur's Seat."

"Why Arthur's Seat?"

"There are quiet lanes aplenty there where a carriage may park with none to notice it. The sort of places where a driver will be content to leave his passengers in peace for a long as they please, if the fare is right."

I feel my face warm with consciousness at what his words signify. There is something so tawdry in the arrangement he describes – tawdrier, certainly, than merchants in the Cloth Market. And yet my palm still tingles with the memory of his mouth pressing against my skin.

"Well?" he says, raising his cane towards the roof of the carriage. "Shall I make one knock, or two?"

When I return home Agnes hands me a note from Katharine Aikenhead, asking me to call with her. She gives an address near the Netherbow, and the hours when she will be at home. It is growing dark, and too late in the day for visiting, so I resolve to call with her the next day. I wonder at what prompted her request – what fresh anger has roused her – and am glad to be distracted by my speculations. It stops me dwelling on what occurred with Dr Maxwell – enables me to dismiss it as something not quite real.

Katharine's lodgings are on the fourth floor of a tall tenement. It is a middling sort of place, for while I am nearly knocked to one side by an ill-fed barefoot child hurtling down the stairs – his mother's cries of abuse echoing after him down the stairwell – I also find my progress across the fourth floor landing observed by a respectable-looking widow woman peering out of her door. It is, therefore, like so many Edinburgh tenements: a place the poor might aspire to, and the genteel descend to.

Katharine answers my knock and ushers me in. She appears calm. I glance discreetly around the room. It is large and bright, with two tall windows, but the furniture is sparse, and there is too little of it for so commodious a space. A door leads off it, but the chamber beyond seems just as empty, from what I can see of it. Still, it is a decent enough abode, and of some value in our overcrowded city. I can understand why Katharine will not willingly give it up to the authorities. "My advocate tells me it may be some time before the matter of Thomas's property is resolved," she says, as if reading my thoughts.

"The law moves slowly."

She gives me a sharp look. "It moves hastily enough when it wishes to."

I remember the brief fortnight between Thomas's conviction and execution. He would likely have been hurried to the gallows even faster had the Privy Council not been compelled to pause for the Christmas season. Katharine has it right.

"So," she continues, "I have determined that I will sell what I can of his moveables, and then if the case goes against me I will at least have retained something."

"I see." I think of my mother's bedchamber in Lauder, its cupboards full of her gowns and fripperies. The notion of sorting through her possessions is scarcely bearable. It must be done at some point, but not yet. Katharine does not have the luxury of mourning as I do. I feel a pang of guilt, both at the ease of my own life, and at the antipathy Katharine's pragmatism stirs in me. "Is there something I can do to help you?"

"No," she says bluntly. "It is merely this." She beckons me into the other room and I follow. There is a narrow bed stripped of all bedding, and a small table with a few tattered books on it. She picks up one of the books and hands it to me. "This is yours, I believe?"

The binding is unfamiliar. I turn to the title page: *A Relation of the Fearful Estate of Francis Spira*. A vague memory stirs. Yes, I remember the tale – an old one, about the wickedness of the Roman Church. Spira had been compelled to recant his Protestantism, and in the process had lost all faith and died in despair. It has been many years since I read it.

"I see from your face that you do not believe me," Katharine says, that edge of anger back in her voice. "Look at what is written on the inside of the front cover."

I do as she instructs. There, indeed, in Robert's neat script, are the words *From the library of Dr Carruth, 1678*. And beneath, in a childish copperplate, *Given to Thomas Aikenhead by Mrs Carruth, March 1682*. This second inscription must, I assume, have been written by Thomas. 1682. The year of my marriage. Those first turbulent months as a wife have left many scars on my memory, but I have no recollection of giving Thomas this book. I remember taking him by the hand and leading him away so that his father and Robert could talk in privacy. He would have been no more than five or six years old, but even then his sharp intelligence was clear to see. Strange that when I think of it now I can remember clearly the ache in my heart as he curled his fingers around mine, and how I had wondered if I would ever have a child of my own to hold my hand, ever have a proper marriage. Why is it that the memory of these feelings is so acute, and yet I cannot recall giving him the book?

"I had planned to sell it," Katharine says, interrupting my reverie, "but when I saw the inscription I thought it might... cause difficulties for you and your husband."

"What do you mean?"

"Guilt by association. The Privy Council are still rooting out freethinkers, confiscating books, sending their spies into the coffee houses and taverns. Perhaps I should have burnt it – Lord knows, I could do with the fuel – but it seemed to me it was not mine to dispose of. You may do with it as you please."

"Thank you." For a moment I consider confessing to her that it was I who had circulated Thomas's speech. It seems ungrateful to maintain my deceit when she has shown me some kindness. But something holds me back. It is partly fear of provoking her anger, but also another less craven motivation. What was it Patrick Middleton said to me that day he'd followed me from Hutchison's bookshop? Something about us not being able to undo what was done. How true that is. What benefit will there be in honesty now? Better to let things lie.

I am confident that Dr Maxwell will not be calling. The game has run its course, and I am glad of it. As each hour ticks by I suffer an increasing oppression of spirit. I steel myself to untie the ribbon on the bundle of letters from my mother. As I read them I remember her as she once was – her sharp, jackdaw eye; her obsession with the right way of cooking mutton; her childlike delight in little vanities of dress. These memories are not sufficient to erase the images of those last terrible days of her life, but they are something, I suppose. A counterweight. I find that I can cry for her now, for the light extinguished.

I sit with the children while Alison reads out loud from the Bible, and bite my lip to stop myself from questioning, criticising, doubting. When I have time to myself, I write frantically in my journal. The empty page is the only place where I can express myself freely. Even then I am gripped with fear – not of a vengeful God, for I am now almost sure that none such exists – but of someone else stumbling upon my words. Alison, perhaps – what delight she would take in exposing me to censure! Each day I rip what I have written from the journal and throw it on the fire. If my words are turned to ash they cannot be used against me. And yet I cannot bear to destroy the book I once gave to Thomas that is now returned to me. I reread it, and a confusion of feelings revives. When I first turned its pages it my faith was strong and I had pitied poor Francis Spira as his own belief fell away. But now I wonder if even then some seed was planted that came to fruition these last few months. The very idea that religious faith could die – I had probably never considered it before first reading this book. Did it work in the same manner on Thomas? He had only been a child when it came into his possession. Even with his precocious talent, it would have been beyond him, would it not? I do not know. I can be sure of nothing.

Mungo

Another knock at the front door. So many visitors. This time there are no voices. Nothing but Mother's painful ascent of the stairs. She carries a package into the room. It's stoutly parcelled up and tied with string. I take it from her. A fair weight. She lifts the tray and leaves the room. No curiosity to know what the box contains.

I set it on my bed, and sit down to be more comfortable while I examine it. Unknot the string, and unwrap it. It contains a black lacquer box. Open it up and find a thick cotton money bag within. My heartbeat quickens. Salvation at last. Reach in and pull out a handful of silver ten-shilling pieces. Enough to buy food and fuel for a month or more. Or to buy my passage away from this place. Not as far as America, I think, but far enough to let me start again. I throw the coins on the bed and empty the rest of the bag's contents alongside it. Mother will be up again soon. Her sharp ears will hear the clink of money. I count the coins, and taste the bitterness of my mysterious benefactor's wee joke. Thirty pieces of silver. Of course.

A daybreak departure, this time. I bid Mother farewell. Promise to write when I'm settled. Promise to send money when I have any to send. I'm leaving her half of my ten-shilling pieces.

This last time, I decide not to skulk by any back way. The Lion of Judah is by my side once more. I'll walk up the road from Leith, through the city, out by the West Port and then westwards towards Portpatrick.

There are others on the road at this time of day. The cold nips my nose, so I pull my muffler up to cover my face. I've an old cloak on, and workman's clothes. They will do well for the journey. I have my better clothes in the bag over my shoulder.

Perhaps I should think of a new name for myself. Start afresh. Who was it once told me of the clansmen who took on the name of Black to hide their true allegiance? Mungo Black. No. Mungo is too memorable. William, then? William Black. Mister William Black, minister of religion.

There's the Gallowlee, up ahead, and the gallows still standing. Bare, thank the Lord. Slower now. Steady. No need to rush past. My heart batters that hard against my ribs I can feel it in my throat. As if it would leap out of me and run on, all the way to the western sea.

Stop now. Be a man. Face it. Remember, the Lion of Judah walks by your side. Turn off the road, up the track to the scaffold. A pair of corbies on the crossbeam. One stretches its wings and gives a squawk.

There's a patch of ground that looks as if it's not long turned. It could be him. Most hangings are at the Grassmarket still, and the bodies returned to the families. No such tenderness for Thomas's remains.

I should speak. Pray. But what words? None come. Not even the simplest.

Back. Back on to the road. Onward.

A last look up at Calton Hill. A last glance at the murky waters of the Nor' Loch. A farewell to the castle. Here's the West Port. The road away from here, to Covenanter country. Beyond it the coast and the sea route to Ulster. Hard people, secure in the safety of implacable belief. There'll maybe be a place there for a Soldier of Christ, such as I.

Isobel

After supper Robert disappears into his consulting room and closes the door. He has been preoccupied these last days, saying little beyond what is necessary and – it seems to me – avoiding my company. I harden my heart against guilt. There is nothing to be gained from it.

I take the children upstairs, and loiter in the nursery until they are in bed. Alison carries on as if I am not there, but I feel that her every word and action is performed for me. I wonder if I could find some reason to dispense with her. Henry is nearly beyond needing a nurse, but Margaret is attached to her. I do not want to give my daughter another reason to fix me with those accusing eyes of hers.

When there is nothing else to be done I return downstairs. Before I go into the parlour I peer over the banister and see that Robert's consulting room door is still closed. Time passes. I have been reading by lamplight for long enough to make my eyes tired when I hear the door to the consulting room creak open. I hold my breath and wait as Robert ascends the stairs and comes to the door of the parlour.

"Are you there, Isobel?"

"Yes. Please come in." I put aside my book and stand up to meet him.

He hesitates in the doorway. "Will you step into my consulting room? There is a matter I must discuss with you." There is a fearful tremor in his voice that makes me sick with anxiety.

Once in the consulting room he bids me sit down. "What is it, Robert? I can see something is wrong. Are you unwell?"

He shakes his head but will not meet my gaze. He kneels in front of one of the low cupboards and unlocks the door, then reaches inside and brings out first one book, then another, and then a third. The books are unfamiliar, but that means nothing. Robert's consulting room is full of books, and he is often in receipt of new ones. He looks up at me. "I am afraid to show you these, Isobel, but I can no longer bear this burden alone."

I am confused. He looks as tortured by remorse as any penitent. I rise from my chair and kneel down beside him on the floor. He hands me one of the books. I open it to the title page. "*Christianity Not Mysterious*," I say.

"Keep your voice low," Robert whispers, glancing at the door.

I take the next book. *The Oracles of Reason*. The third book is *A Critical History of the Old Testament*. "I don't understand," I say. "What are these books? Why are you so concerned about them?"

"These are the very titles that inspired Thomas's free-thinking. The ones the Privy Council is determined to suppress. If Campbell and Hope had only known they were sitting but a flight of stairs away from the very volumes they deem blasphemous! I should have thrown them on the fire the moment they left, but I could not bear to. How could I see the words of our best thinkers reduced to ashes? And yet I should have done it, had I valued our safety. I have been tormented by the thought of them hidden here, and you, all innocence..."

I push aside a pang at Robert's misguided view of me, and turn the pages of *The Oracles of Reason*. I pick a line and read it out to him. "'I myself could shew a catalogue of doubts, never yet imagined nor questioned, which are not resolved in Scripture,'" I quote. "I am sure the Privy Council would understand that a learned Christian gentleman might want to familiarise himself with such works, in order to refute their thesis."

Robert bows his head and covers his face with his hands. "Don't you see what I have done?" He pauses, striving to control his emotions while I struggle to understand what it is he's telling me.

"Calm yourself, Robert. There's no harm done. No one but you and I know they are here."

"Mungo knows," he says, so quietly I barely hear him.

"How?"

Robert carries on as if he had not heard me. "We only spoke of it the once. I was showing them – him and Thomas and Patrick – my collection. Showing off, I suppose. There was something in Thomas that irritated me, made me feel that I had to remind him of my standing. Then we were called for dinner. Mungo and I lingered a moment, and I let him see these books. I don't know why. Perhaps I saw something of myself in him. He had none of Thomas's spark and fire, but yet..." He looks over at me, haggard with remorse. "If I had known what those moments would lead to..."

And Mungo had spared me this knowledge. Or perhaps he had withheld it, not from delicacy towards my feelings, but out of some echo of sympathy with Robert.

"You cannot attribute Thomas's downfall to your discussing these books with Mungo," I say.

"Can I not? Thomas said it was Mungo who first led him to such conversations."

"Thomas had been a sceptic since childhood. He said so himself in his gallows speech. It was not your books that put the doubt in his heart."

"But I drew Mungo's attention to such works. And doubtless that drew him to the university library where he and Thomas could read them at leisure. These books gave Thomas the words to express his ideas, and the encouragement that he was not alone in entertaining them."

I turn another page of the book in my hand. There *are* others who think as I do. These books are evidence of it. The men who wrote them would not have been shocked by my doubts. And what of Robert? I take a deep breath and speak. "When I first read of Thomas's notions I was appalled," I say.

297

Robert looks intently at me. "What do you mean, Isobel?"

I hesitate, gathering my thoughts. "Do you believe in boggarts, Robert? Or brownies? Or silkies?"

"Of course not. Those daft tales are for cottars and auld yins in the country."

"What of witches? There's many a wise man will hunt them down."

He makes a dismissive gesture, very much the man of science. "I wouldn't call any man wise who burns a half-dozen crones because some farmer's cattle get the head-staggers. People will sicken and die, and crops will fail, but it's nothing to do with some old bizzum chanting spells."

"These are foolish notions for simple-minded people, yes?"

"Yes indeed, but Isobel…"

My heart is beating hard in my breast, but I force myself on. "What of water being turned into wine, then? Or a storm being stilled with a few words? Or the dead rising?" Robert seems frozen, staring down at the books, but I continue in a whisper. "Are these not foolish notions too? They make as little sense as spells and boggarts." He nods slowly. "What think you of the notions written here in these books?" I lay my hand over his. "Please be honest with me."

His eyes search my face in a kind of panic. At last he says, "I regret to say… I share the views of their authors."

It is as if I have been released from an unbearable burden. The oppression that hemmed me in at every turn melts away. "As do I," I say, watching him to see how he will respond.

He frowns, and stares as if he fears he has misunderstood me. I nod slowly to confirm that he has heard right. "For how long?" he says.

"I cannot tell. Once I believed, and now I do not. My mother's dying days, I think, were the final end of my faith. And you?"

"For nearly as long as I can remember. The more I observed of the world, of the arbitrary workings of nature,

the less I believed they were directed by any higher power."
He squeezes my hand gently. "We must tell no one."

"Of course."

"We will go to kirk on the Sabbath. Continue with our daily Bible readings and prayers."

"Yes. And never let the children see our doubt. Never."

Robert looks at the three books. "We have to burn these. I'll not rest easy until they are gone."

I do not reply, but lift the guard away from the fire. Robert begins tearing pages from one of the books and throwing the leaves on to the fire. I take another and do the same. The flames flare and die down quickly, as they will when burning paper. We work diligently until we are left with three empty bindings. Robert rips each of them in two along the spine, and adds them to the fire, one at a time so as not to overwhelm it. When it is done he stands up stiffly and sits in his chair. "Will you sit beside me, Isobel?"

I pull the other chair alongside him, and sit.

"Did I kill Thomas?" he says.

"No," I reply. "No more than any of us." I think of the book Katharine gave me. I will not destroy it, whatever the dangers of keeping it in my possession. It is hidden where not even Margaret will find it, like a secret, silent cry of defiance against those who would suppress free thought. I take Robert's hand and hold it tightly.

So we sit, hands clasped as if we fear we might fall without the other to cling to. The fire crackles, but I am chilled by the knowledge that beyond our shuttered window lies the dark city, and above it the endless fathoms of the heavens. Some might look up at the night sky and discern the hand of God in the pattern of the stars. Not Robert and I. If we see patterns they are the product of our own longings. All that is real is contained in this room, at this moment. The warmth of skin on skin; the consolation of a hand holding mine; the knowledge that I have, after all, a true companion for the short and troubled journey that we call life.

Acknowledgements

Among the many people who have helped me in writing this book are some who have been dead for over three hundred years; those seventeenth-century Scottish men and women who put pen to paper to record their thoughts, fears and domestic minutiae. Their compulsion to make a record of their lives, and the efforts of the archivists and scholars who have preserved and interpreted them, make the novelist's guessing game a little more rooted in historical evidence.

Most of my thanks, though, must go to the living. I'm particularly indebted to Linda Anderson and Derek Neale, who supported, guided and challenged me during the several years I was working on the novel. Forthright critical friends are invaluable to any writer, and I am grateful to count Linda and Derek as mine. Other friends and colleagues assisted with their interest, suggestions and questions that got me thinking. My thanks to Sara Haslam, Fiona Doloughan, Peg Katritzky, Janice Holmes, Sara Jan, Encarna Trinidad Barrantes and Jennifer Shepherd. Mention must also be made of Professor Michael Green, who pointed out, in the kindest way possible, that the novel's original title was terrible and it would never get published unless I changed it. I will undoubtedly have left out some names that should be included, and can only apologise for my faulty memory.

Finally, thank you to my family: my father Tom, late mother Evelyn and brother Gary for all the years of understated Northern Irish cheerleading. Most particular thanks go to my husband John, and sons Isaac and Leon. They keep me entertained, infuriated and – crucially – supplied with vast amounts of tea.

Images

The two woodcut images contained herein are reprinted under a Creative Commons Attribution only licence from Wellcome Library, London:

Woodcut 1: "The figure explained: being a dissection of the womb…" wood engraving showing woman dissected to expose child in womb. From *The Compleat Midwife's Companion: Or the Art of Midwifery Improv'd*, by Jane Sharp (London: J. Marshall, 1724).

Woodcut 2: Andreae Vesalii Bruxellensis, scholae medicorum Patauinae professoris De humani corporis fabrica libri septem. From *Andreae Vesalii Bruxellensis, scholae medicorum Patauinae professoris De humani corporis fabrica libri septem*, by Andreas Vesalius (Basel: Joannis Oporini, 1543).